The Secrets of Arguris
By Dianna L. Ortiz

ISBN: 979-8-504978-27-7

Secrets of Arguris by Dianna Ortiz

You are whoever you say you are. But I tell you, you're so much more.
-Dianna L. Ortiz

1

She watched her uncle enter the room, not even bothered by his odd stride. Samantha had gotten used to it since the first time she met him a few years ago. His blue damask banyan hid his legs. He was always dressed like the locals from whatever country he had been to recently. He never appeared in the same garments. Samantha secretly wished a gust of wind would push open a window and reveal in what ways his legs were crooked. Her mother had said his legs weren't the only things that made him crooked. She didn't like her spending much time with him, but she loved his stories of places he had traveled, and he relished in the opportunity to relive his adventures.

Sometimes he'd return from a long trip and bring back an artifact to donate to Chraimyth's library. He'd send word for her immediately and she would drop everything to see it before he packed it up again. Sometimes he'd get so wrapped up in explaining where the artifact came from, it was as though he had lived through the historical event himself.

"Oh, Samantha, the places this has been, the hands that have held it," her uncle would say. She would beam at him in wonderment, letting her imagination take her to far away places. It was easy for her to dream about places around the world even when he wasn't telling her about them. Her uncle let her look at all his atlases and she'd always wonder, "In which one of these places do I belong?"

No one knew how she had come to Chraimyth. She woke up one day at the doorstep to an orphanage with the housemother and a young girl picking her up and dragging her inside. She didn't know her name, where she had come from, what she was doing there, or how she had gotten there. The only belonging she possessed was a golden cylindrical object with engravings on the surface. It didn't open and no one seemed to know what it was. The housemother took her in and gave her the name Samantha, after a stray that kept returning because one of the younger orphans wouldn't stop leaving food out for it. Samantha didn't like it, but she had no other name to claim. The doctor had visited and told her her memory might return in time, but he had no other advice for her. The housemother had been angry. Another mouth to feed and no donations on her behalf. Samantha made it a point not to complain and found she was never hungry much anyway, so it didn't bother her when she noticed her portions were smaller than the other girls. She would lay in bed at night and fumble with her golden trinket, trying to figure out what it did, where it might open. It never did anything. Still, she held onto it as it was the only thing that linked her to where she had come from.

She stayed in the orphanage for three years before being approached by Sylvia and Marcus Roeker. They were an older couple, and unlike the younger couples that came in, they had no interest in the little girls. Instead they wanted one of the older girls. They had explained to her they felt it made the most sense, that they were too old to raise a child and wanted to open there home to a girl who would appreciate the family name and pass on family traditions. The housemother had sent them straight to Samantha, and she knew it was best to go with them than wait for the day she was packing her bags to work at the factories she had heard about.

She had never asked why they never had children of their own, though they could have, she supposed, and the child might have died. She thought it better to leave the topic alone. Over the next few years Sylvia, a short, stocky woman, made it her mission to teach Samantha how to be a proper lady. She had dark hair that was showing gray though she tried to hide it by pinning her hair in a ridiculously large bun. It looked more like a hat than her hair, and it didn't hide the gray at all. Her blue eyes were always sparkling when she looked at her daughter. Samantha loved being looked at like that, but it made her heart ache to think her real mother could be looking for her right now and she might have looked at Samantha that same way once. And perhaps Samantha had already been a proper lady and no one had to teach her how to pick up a fork or lay a napkin on her lap. Maybe she already had maids that wouldn't allow her to dress herself. She also considered that something may have happened to her mother, just like something may have happened to any children Sylvia and Marcus may have once had. Samantha appreciated the effort Sylvia put into making sure she was proper for the upper class society of Chraimyth, but she couldn't ignore the emptiness. The constant reminder that something that was once there before was missing. She had questions no one could answer.

Marcus was always impressed with her intelligence and had
even remarked that she must have completed her schooling
some time ago. They had sent her to the school house for a
few days so the teacher could test her and hopefully give them
a better idea of how old she was, too. The house mother had
told them she thought Samantha to be about 17, but Marcus
was confident she was much older. "You don't act like a child,
my dear," he had said, "You act like a young lady that has seen
the world and knows a thing or two about a thing or two." He
puffed on his pipe as he said it and his mustache twitched.
Samantha sat next to a young girl at the school house who kept
smiling at her and touching her hair.

"You're pretty," she said with grin.

Samantha shushed her, quietly saying thank you, then looked
straight ahead so the little girl would do the same. She noticed
some of the other kids were doing the same. There were boys
and girls of all ages seated in twos down four rows in the small
room. They all kept looking at her, curious about her. The
afternoons were stuffy and Samantha was happy school started
early in the morning when it was still cool. They'd open the
windows and the brisk air kept the room from suddenly
feeling too small like it did just before they were all sent home
for the day. Everyday the teacher would give Samantha a
special set of questions to answer, or ask her to display various
sets of skills in math and science and reading. Often times

Samantha found herself completing each task with ease, unable to explain where she had learned her methods. The teacher questioned them often, letting her know that while her answers were right, it wasn't how any of her students in Chraimyth were taught, or any student from any of the neighboring towns. When the week was over and the teacher gave her report to Sylvia and Marcus, she told them, "Samantha is smart. She has a good head on her shoulders and I'm sure if I retired today she could take over and every child in there would be just as well off, if not better." Marcus had beamed. She went on, "Her methods are very old fashioned, in my opinion. *Very* old fashioned and I found it quite refreshing and amusing. Samantha is definitely not seventeen. Just looking at her in the classroom next to the children you can tell she is well into her twenties. I'd say at most twenty-three or four."

Sylvia and Marcus withdrew her from school immediately and that was when Sylvia decided to prepare Samantha for the life of a woman ready to bare children and run a home for her husband.

"You grew up on us even faster than we expected," she had laughed. "Now we need to see you married."

Samantha had tried to make other suggestions for how she could use her time but Sylvia wouldn't consider any of it. She insisted Samantha needed to marry and start having children while she was still young, before others would start calling her an old maid. Samantha remembered why they wanted a child in the first place and knew there wasn't much point in arguing with the woman.

She began taking her to dances and picnics, which Samantha was relieved to find were mostly held at Uncle Nicolas' estate. She knew all the hiding spots and was able to avoid her parents when their determination to introduce her to every man in the room became too much. Her uncle owned the largest piece of land in Chraimyth and people would often make deals with him in exchange for hosting various gatherings. Samantha learned how to dance and met other young men and women her age. One young woman, a giggly blonde with dark green eyes named Celeste, became friends with her quickly. She mostly loved that she could tell Samantha any story she wanted about Chraimyth and the people who lived there because Samantha wouldn't know if they were true or not. Sometimes they'd make a game of it, especially stories about the young men. Samantha would point one out at a picnic and Celeste would tell her one awful thing they had done and one normal or funny thing they had done and Samantha had to guess which was true. One day she asked about an especially well dressed young man who she noticed kept looking her way while she was standing with her parents who were introducing her to Chraimyth's mayor. The mayor was fat and his laughter couldn't hide the scowl that was his face. She had looked away and noticed Edward nearby sneaking glances at her. Her cheeks became warm and she looked away, but couldn't help looking back at him. She was glad when Celeste had stolen her to the drink stand.

"Oh, that's Edward. Chraimyth's main bachelor. My parents already tried to make us a match but his parents weren't impressed with my overly-optimistic spirit," she laughed, "but oh, I bet you could snag him." She pointed to where Samantha's parents were now talking to another couple, "And from the looks of it your mother thinks so, too. Just promise I get to be the maid of honor."

Celeste had been right. Over the next year, Sylvia and Marcus had taken every opportunity to make sure Samantha was available every time Edward showed up at the door. At first she found him annoying and it was hard to find things they both enjoyed talking about. Edward seemed to take it all in stride. He was good at filling the silence when she didn't want to talk. She enjoyed listening to him. His voice was deep but youthful. Sometimes they would stroll along the streets in silence, turning to smile at each other occasionally. One time he asked her what it was like to not remember an entire life and she didn't know what to say. What was it supposed to be like? She felt lost. Someone like Edward wouldn't understand that. He had everything. He knew where he was from and where he was going. Samantha felt like she had been swept up in a cyclone that wouldn't put her down.

As the months passed Sylvia became more attentive and Samantha found herself feeling like a horse training to pull a carriage. Her dresses were strategically planned, and while she was being dressed her mother would go over the etiquette of courting and appearing in public with a man she wasn't married to. She was insistent Samantha make no mistakes, pointing out that their entire reputations lay in her hands every time they left the house.

Her uncle was her only escape. No one bothered finding her there when she went to visit. Samantha found herself visiting her uncle more than before. She had met him at the first ball Sylvia and Marcus had taken her to. She thought his home was beautiful. It was twice the size of theirs and everything looked like white marble. She was especially impressed with the things that decorated the walls and shelves. There were books everywhere and every wall held a different theme. There was a wall decorated in colorful kanthas and a large elephant tapestry. One wall was covered in shelves full of African sculptures made from stone, clay, and even bone. Her favorite was a stone dragon. She hadn't read any stories yet of dragons in Africa, and she enjoyed the mystery the piece gave her until the day she would come to those tales if they existed.

Beautifully painted portraits decorated other walls, with tables displaying small trinkets and jewelry her uncle claimed were once worn by great leaders from that area centuries before. Samantha knew better than to believe all his tales, but they were exciting and she did love to look at them. Her favorite room was the room where he kept weapons. Her mother had made it clear she wasn't allowed in the room, but her uncle encouraged it. He taught her the names and where they had come from, most of them being from ancient Greece and Rome. He let her take home books about the old Greek gods then quiz her on them. In the same room were head statues of kings and queens and he'd share their stories as if they were his own. She fell in love with the world he lived in and wished she could go with him on his journeys.

"Can I go with you the next time you leave?" she ask him today. He walked to where she was standing in front of the row of spears and studied her face.

"You know you can't do that Samantha. You're a young woman, and you need to start a family before it's too late," he said and Samantha was disappointed that he sounded like Sylvia.

She picked up a spear and examined it. "Do you think only men managed a spear in the hands?" she asked as she examined the tip of the blade at the end of the long stick.

Her uncle twitched nervously and held his hand out for the spear. He looked like he was suddenly afraid and Samantha wasn't sure why. Did he really think she would hurt herself? She rolled her eyes and shoved the spear at him. He put it back on the display rack and put his hands on both of her shoulders.

"My dear, the weapon you wield is greater than any of these. It is one no man can ever claim, and most certainly never master," he told her.

Samantha could feel her heart beating faster and her face turning red. She was tired of being reminded she was expected to be a woman. A very limited woman whose reach into the outer world would be determined by the hands of her husband.

"I don't want to *wield my weapon*," she mocked, "I want to wield those weapons. I want see the places they were forged and walk the battlefields where those soldiers fought. I want to see Athens and visit Rome. I want to ride an elephant and smell the spices of India. I want to be all the places you've been. Edward won't take me to any of these places, Uncle! He's told me so. He thinks just like Sylvia and Marcus, and you." She saw the pain in her uncle's eyes when she mentioned him and the guilt felt like a knot in her stomach. He had always been there for her when he was around. She though of all the people she knew best in Chraimyth, he would be the one to encourage her to seek her hearts desires. But he was just another rich man in a small town that was too content in minding only the business inside the city's walls and the attention it gave him.

She had spoken to Edward the night he asked for her hand in marriage. It was one year to the day after they began courting. Her parents had of course already given their blessing. The two had become good friends over the year and Samantha enjoyed Edwards company. He was good at telling jokes, though they were always the same and he did his best to try to tell it differently every time. Sometimes that alone was enough to make her laugh. He spent a lot of time talking about his father's business adventures and how his family had built their wealth mostly on wise investments. It would soon be Edwards responsibility to maintain those relationships and he explained what he would expect of Samantha as his wife. When she had asked him if they could make time to travel, he made it clear he intended to make her far too busy with their children to even have time to think about the rest of the world. He had meant it as a tease and affectionate to mention children and them becoming a family one day, but it broke her heart and she had to excuse herself so he wouldn't see her cry.

And now her uncle was pointing her in the same direction. No one seemed to see any alternate future for her, and they especially didn't want to hear any of her own ideas about it.

She stormed out of the room and walked out onto the patio looking over the acres of land spread out before meeting a forest that stretched for miles beyond. That was all the surrounded Chraimyth, trees. She made her way to a row of head statues of various philosophers. She tapped Socrates' nose, and hearing her uncle's odd footsteps behind her she said, "Why were they all allowed to think outside the box, and we admire them, but I'm not? Why don't I get to be unlike the rest when I feel myself pulled in a direction away from the one everyone wants me to go?"

Her uncle didn't speak. He thought for a long time and she walked from one statue to the next, waiting to hear what he would say.

"I know you want to find your family, Samantha," he finally broke the silence and sat down where they had shared an afternoon tea many times before. "I once felt the same way. I wanted answers."

Marcus had explained to Samantha early on that Nicolas was not actually a part of their family, but they had been friends ever since Nicolas first arrived in Chraimyth several years before and he had come to feel like family and they often introduced each other as *brother*. Marcus had even introduced Nicolas as *Uncle* Nicolas. Samantha wondered if that's what he meant. He didn't have any other family in Chraimyth aside from them. She hadn't really thought about it before, maybe she just assumed he visited family during his travels.

He went on, "There's a lot of those other girls who have moved on from that orphanage who weren't as lucky as you. They're working in factories, saving up every spare penny in hopes of someday living in the manner that was handed to you on a silver platter. Maybe Sylvia and Marcus chose the wrong girl." He shrugged his shoulders and Samantha understood what he was saying. They had given her everything but it wasn't enough for her. Any other girl would have been satisfied and would have no argument to marriage or family. They'd love Edward and they'd feel like princesses in the wedding she knew Sylvia was planning for her.

She wished she could be so ignorant so she could fit in with no doubts about the flutter in her heart that told her to run and live. In Chraimyth you could only run so far and living was the same on every part of its borders.

"Uncle, what do I do?" Samantha asked quietly, sitting across from him. They both stared out over the large lawn.

"The way that I see you may not be you at all, and it's not for me to decide. You see me in your way, but it may not be who I actually am. You have to decide which version of you is best for you to be. What they see, or what you see. Then you have to decide what you're going to do about it." He looked across the table at her as if he were daring her.

"The rehearsal dinner is tonight," Samantha said, and just then one of the maids walked out and announced the flowers had arrived. Uncle Nicolas was, of course, hosting the rehearsal dinner and Sylvia had decided it was necessary to invite the whole town though they'd all be gathering the very following day for the wedding.

Her uncle stood up to leave and turned to her, "I suggest you have a heart to heart with yourself there, and make up your mind pretty fast. Either way, there will be a party tonight at least. It's too late to cancel now."

Samantha watched him disappear inside, pointing down the hallway and three men carried two boxes each filled with dark pink carnations. Sylvia's favorite color.

2

The priest rolled his eyes at Sylvia as she kept getting out of the pew to rearrange Samantha's skirt, as if the wedding were happening right now. Samantha stood with Edward in front of the priest and barely noticed. Her uncle's words kept racing through her head. She stared at the cross hanging on the wall behind the priest, at the man nailed to it with thorns on his head. He had suffered for the purpose he believed he served, even giving his life for it. Marcus had explained that he had even given his life for her though there was no way he could have ever known her so many years before she was even born. Supposedly his act forgave her sins. What sins had she committed? Was that how she had come to Chraimyth? Was she running away because she was a criminal? She didn't feel like one.

Her thoughts were interrupted when Edward grabbed her hand and squeezed it. The priest had been asking her if she had memorized her vows or if she needed to repeat them after him. He was sweating and she felt sorry for him being stuck in his heavy robe.

"Yes, please, I'll repeat after you," she said.

She faced Edward, who looked at her with a wide smile across his face. She tried to force one but it felt awkward so she turned her attention to the priest. He went over every section of the ceremony, then had Edward and Samantha practice their lines. Edward had memorized his. That annoyed Samantha. It would make things easier if he wasn't so excited. They could mutually agree to call the whole thing off and go their separate ways. She listened to his vows and watched him as he looked at her, speaking as though it was the real ceremony and was ready to say *I do* that day. Everything about him was agreeable. Aside from his family's money, which Sylvia had explained was important in any marriage, Edward himself was a good man, and he was handsome. His dark hair was always neatly combed with just a few strands that fell over his forehead. His dark eyes, with his lips that always seemed curled in a smile, made him look playfully mysterious. That was what Samantha liked most about him when they had first met. But she had read him wrong. He could be playful and she enjoyed the way he flirted with her, but he was predictable and she could see his whole life from beginning to end as he said, "until death do us part."

Her mind flashed back to her uncle's face daring her as he said, "You have to decide which version of you is best for you to be."

Just then she knew exactly who she wanted to be, and every bit of her was ready to escape that room and that town, but she wasn't trying to make a scene of it and she knew running off aimlessly wouldn't get her far. She would need to plan. It would have to be somewhat spontaneous because there wasn't much time before her mother was sewing her into her wedding dress tomorrow.

The rest of the rehearsal she went through the motions of a happy bride-to-be. When it had ended, she barely noticed Edward's mother pull her aside, her words sounded distant and mumbled except when she said she admired her son *taking a chance on a young lady who could be a miscreant for all they knew.* Samantha laughed with the woman, saying, "Oh thank you, Mrs. Hamilton, you're so sweet." Mrs. Hamilton gave her an odd look and Samantha walked away.

Everyone made their way back to the carriages to meet again at Uncle Nicolas's house for the rehearsal dinner party. Sylvia made their driver wait, saying it was appropriate for them to leave last so they could make an entrance. Samantha stared out the window as the carriages passed. She looked at the people in them, Edward and his family, Celeste with her parents. She had, of course, been declared the maid of honor. A hand waved out the window of their carriage and Celeste was smiling over at her. Samantha returned a weak smile and barely waved back. Celeste frowned as they disappeared from view.

They followed behind the long line of carriage wheels and her mother carried on excitedly. "I can't believe it," she squeezed Marcus's arm, "tomorrow our daughter is going to be Mrs. Hamilton!" She squealed and reached over and grabbed Samantha's knees, her fingers digging in as she shook her legs. When Samantha didn't smile back her face dropped and she sat back.

"Don't worry about cold feet, dear," she was calm now, "it happens to every bride, even grooms sometimes."

"You'll make Edward a wonderful wife, Samantha," Marcus chimed in. She could see the pride in both their faces, and she wished for a moment that she had been their real daughter. Then all of this might feel natural and she wouldn't be questioning all of it.

They chattered on about the wedding day schedule and Samantha stared out the window. It had gotten dark and the sky was clear, revealing a cast of constellations. Samantha could identify many of them. Uncle Nicolas had a large woven map of constellations hanging in one of the guest bedrooms and it was her favorite one. She chose that room for herself for tonight's occasion. Her uncle had insisted they stay the night so they would get a good nights sleep after the party and not have to worry about the travel home, though it was less than half an hour away. If Samantha ran, she could get there in even less the time than the carriage would.

She looked at the stars and identified the constellation Gemini. Two of the same. She understood that. She felt that there were two of her. The Samantha Chraimyth had made her to be, and then the girl she had entered the world as, the one she had lost. She reached into her dress pocket and fumbled with her golden trinket. It was always in her pocket, she never left it anywhere. She tried to remember the names of each of the stars in the constellation. Pollux, Castor, and Athena. She couldn't remember the names of the others. Her uncle would most likely give her a book on astrology to study to make sure she didn't forget.

She didn't want anymore books though. She looked down the road and the house was just up ahead. Guests were climbing out of carriages and she could spot her uncle welcoming them at the door. Samantha had decided she would let her mother parade her around for a few minutes, then make a couple rounds with Edward until she could make an excuse to go to her room. There she would think of some way leave the house tomorrow unnoticed. She was sure she wouldn't get a moment to talk to her uncle again, and Celeste and Edward definitely weren't going to listen to her. She would have to decide, tonight, what the rest of her life was going to look like and she would have to be content with whatever it was going to be. Her parents helped her out of the carriage and walked on either side of her until they reached Edward and his family. Any other night she wouldn't have thought anything of it. They always walked on either side of her. Tonight she felt like a prisoner being escorted to the jailhouse. Edward stood next to his parents and Uncle Nicolas, engaged in chatter. Mrs. Hamilton was going on about how well the rehearsal went and how beautiful the estate looked. Edward smiled at Samantha as Marcus took her hand and pulled her to his arm, clearly practicing for his one part tomorrow. She had to laugh. Their parents followed the couple inside where they were greeted by guests, many Samantha had only seen in passing around town, and others she recognized from the many dances Sylvia had her attend. All the women were dressed in beautiful gowns and she wondered if they planned to show up in the same garments tomorrow. Celeste approached, hugging them both and kissing their cheeks. She whispered in Samantha's ear, "Don't these women look ridiculous?" She motioned toward a group of young women standing together, mostly frowning in their direction. She had to agree, they seemed a bit overdone on jewels and cheek color. They looked as though they had just come from a play rehearsal and she was tempted to ask them so.

"Edward, do you mind if I steal your bride away?" Celeste was already pulling Samantha toward the hallway. She followed her friend into a room where her uncle had paintings of European kings and queens from centuries ago. They sat down on a bench across from them. Celeste leaned in close and though they were alone she whispered, "Are you okay?"

Samantha didn't want to open up to her friend. She assumed Celeste would scold her and maybe even drag her to the alter herself if she tried to run away. She looked at the portraits. The kings with their stern expressions, the queens smothered under materials and jewels.

"Do you think they ever wanted anything other than the roles they were given by their parents?" Samantha asked.

Celeste glanced at the paintings, then back at Samantha. "Don't worry about cold feet, my mom said it happens to everyone. She even told me you might be having them tonight and here you are, flustered," Celeste laughed and Samantha smiled.

"Celeste, can I tell you something in confidence? You won't tell anyone?" Samantha decided to take a chance. She needed another woman to talk to freely and who better than her best friend.

"Of course! I can't believe you're hiding something from me. Spit it out," she shifted in her seat, getting excited and curious. Samantha straightened herself and hoped she wouldn't regret this.

"I don't want to marry Edward. I want to leave Chraimyth and travel the world, to places like my uncle has been. Maybe even learn something about where I'm from." Samantha spoke softly so guests roaming down the hall wouldn't overhear. Celeste's face dropped. She looked confused and disappointed. Samantha waited for her to say something.

"I don't know what to say," Celeste shook her head as she stared at a painting of queen Elizabeth I. "So you want to go at it on your own? No man, no children? Just you and yourself out there?"

She was scolding her. Samantha knew it was better to say nothing and she stood, ready to say something before leaving the room but Celeste pulled her down, a smile on her face. It was Samantha's turn to be confused.

"I always knew you were incredible!" she grabbed Samantha by the neck and hugged her tight. Samantha was shocked, but relieved. She had underestimated her friend.

"Oh thank god, I wasn't sure how you'd take that, I was so afraid of telling you."

Celeste's face became stern and she leaned away from Samantha. "I'm your best friend. This is something you should have been telling me a long time ago. We have less than twenty-four hours to come up with an escape plan. I assume you have a plan on such short notice?" Celeste began pacing the room with her hands on her hips. Samantha was surprised. Celeste never seemed like the courageous type.

A couple walked in and hugged Samantha when they spotted her, congratulating her on the coming wedding. They strolled along the room, admiring the paintings while Samantha and Celeste quietly looked at each other.

"Come on, I know a good place we can think," Samantha pulled Celeste upstairs to her room and shut the door.

"Your mother's going to come looking for you, you know that right?" Celeste said as she locked the door.

"I know." Samantha said as she sat at the edge of the bed. Edward would no doubt be looking for her, too.

Celeste sat in the chair in front of the vanity and they both looked at each other, then at the floor, and at anything else in the room. It was quiet for several moments and Samantha wondered if she would end up marrying Edward because she couldn't find the courage she needed to walk right out the door. If she couldn't do that much, how would she manage herself anywhere else? Celeste jumped up and went to the wardrobe, throwing the doors open, showing a few dresses

Sylvia had hung for her and an extra pairs of boots. They were only staying one night, but Sylvia said it was better to have a little extra for the weather. One dress was heavier for cool nights, the other lighter for warm days.

"Get your bag, you're leaving right now." Celeste said as she yanked the dresses out of the closet and began carelessly rolling them up.

Samantha's heart raced as she pulled her bag from under the bed and opened it. She watched Celeste shove her things inside and began laughing.

"Have you been wanting to get rid of me the whole time Celeste? Am I a threat?" Samantha asked as she began laughing harder. Celeste stopped and stared at Samantha as though she had just lost her mind, then she looked at the bag, then the dress wadded up in her hands. She burst out laughing, too, then dropped the dress in the bag and walked over to Samantha, hugging her again.

"No, you could never be a threat. You're my friend and knowing you're out there in the world, I can live vicariously through your letters that you're going to write every day. And the day the letters stop coming is the day I'll have to leave Chraimyth myself to come find you." Celeste reassured her friend.

Samantha was grateful for Celeste. She pulled her in and hugged her again, "I love you, Celeste."

"I love you, too. But we're not going to stand here and cry because your mother will hear us and come running with every nurse and doctor that's down there," Celeste laughed and pulled away, wiping a tear from her eye. "Does anyone else know how you feel?"

"My uncle," Samantha replied as she found room for her boots and gloves. "He said I have to be the best version of me."

Celeste nodded in agreement, gathering items from the vanity and tossing them on top. When the bag was closed and Samantha had her shawl they both stood next to the bed and stared at each other.

"What now?" Celeste asked.

Samantha had to figure out how to get out of the house unnoticed. She wouldn't even be able to reach the stairs without someone seeing her, and they'd most certainly question her carrying a bag and a shawl wrapped around her shoulder when the party was only beginning.

There were footsteps outside the door and Samantha's heart raced again. A soft knock was heard and Sylvia's voice, "Samantha, come down, the guests are waiting to see you."

Samantha looked at Celeste who shrugged her shoulders at her. Neither one of them knew what to do. They looked around the room but there were no other doors. Only a small window next to the night stand. Samantha went over to it and quietly opened it.

Sylvia knocked again, louder. "Samantha, open the door. Are you okay, do you need your corset loosened?"

Samantha ignored her as she handed her bag to Celeste. She looked out the window and saw the rooftop extending a few feet under the window. Below, the grass was dimly light by the window on the floor below. She saw no shadows, indicating the room below was empty, and no one would be roaming around in the dark on this side of the house. She climbed out, then turned as Celeste was holding the bag out to her. Sylvia was knocking louder now, her voice sounding upset and concerned. Samantha felt a little bad, but she knew if she opened that door it would be the end of it. Celeste leaned out the window and kissed Samantha's cheek, "Enjoy your adventures, and don't forget to write," she said before slowly closing the window. Samantha watched as Celeste crumpled the blankets on the bed and rubbed her hands over her hair so it looked like she had been sleeping. Samantha smiled, then slowly made her way to the edge of the rooftop, her bag hanging over her shoulder and resting on her back. She looked to the ground below and her jaw dropped when she saw her uncle standing there with one of his staff. The man was large and muscular and they both stared up at her. She wondered if they had been expecting her or if her uncle had some business with the man and she had interrupted.

"Um, hi Uncle," she waved, feeling like a child that had just been caught stealing candy from the store.

"Well come on child, we don't have all night," he waved her down and the man next to him reached up to her.

She then understood why they were there. She dropped her bag to him and he set it on the floor. As she reached her legs over the edge of the roof he reached up to her again and she closed her eyes as she pushed herself off. The man caught her with ease and gently put her feet to the ground, putting the bag back on her shoulders so it rested on her back.

She looked at her uncle, unsure what to say. Was he going to take her back inside?

"If you follow the road from Chraimyth down that way," he pointed to the southern road near the school house, "it'll take you to the next town. There you'll give this to a man named Jesup. He'll take you from there wherever you want to go." He handed her a note with a handful of dollars, then gave her a bundle of books, including her favorite atlas. She threw her free arm around him and he held her tightly.

"Thank you, uncle." Samantha said. She began to walk away but her uncle stopped her.

"Please, let my man here take you there. It's dark, and there's little light along that road. You should be escorted," her uncle motioned to the man then waved Samantha off to follow him. There was a horse already saddled and the man took the books from Samantha and shoved them in a sack then climbed on, pulling her up behind him. Her uncle waved as they passed. Samantha looked up to the window but didn't see anyone. She waved to her uncle then looked on to the dark road ahead.

3

They rode slowly down the southern road with only the moon lighting the way. The man in front of her was quiet. The only sound heard was the clopping of the horses hooves and an occasional snort. Somewhere in the forest an owl called out into the night. Samantha didn't mind how quiet it was. Her thoughts were racing. She looked up as a shooting star streaked across the spotted sky. It was a sign, she thought to herself, a symbol of good things to come.

"Do you mind if I ask where you plan to go," her escort asked. She hadn't thought about that. She figured she'd find a room tonight and study the maps in the morning. She knew she would have to be quick. Her parents would be out looking for her and if they found her, Sylvia wouldn't let her out of her sights until she said *I do.*

"I'm not sure. Any suggestions," she asked.

He thought about it a moment then looked back and said, "California, I think they have some gold left."

They both laughed.

Of all the places her uncle had told her about, he never spent much time talking about the states. She found their history boring and self-serving. She had no desire to visit California or New York or any of the regions of that country. She wanted to see places further away than that. Places on the other side of the world. She hoped Jesup could help her with that.

The road wound to the left and they followed it, the trees growing thicker and the moon light dimmer. Samantha thought she saw light coming from the woods and pointed it out.

"What's over there?"

Her escort looked in the direction and shrugged his shoulders, "No idea."

As they came up beside it they could see the light was coming from candles sitting on posts nailed to the trees. They went on in a row into the forest and they couldn't see where it ended. A gust of wind blew and Samantha was sure she heard a woman's voice.

"Hello?" she said quietly.

"Hello." her escort replied.

"Did you just hear a girl?"

"No, did you?" he looked back at her, then toward the candles, but saw no one.

Samantha asked him to stop and he offered his hand as she eased herself off the horse. The wind blew again and she could hear the voice. It was clear this time. She was sure it was a woman's voice, but she couldn't understand it. Like it was speaking another language. She stepped off the road and approached the area where the candles were burning. She noticed the ground was bare and a path to walk could be seen clearly.

"We should keep going, it's not safe in the woods at night," her escort called softly as he jumped down from the horse and waved for her to come back. She could barely see him in the dark night.

She held her finger up to him, motioning for him to give her a moment longer to investigate. She stepped up to the first two candles. They sat a few inches higher than her head and they were much bigger than they appeared at the road. She wondered who lived in the woods here that would come and light these every night. *They must be very tall*, she thought to herself. She looked down the candlelit path for the woman she had heard but no one was there. She couldn't see into the dark woods past the candle light. She stepped forward. As soon as she did, a gust of wind roared around the first pair of candles, smothering the flames. She looked back to her escort and the horse but it was harder to see them now. She knew they were there, so she moved ahead. As she past the candles on either side of her, the wind choked the flame. She wasn't sure how far she had gotten from the road, and she couldn't hear her escort calling out to her, so she guessed he could still see her. She kept walking, hearing the wind blowing behind, she followed the trail of candles for several minutes until there were only two left. She looked behind her and saw nothing but darkness.

"Hello," she called out. No one called back. "Hello," she called louder, but still nothing. She wanted to go back, but it was too dark and she worried she'd turn the wrong way and get lost. She tried to take one of the candles but they stuck to the wood and she couldn't pull either of them down. Her bag and books were back with the horse and escort. She looked around and grabbed a stick from the ground and tried to light it. Nothing. She threw the stick down and looked ahead past the last two candles. She noticed in the dim light what looked like a door. A very large door, about twice her height and wide enough to fit five or six men walking side by side. Samantha moved closer to examine it, hoping someone might be home who could give her a lamp to guide her back to the road. As she got closer, she squinted as she saw peculiar statues on either side of the door. Two large snakes, long and thick stood coiled up the height of the door. Samantha knew if they were real they could swallow her whole. She couldn't tell in the dark if they were made out of clay or stone, though she was sure it was clay from the dry, cracked surface. She rubbed her hands along the scales of one and admired how realistic it looked. She had never heard of an artist living outside of Chraimyth in the woods, but then she considered maybe she had reached an old building that was no longer in use. That wouldn't explain the candles lit this time of night. She walked across the door and examined the other snake. They both looked the same, standing several feet above her, their faces stared straight ahead into the dark. She looked for a knocker on the door, or a bell somewhere, but found nothing. She ran her hands along the wood and the moment she did so there was a low rumbling sound that quickly grew and Samantha realized it was coming from the statues.

"Well, that's just great", she said to herself.

She took several steps back and watched as two large anacondas shook off the clay and dropped to the ground. The light reflected off the gold laced throughout their scales and their eyes glowed yellow. Each one wore a gold-trimmed hat with a beautiful embellishment on the front. Their tongues lashed out as they slithered forward, stopping a short distance in front of her. They both stared at her, and she wanted to run, but she couldn't make her feet move. They watched her quietly, standing perfectly still, only their tongues flicking in and out.

She watched them, helpless. If she ran, they would most certainly strike, but if she kept standing there, one might strike anyway. They watched her, not making a sound, not moving. Samantha looked at the door behind them, then glanced over her shoulder at the darkness where somewhere her escort was waiting for her. She looked up at each snake, into their bright yellow eyes, trying to figure them out. When they only stared back, she gathered her courage and took several steps forward. Her hands were shaking as she came right in between the two large serpents.

One turned its head toward her and she almost screamed. She stood still, staring straight ahead at the door. Hoping someone would open it and let her in. She hoped if they planned to eat her that it would be over quickly. The snake lowered it's head until it was right in front of her. He stared at her and she thought she could see it smiling. It flicked its tongue, then raised its head and nodded. The other serpent nodded in return, then they both turned and slithered back toward the door. She shuddered as she felt their scaly skin rubbing along her legs. They were almost as thick as her legs were tall. When they reached the doors they each picked one side and began climbing, making a knotted pattern against the wood as they went. Their bodies twisted and turned and she wondered how they didn't fall to the ground. One of them looked at her and winked just before both of their bodies became one with the door. All that was left was a carving in the wood resembling the shape each anaconda had taken. She gasped and cried out, looking around into the darkness, hoping someone else had witnessed what she had just seen. She stepped forward to examine the door. As she reached her hand forward to feel the surface, she heard a loud banging sound and the doors began to slowly open away from her. She jumped back as branches fell and long vines of white ivy floated to the floor. As the doors opened, she noticed the engravings on them began to disappear, and the anacondas slithered from right underneath the wood and past her, back to their posts and watched her. She looked back as the doors stopped moving and stared ahead. She didn't understand what she was looking into because it was too dark, but she was sure she saw a shadow moving. She heard something roar, then the shadow flew over. She was suddenly light headed and the candle light faded away as she fainted and fell to the ground. She didn't feel when the anaconda lifted her and carried her away.

It held her carefully coiled in it's body, rolling her along in the darkness until it reached a doorstep. There was a light coming from inside and the serpent banged on the door with its tail. A creature emerged, its face hidden in the dark and it stared at the snake. The snake flicked its tongue, then nudged at Samantha's body with its nose. The creature bent down and examined her face, rubbing a smudge of dirt off her cheek. "Who is she? Who are you?" the creature asked but the snake only stared back. "Okay, I'll take care of her for tonight, but then she goes home tomorrow."

The creature pulled her inside and the large snake slithered away. It dragged Samantha into a small room with a bed and looked at her a moment. It grabbed one of her shoes and gave a funny look and tried to pull it off but it was tied on tightly. It tugged at the laces until the foot was free, then took off the other one and placed them neatly against the wall. It watched Samantha for while, touching her dark hair and smelling it, giving a funny look at the unfamiliar scents. Grunting, it walked into a small kitchen and used a ladle to pour water into a cup and took it back to the room, sitting it on the table next to the bed. It walked to the main room and pulled two chairs together. Grabbing a large fur from the floor it laid out over the chairs and covered itself, grumbling under its breath before falling asleep.

4

Chimera prowled along the road that ran parallel to the
border. It was night, but her eyes let her see clear enough to
make her way through the dark. It had been at least a year
since she had been to this part of the wall, but she knew it
would be just as it had been before. The border walls were
made of branches tangled together and they climbed far into
the sky where their end couldn't be seen.   She had watched
the flying creatures and saw they never left, so she knew there
was no way out. She looked at the high brush and vines that
had grown along the walls. The branches could barely be seen

near the ground anymore through the ivy and tall grass. Brush had grown thick all the way up to the roads edge.

Reluctant, she stepped off the road and crept through the brush toward the wall. She could hear the scurry of mice running off as she approached. She turned to the left and followed the wall a moment longer until she came across Speranta, two large towering wooden doors that never opened. They were the only reminder that there was more to the world than what she had been forced to call home. She remembered a long time ago when creatures from all over had come to tear the doors down, but no matter the creature, none were strong enough or clever enough. Some had tried cutting them down, only to destroy their tools and weapons. They had tried setting them on fire and burning them to the ground, but the blaze chased them into the rocky hills nearby. They had looked for ways to take the doors apart but found no hinges. Along the wall on either side, bare patches of ground could be seen where the earth had been dug up over the centuries, mostly by Chimera herself, hoping to find her way under the wall, but the roots extended too far into the earth, just as they did into the sky, and she had never found their end. Chimera stared at the doors, and tried to remember who had named them. *Speranta*, hope. There was no hope here. Hope had been lost. They were trapped within this hollow mountain of branches, waiting for eternity to find its death so they could all

perish if they couldn't be free. Most of the creatures that had
been here since the beginning had forgotten all about them,
and those born here found them of little interest, except to
practice their tricks and test their strength.

Chimera stared at the doors a moment longer, and just as she
began to turn away, she heard a large bang, then the breaking
of branches. She turned and saw tall blades of grass fold into
the ground, shrubs cracked and fell over as light poured in.
The doors were opening. She froze, not sure if she was seeing
things, or if it was really happening. She felt her heart begin to
race. Freedom was finally inviting her out. She crept forward
slowly then stopped when she noticed a figure on the other
side. A young girl in odd clothing stood staring at her, looking
horrified. Beyond her was a dim light, then darkness. She
couldn't tell what was out there but she decided to take her
chance before it was too late. She pounced, jumping through
the brush and leaping over the girl. As she did, she saw the girl
faint, falling to the ground. Two large snakes launched forward
to catch her. Chimera landed between two large candles above
her. Their flames beginning to dim. She heard the sound of
something rustling in the trees around her, then she realized it
was the trees. Their branches gathered around her, closing her
in. She tried to push through with her strong forehead but the
wood was strong, just like the wood of the border walls and it
pushed back. She turned around, retreating back to the other

side, and watched as one of the snakes coiled around the girl, creeping into the darkness with her. The other snake watched Chimera as she passed and hissed at her. Chimera lifted her tail, which hissed back, surprising the towering snake and it flicked its tongue at her. She glared at him and watched as the doors closed between them. Her opportunity was lost. She roared into the night, clawing at the ground and shaking her mane, her tail hissing and snapping at the air. She stopped only when the bare stump on her back began to ache. She lowered her head, panting. Then she looked again at the doors. They looked as they always had. No one would know they had opened, nor would anyone be likely to believe her if she were to tell them what she saw. She ran ahead looking for the snake and the girl, but they had disappeared.

Chimera paced back and forth, exploring all the possibilities of what she had just witnessed. No one since the Anemoi had been in or out of this place. There has never been a report of the doors opening before. She thought of the snakes on the other side. They were uniformed. "Those were guards," she said. She roared again. "Why would creatures of the gods need guards?"

She thought about the girl. Who was she? Where had the large snake taken her? Arguris was a large place, but she knew it well and would spend months if she needed to, tracking the girl down.

"Has it been so long that you don't remember her face," her tail crept forward, hovering her snake head above her.

"Whose face, Paphene?" Chimera asked.

"Nova, think. You know that girl." Paphene said. They used names only they knew among themselves. To everyone else, they were simply Chimera.

Nova tried to remember what the girl in the doorway looked like. Most of her features were hidden under her clothes and hat, but as she thought about the girl standing in the doorway, Chimera began to realize who Paphene meant. It was possible. But after all this time, it was unlikely.

"That's no goddess," Chimera roared, "she was a frail human, you saw her fall."

"Head to Cyrene," Paphene hissed.

"Yes," she agreed, "We'll visit the dark woods as well, see what we can find out." She sprinted off, wondering if it could be true. If it was, there were many questions to be answered, and one thing for sure to be done. Chimera's face hardened and she roared again at the night. Freedom might be within these walls at last.

—

Samantha opened her eyes to see a warmly lit room. She was laying on a bed of fur, covered with a large hand woven blanket. Her boots had been removed, and her hair had been let down. She quickly checked under the blanket that nothing else had been removed. Sure that nothing had, she sat up and examined the room. The bed was large and stood a bit higher than her own. Her feet didn't touch the floor when she sat on the edge. The walls were made of clay and decorated with dried flowers and vines. There was little furniture, aside from the bed and a beautiful wooden table with carvings unlike anything Samantha had seen. There was a wooden cup filled with water sitting on it. She picked it up to drink, but when the odor filled her nose, she changed her mind and put it back down. On the other side of the room the wall was adorned with hooks that looked like they may have been made from ivory, and garments hung from each of them. Her boots sat on the floor below them. The floor was dirt, with no coverings. She spun around checking for bugs crawling across, but only found smooth surface. Above her hung a glass plate with dried wax hanging over the edges. Several wicks were lit, giving the room its warm glow.

Samantha grabbed her boots and began lacing them. As she did, she tried to recall all the events up to now. The party, climbing out the window, the escort, the candles and the snakes, and that dark figure. She froze as she remembered the creature she had seen on the other side of the doors. It was only a shadow, but it had come straight at her. She examined herself once more, and saw there wasn't even a rip on her clothing, so the creature hadn't touched her. Where had it gone then? She thought of her family out looking for her and what if that creature managed to roam into Chraimyth. She considered returning home to warn them. It was the last thing she wanted to do and there were many other directions the animal could have gone. Still, she didn't want to run off knowing she had left them in danger. They would need to know about a creature in the woods. Of course, she told herself, it could have just been a wolf or coyote, something that belonged in the woods and therefore nothing to be concerned about. She remembered the sound it made, the loud roar as it leapt. "That was not the sound a wild dog makes," she mumbled to herself.

Samantha had just finished lacing her boots when the door opened. She looked at the tall, bulky figure walking in and gasped. A woman stared back at her, her face filled with confusion. Her skin was green and smooth from head to toe aside from scars visible on her muscular arms and her brown eyes were deep, curious, intimidating. She had no hair on her head and she wore a simple brown smock held up with a thin rope that was tied under her breasts. Another rope hung loosely from her waste with a large satchel at her side. Her feet were large and bare.

Samantha's mind raced through everything she had learned from her uncle. Of all the places and people she had read about in the books he gave her, the woman in front of her didn't match any of them. But there were other creatures and monsters she had read stories about, too. The stories that weren't meant to be real. Just tales to amuse the mind and pass the time. Yet one of them was standing right in front of her. An ogre was an odd assumption to make so quickly from the looks of the creature that stood in front of her. If she were an ogre then that meant Samantha was her next meal. Whatever she was, it didn't matter. As soon as she could get out of wherever she was, Samantha would return to the road and keep moving forward.

The ogre rubbed a hand over her bare head and closed her mouth that had been gaped open. Samantha hadn't realized her own jaw had dropped open until she closed her mouth, her lips smacking together. She stood, unsure what to do. The ogre took a quick look around the room, grabbed the cup from the table and frowned, then said, "Are you hungry? There's food waiting." Her voice was deep and rumbled, but it was kind and inviting. Samantha nodded and followed her hostess. She wondered if she was dreaming. She didn't remember drinking anything at the rehearsal party. She didn't have time to drink. She was too busy climbing out the window instead. What was happening? Where was she?

The rest of the house looked much the same as the bedroom. Candles hung from the ceilings on glass plates, dirt floors, and the walls only decorated with useful items and vines that looked like they were growing right out of the wall. The ogre led her into a room with a large table and three large chairs. She paused beside the table and stood quietly, not sure what to say. Sylvia had never taught her the proper etiquette of waking up in the home of a story book character.

The creature pulled out a chair and motioned for her to sit down. Samantha sat and listened for sounds of anyone else living there. It was quiet. She watched the ogre move about and noticed the smells filling the room. They reminded her of holiday feasts when her mother would help the cooks and make the turkey herself. Her stomach began to rumble and she watched eagerly, hoping to be brought a plate full of turkey and potatoes with carrots and other vegetables.

The ogre walked over with two large plates and placed one in front of Samantha, then dropped into the next chair. She let out a heavy sigh as she picked up a large wooden fork of sorts and began poking at her plate. Samantha expected to hear loud obnoxious chewing, but she ate quietly. She looked at her plate. The roast and vegetables looked appetizing, but there was something lumpy and gray she wasn't sure of. She picked at the food with her fingers since the fork was too large and watched the ogre. She followed the creature and dipped her meat into the gray stuff and ate. She gagged at first, until the taste filled her mouth and she could forget the texture. She had never tasted a gravy like it, but enjoyed it and continued eating.

"The name's Phoebe." the creature said.

Samantha looked up to see Phoebe staring at her.

"Samantha."

"Don't they teach you how to act right where you're from. Someone puts a plate of food in front of you, you're supposed to say thanks," she was frowning, but continued eating.

Samantha was suddenly embarrassed. "I'm sorry, thank you so much for the meal. It's delicious and I'm very grateful," she stretched her arm across the table and Phoebe jumped, as if she were a snake trying to bite her. She pulled her hand back and apologized again.

"Where are you from anyway? You should think about heading home soon." Phoebe said as she stood up and cleared their plates. Samantha was about to protest so she could eat more, but she chose to answer her questions instead.

"I'm from Chraimyth, and I'm not sure how I got here. I'm rather confused about all of it actually, and I'm wondering the same about you," she paused then added, "and that creature I saw before. What was that? I need to make sure my family is safe. They might run into it."

Phoebe sat back down at the table, looking confused. "I've never heard of any Chraimyth, and what creature are you talking about?" she tapped the table, looking a little impatient.

"I'm not sure, it was dark and I only heard it growl or roar or something, like a lion," Samantha waved her hands around as she spoke. She wished she could give more details about what she saw. No one that she knew of had ever heard of a lion roaming the woods around town. It seemed out of place.

Phoebe was quiet for a moment while she watched Samantha. "I think that was Chimera." She continued to tap her fingers on the table and Samantha thought maybe she was wearing out her welcome. She wanted to ask the ogre more questions but thought better of it, figuring maybe she had hit her head the night before when she climbed off the horse and she must still be dreaming. It seemed a good time to thank her host for her generosity and find her way back to the road.

"Well, Phoebe, I'm delighted to have met you, and thank you for your hospitality, you've been a wonderful hostess, and I hope one day I might be able to return the favor," she rambled as she looked around for the door, "but I should really be on my way now."

She got up and reached her hand out for Phoebe to shake. Phoebe just sat and stared at her. Then she took a finger and pushed Samantha's outstretched arm down and laughed.

"Deary, that isn't how things work around here."

Samantha felt her stomach in her throat and the panic build. *So this is a nightmare*, she stiffened as she waited for the ogre to explain.

48

Phoebe continued, "They don't just let anyone walk in here, and they definitely don't let anyone out. You say you're from some place called Chraimyth. I know every place around here and I've never heard of Chraimyth," she said the name of the town mockingly and Samantha gave her a dirty look. The ogre went on, "So I'm thinking you're either a little scattered in the head, or you're from outside these walls, which doesn't happen." She smirked at Samantha, teasing her. "And you don't have to worry about Chimera, I doubt she went anywhere."

"What do you mean?" Samantha asked, "Who's *they*?" Phoebe studied her for a moment, then leaned back in her chair and folded her arms.

She said, "I think we better find Kuma."

Samantha needed to know more about where she was, and especially about the strange creatures she was running into; large anacondas, whatever a chimera was, and the impatient ogre in front of her.

Samantha sat back down and they both watched each other in silence. The ogre tapped her finger slowly now and Samantha wished she would stop. As she watched the green woman, she tried to remember all the facts she could about ogres. Still not sure, she asked, "You're an ogre, aren't you?"

"That's right," the ogre pulled a dagger from a box on the floor next to her, then pulled a rag from her apron and began to wipe the blade. "Is that an issue for you?"

Phoebe stared at her as she sharpened her blade and Samantha felt her hands begin to shake, "No, it's not. It's just that where I come from ogres are only heard of in stories. They're not real."

Phoebe put the dagger on the table and leaned back in her chair, studying Samantha, turning her head from side to side, trying to size her up. Then she got up and pushed in her chair. "Like I said, we need to see Kuma."

"What about Jesup," Samantha remembered the name her uncle had given her. "Do you know where I can find him?"

Phoebe raised an eyebrow at her, "Let me pack and we'll head out."

Samantha wondered what she had to pack for, and she wished she had her atlases so she could figure out where she was.

5

"Couldn't we have taken a carriage?" Samantha hollered as drops of rain fell on her face. A leaf drifted down and stuck to her forehead and she pulled it away. She looked up at the trees but there were none. Just a clouded sky above her and the rain lightly falling over them. She wiped her face and stomped up the hilly road after the ogre.

"You won't find chariots here" Phoebe hollered back. She wore a brown knee length dress with a silver decorated breastplate that had dents and scratches on it. Rust covered some spots. The belt around her skirt clanked with long metal strips. Her feet and calves were covered in long boots made of leather and fur and tied with leather straps. Samantha was quite impressed, compared to the rag she first saw her in. A long scabbard swung at her side and she held the handle of a long sword as she walked. She hoped later on the ogre would let her look at it, if she hadn't decided to eat her by then. Samantha still wore the same dress, and every layer was now soaked through. She wished she had her bag of clothes she had left with the horse. They had been walking for a few days already and every time she demanded answers about where they were and where they were going, Phoebe always answered the same. "We're going to see Kuma."

Samantha had tried to turn back once, and the ogre let her. She had gotten as far as the ogre's house and then realized she didn't know where to go from there. She walked back alone, thirsty and hot. It had taken a few hours round trip and she didn't know how much further they had to go.

The ogre sat in the grass waiting for her. She had said nothing, just handed Samantha a canteen, then they went on their way.

The road looked unfamiliar and she hadn't caught any glimpse of the large door. She assumed since the ogre hadn't eaten her yet that she owed her a certain level of trust. But she thought it was odd they would be walking for so long. She tried to remember what her uncle had told her about the next town, but she couldn't remember how far away it was. It could have been a week's worth of travel, she had no idea. If so, then it made sense, especially since they were on foot. She wished her driver would pull beside her and tell them to get in. But her driver had no idea where she was. He was probably carrying her parents around town right now looking for her. Certainly her escort had returned and would lead them to the place he last saw her. They would probably be on their way to find Jesup. But Jesup wouldn't be able to help them.

She had asked Phoebe to take her to the police station, but Phoebe only gave her a funny look. When she asked her to take her back to the place she had found her, Phoebe only shared that she wasn't the one that had found her. That another creature had dropped her on her doorstep with no explanation.

The rain continued for hours and there was no sign in the sky above that it was stopping soon. Samantha looked around for shelter but there wasn't much to see in the scattered trees. Everything had looked the same since they left Phoebe's house. Phoebe lived very much alone. There were no neighbors and her house sat on a boulder that seemed out of place in forest of pine trees and elms. She had a small garden that she pulled vegetables from and put in a bag, and a cage of chickens she pulled eggs from. She had seen no one else, or any other town, not even a single building since. That made sense. Who would want to live near an ogre. Only her uncle came to mind.

When they came to a crossroad, Phoebe stepped off the path, waving for Samantha to follow her. They walked toward some low rocky hills and they could see an entrance to a cave between two pine trees. A cave. Is this were Kuma lived? Either way, Samantha was relieved and picked up her wet skirt, ready to hurry on. Phoebe stopped them both a few yards away.

"Wait here," Phoebe said, pointing to the tree as she pulled her sword from her side and crept inside the cave. Of course. She'd want to warn Kuma, hopefully telling her, or him, not to eat her. Samantha had become comfortable with the idea that Phoebe didn't see her as food and she forgot for a moment to consider the danger she was still in around another hungry ogre.

Samantha rolled her eyes and moaned in frustration. She hugged her arms and looked around. Pine trees were scattered down the hill side, and large boulders were piled over the cave. She looked around for mountains but didn't see any. She wondered where the boulders had come from.

There was a loud shriek from the cave, but through the rain Samantha couldn't tell if it had come from Phoebe, or Kuma. She slowly approached the cave, hoping to see the ogre walk out and not some other hungry creature. She wasn't ready to be on her own, let alone fight a vicious monster, and she figured Phoebe knew how to handle herself. Just as she touched the wall and leaned forward to peek her head in, Phoebe emerged with three dead deer. She could see it was a doe with her two babies. She looked at Phoebe, feeling mostly relieved but also confused.

"It's food, and we'll need it," Phoebe turned back to the cave and Samantha followed her inside. She couldn't disagree about food. They had eaten raw potatoes and carrots every day and Samantha couldn't stand the taste anymore. Phoebe had tried to get her to eat a raw egg but she couldn't bring herself to do it. It was hard enough trying to eat what Phoebe gave her while the ogre poured the slime right out of the shell into her mouth.

The cave was small, but warm and dry. It was clear from the emptiness that they hadn't reached Kuma's home yet. Samantha sat on the floor and watched as Phoebe examined the room.

"I think they're all dead." Samantha teased.

Phoebe snorted.

Samantha watched her gather things to use as kindling and pile them in the center of the cave. Then she grabbed a rock and held her sword to the ground. Sparks flew out as she stroked the stone along the face of the sword, giving the cave a brief glow. Samantha covered her mouth in case her breath should blow away any emerging flame. She was desperate for warmth. When the kindling was lit, Phoebe untied one of her boots and cut several inches off the leather straps. She wrapped them into tight balls and sat them beside the flame.

"How much farther do we have to go" Samantha asked as Phoebe pushed the straps into the flames. The fire grew and Phoebe turned her attention to the deer.

"We will be there tomorrow," Phoebe said.

Samantha pouted as she wrung her skirt. Then she asked, "What is this place exactly?"

Phoebe smiled, not looking away from her work. "Depends on who you ask. A retreat, a prison. Some call it sanctuary." She carried meat over and laid it by the fire then went on, "Those who were born here call it home."

That confused Samantha. "Where were you born?" Samantha asked.

"Not here." Phoebe replied.

"So, is this a secret home for ogres? Is Kuma the king ogre and I'm the sacrifice for some ritual?" Samantha felt ridiculous asking but she was trying to figure it all out. She knew she wasn't far from Chraimyth. At least she hadn't been a few days ago. No one there had ever mentioned a forbidden area of the woods where story creatures lived. Not even her uncle and she wasn't sure he'd be able to keep his mouth shut about a secret like that. Not from her.

Phoebe laughed as she used her dagger to cut strips of deer meat. Samantha had to look away. She focused on squeezing as much water out of her dress as she could.

"Yes, there are other ogres here but Kuma is not one of them. There are many species here and," she looked at Samantha and laughed, "if I worry you, you may want to brace yourself for what else roams within these walls."

"Walls? What walls?"

Phoebe just shrugged.

Samantha was disappointed none of her questions were being answered. She had no idea where she was. Only that she was several miles away from home, in some place that she supposedly couldn't leave of her own free will. Not too much unlike home. She thought about finding her own way out, but she wasn't stupid. She didn't want to accidentally stumble upon another ogre's house who *was* just like the story ogres. And she feared coming across that creature again, Chimera. Even in the dark it had scared her. She was sure it was attacking her and simply overshot its jump because it was too dark. Samantha had been lucky.

She thought about Celeste and hoped she wasn't in too much trouble with Sylvia and Marcus. They shouldn't be mad at her, she was being a good friend. She thought about her uncle and and knew he'd be there to comfort the sweet blonde. She wished she could have seen Sylvia's face when she finally got into that bedroom, and wondered if Edward was okay. She knew she had hurt them, but she couldn't think of any other way.

"I was supposed to get married a couple days ago. But I ran away from it all." Samantha shared as she gazed at the growing fire. When Phoebe didn't offer a reply she said, "Can you show me how you started the fire like that?"

"Why would you be so stupid?" The ogre asked as she pierced the meat with her sword and held it over the flames.

"To want to start a fire?" Samantha was a bit taken aback.

"No, to get married." Phoebe rotated the sword, as the meat cooked.

"Because that's what women do." Samantha said it more like a question and watched Phoebe curiously.

"Hmph," was her only response. Samantha smirked and considered she might like this ogre after all.

As the rain continued to pour outside, they ate deer meat inside the cave next to the warmth of the small fire. When she was done, Samantha laid on the floor, still wet and cold, resting her head on her arm. As she drifted off, she hoped once more, like the nights before, that when she woke this dream would be over.

The next morning Samantha woke up on the stone floor and Phoebe was cooking the deer meat and packing it away. She was disappointed as she stood and brushed off her damp skirt.

She was quiet as they returned to the road, continuing in the same direction, north, at least she thought it was north. Phoebe carried the bag over her shoulder and Samantha followed behind. Though she couldn't see the sun, it was light out, and she could take in her surroundings. Hills and trees covered the ground for miles around her. Oaks and pine trees. Though they weren't as thick as the trees that surrounded Chraimyth. She saw a creek in the distance running off to the east and thought she saw full baskets floating in it.

"What's that?" she pointed.

"No idea." Phoebe said.

Samantha rushed in front of Phoebe and blocked her path, "Do you ever explain anything? Please, tell me where I am. I had expected to wake up anywhere but here this morning, yet here I am, with an ogre, in the middle of nowhere looking for someone named Kuma," Samantha ranted and threw her arms around, then looked at Phoebe impatiently. "I see nothing familiar, you say I can't leave yet we're out in the open which is hardly a prison I think, I've seen creatures I've never even heard of before, and as nice as you are to help me and not eat me, you're not telling me anything. I'm not sure I can believe you're helping me at all."

She waited for Phoebe to explain, but the ogre just brushed her aside and kept walking.

"I told you, we need to find Kuma."

"Yes, Kuma. Who *is* Kuma?" Samantha stomped beside her, determined to get something out of her.

"Someone who can give you answers." Samantha stopped and let out a loud shriek. She noticed a smirk on Phoebe's face and realized she was having fun irritating her. Samantha shook her head, giving up, and continued to follow.

It was a few hours before they reached a small village. Samantha was aching to get out of her clothes and into something clean, dry, and presentable. She was furious with Phoebe for taking her who-knows-where. She was scolding herself for agreeing to follow the ogre instead of trying to find her own way back to the door. She decided whatever fate waited for her here she deserved.

As they walked through the village, Samantha was greeted by more strange creatures. She looked at them in astonishment, and most of them looked at her the same, especially at her clothes. She wondered what it was about how she was dressed that grabbed their attention. Most of them wore next to nothing, at most a robe, or just a strap across their chest with a dagger or sword. She recognized some of them as monsters from books. Satyrs, and more ogres walked passed them, darting to the sides of the street as if they were a large procession passing through. Some whispered while others just stood and stared. There were other creatures Samantha had never heard of, and winged creatures that looked like they were made from different animals put into one. They lay crouched on rooftops, staring at her with solemn expressions. Small fairy like things flew in a swarm and followed them awhile before scattering across the sky. She stayed close to Phoebe and followed her to a large hut.

Phoebe banged on a tall door and waited. They listened to heavy footsteps approaching, then a tall, dark figure opened the door. Samantha stared up at the towering giant. It stood even taller than Phoebe, examining them both. Samantha thought it must be at least ten feet high. It's head hunched over so it could see under the doorway. It portrayed all the same characteristics of a large bear, except its human hands, the size of her torso, with long claws. Instead of a large round belly of fur, it bore muscles. Its eyes were dark, and full of expression. There were scars along its snout.

"Why are you here?" its voice was deep, and rumbled like thunder. *So it's a boy,* Samantha thought as they followed him inside. The bear snorted as he led them in. Phoebe handed him the bag of meat and he threw it in a deep pot sitting on the floor next to the fireplace.

"Something's happened I think" Phoebe motioned to Samantha and dropped herself into a seat. The bear stood in front of Samantha, twice her size, and it hurt her neck to look up at him. They studied each other for a moment. Looking up

61

at the fantastic beast, she felt something stir inside. Not the fear that should be overwhelming her, but something else.

The bear said, "Well, let's hear it." He sat down in a large chair covered in blankets and Samantha almost laughed at the strange sight. *Bears in chairs. What would Celeste say?*

The ogre and the bear looked at Samantha, waiting for her tell her story. And she did. She ended with the large anacondas, and the creature she saw just before she fainted. They both sat expressionless, quiet, as she spoke. An occasional groan coming from the bear.

When she was done they stared at each other a moment, then Phoebe said, "What do you think?"

The bear looked to the ground, then at Samantha. It was hard to tell what he was thinking. She wasn't sure how she was supposed to read his expressions. He asked, "You came alone?"

She had already made it clear she had.

"I'm sorry, but I've been here several days already and I still don't know where I am. Can you please tell me?"

The bear looked at Phoebe who just shrugged her shoulders. He rolled his eyes at her and groaned.

"What's your name?" he asked.

"Samantha."

The bear studied her a moment, his eyes squinting as though he were trying to look through her.

"My name's Kuma," he finally said, standing up to shake her hand. The last thing she wanted to do was touch the monster. His large hand was stretched out to her. Samantha reluctantly pressed her hand against the palm of his. Her hand was too small for a proper shake. Aside from the large size, and the claws at the ends of his fingertips, his hands were like any other mans. He wrapped his large fingers around hers and shook gently. She looked him in the eye and when he stared back she found it weird that something about him seemed almost familiar, like they had met before.

He returned to his chair and motioned for her to sit down. She didn't want to sit on his clean blankets in her filthy dress, but she was too tired to stand anymore.

"You're in Arguris, and this is the city Cyrene," Kuma told her.

Samantha new all the local maps. Though she preferred to study maps of ancient worlds, she was familiar with the names of towns outside of Chraimyth, and Arguris was not one of them. Neither was Cyrene. Seeing her confusion, Kuma said, "Maybe you can tell us where we are."

She found that odd and looked at Kuma, thinking perhaps he was picking on her. But his expression remained fixed and she knew he was serious. Maybe it was a test.

"Um, you're south of Chraimyth, it's a small town in the northwest territories of Canada, at least from the doors I came through. We've been walking north for so long I don't know how we haven't come back to it yet." Samantha hoped they would have an explanation.

Kuma looked at Phoebe again, she shrugged again and looked at Samantha, waiting to hear more. Samantha, seeing they were wanting answers just the same as herself said, "This is my first time outside of Chraimyth. I've only lived there a few years. I don't really know what would be useful to tell you. It's just a small town."

"Where were you before that?" Phoebe asked, leaning forward like she was being told an intriguing story.

Samantha folded her hands over her chest and stared at the floor. She had always wondered that herself. She assumed that was why she always wanted to travel and explore.

"I don't know," she sat up straight and went on without hesitation, "I was found at the doorstep to an orphanage. When I woke up I had no memory. Just a toy." She put her hand over the pocket holding her golden trinket and the ogre's and bear's eyes went to it.

Just then a little boy peeked through the window next to Kuma. Little horns grew from his head and he looked at them mischievously. Kuma grabbed a soft object and threw it at the boy who giggled and ran away.

Samantha leaned toward Kuma and said, "I'm sorry, do you guys not know where you are? I mean, it looks like you've been here awhile."

Phoebe stood and began slowly pacing the room, running her hand over her head. Then she stopped and put her hands on her hips, looking at Samantha, "You're sure you don't remember anything before Chraimyth?"

Samantha shook her head, wondering why that would matter. The ogre paced a little more then fell back into her chair.

Kuma stared at the unlit fireplace then said, "Have you ever heard the story of the four winds?"

Phoebe looked at him, and Samantha noticed the sudden expression of sadness and anger in her eyes.

"No." Samantha said.

"Kuma, hold on. This human needs to get cleaned up. I'm not sure I can stand smelling her much longer." Phoebe jumped out of her chair and grabbed Samantha's arm, pulling her toward the door before the bear could say anything else. He just grunted and waved them away.

6

Phoebe took Samantha to another small house where a family of ogres lived. They seemed happy to see Phoebe, and let her rummage through garments while they took Samantha to a large tub behind the house and made her strip down and get in. She tugged at the dress before the ogre could take it away and pulled her golden trinket out and sat it on the ground beside the tub. They handed her a bottle of oil and a cloth and let her bathe. The water was too cold but Samantha didn't care. She wet her hair and poured a small drop of oil onto her hands and rubbed it over her hair. The ogres were washing her dress in a smaller tub not far away. An older ogre with thin gray hair that stuck to her face watched her, grumbling under her breath, then dropped the dress and stomped to the side of Samantha's tub. Samantha jumped when she opened her eyes and the large ogre was scowling at her. Samantha knew she shouldn't have let her guard down. This was how she was going to die. Naked and drenched in bath water. Ogres had horrible taste apparently. The ogre grabbed the oil out of Samantha's hands and poured the entire bottle over her head, taking her hair and rubbing the oil in, then grabbing her arms, spreading the oil out across her skin. Samantha tried pulling away, her breathing becoming heavy as she panicked.

"We're the same miss, we just got more of it," she laughed, misreading Samantha's body language, and looked over her shoulders to the other ogres as she said it and they laughed with her. When the ogre was satisfied that Samantha was fully lathered and clean, she held out a blanket and Samantha climbed out, letting the ogre wrap her in it. She grabbed her trinket and the ogre lead her inside.

"That's much better," Phoebe said as she sniffed the air when Samantha entered a small bedroom room, much like the one she had woken up in a week ago. The other ogres followed her, crowding the hallway in front of the door.   They whispered as they watched Phoebe show her different materials, and Samantha could see how surprised and curious they were. She wondered if they had ever seen a human before, or if there was just something odd about her. They were dressed in simple tunics tied with belts. Satchels hanging from the sides, and some with scabbards like Phoebe's. She was still having a hard time taking it all in, and despite their generosity, she was nervous being surrounded by so many ogres. As far as she knew, ogres were dangerous creatures, barbaric and unpredictable. But these creatures were civilized, no different than anyone living in Chraimyth. She thought Phoebe could be vexing, but she imagined if Celeste was behaving in the same manner she'd probably find it playful and not so irritating. They seemed to live the same way she did. Perhaps with less means, but they had homes with an order to things just as she did. And where were their men? If they were that much like Chraimyth, the men were away working and would be back soon.

She pointed to some pretty dark blue material and Phoebe helped her create a neck line and sleeves. She was impressed by her skill to turn a simple piece of fabric into a functional garment so quickly and with so little. They wrapped the material around her, cutting and tying knots, and one of the ogres gave them gray cords to tie around her waste to hold it all together. There were no mirrors for Samantha to see her reflection, but the crowd pushing each other to peer in the door seemed pleased, and she trusted she looked well enough. She knew her mother wouldn't approve, and that made her appreciate their expressions a bit more. One of the younger ogres brought her a pair of shoes that Samantha assumed must have been her own, the child looked happy to give them to her, so she smiled graciously and let Phoebe help her fit them to her feet. They were too wide.

Samantha was about to take them off and hand them back when the older ogre stepped forward and pulled a knife from her tunic. Samantha jumped and stumbled backwards. Phoebe caught her and looked at her, shaking her head. "Sorry," Samantha said feeling embarrassed. She stood up and let the creature approach.

The old ogre bent down to Samantha's feet and grabbed the edge of one shoe. Using the knife to pierce holes in it, she held out her hand, and without saying a word, one of the others handed her a handful of leather strips. She separated two long strands and wove one through the holes, and the remaining around her ankle before tying it. She did the same with the other shoe before standing up and smiling at Samantha gently, her eyes sparkling.

"Thank you, I really appreciate this," Samantha said. She appreciated them not eating her, too. The old creature nodded and smiled and stepped back as the younger ones pushed their way closer to Samantha. They gave her a bag with a few other items of clothing, including a shawl and blanket and a couple smaller bags. Samantha began to thank them and say goodbye, but one of the ogres asked them to wait. She dug into a chest and pulled out a beautiful golden leaf diadem and placed it on Samantha's forehead. She tried to resist, but the ogres insisted. She noticed Phoebe giving her a strange look, as though they hadn't met before. In fact, she looked downright shocked. Maybe even horrified.

"Thank you, we must leave now." Phoebe said quickly, throwing the extra bag over her shoulder and grabbing Samantha's arm. The ogres protested, asking them to stay, but Phoebe already had them to the street, walking back to Kuma's hut.

Phoebe pulled her along quickly, and Samantha wondered what had suddenly changed. Was the diadem hers?

"You can have the tiara if you want, I don't mind, really." Samantha puffed as she tried to keep up.

"I don't want it. It's yours." Phoebe replied. Samantha noticed a satyr staring at her, then holding his hand over his heart he bowed respectfully. She thought he was being polite, and she smiled back.

Phoebe barged through the door when they reached the bears house and dropped the bag next to the door. Kuma was filling bowls with a thick stew and they joined him at the table.

"You smell better," he said as he looked over Samantha's new attire. "Nice head piece."

Samantha said a quick thanks and waited for Phoebe to explain herself but she just quietly sat down and took a bowl Kuma handed her and began eating.

"Phoebe, what is wrong with you?" Samantha asked impatiently. She wasn't sure she had ever met anyone as frustrating as Phoebe.

Kuma handed her a bowl and they both sat down and began eating. Samantha watched Phoebe stare at her bowl and Kuma paid no attention to either one of them. They ate quickly and quietly.

Kuma left his empty bowl on the table when he finished and sat back in his chair by the fireplace. Phoebe did the same, giving Samantha an odd glance as she pushed her chair into the table. Samantha huffed and followed her.

Kuma began to tell Samantha about the four winds. Phoebe watched her with the strange look on her face and Samantha decided to ignore her and listen to Kuma.

"The doors you came through haven't opened for anyone. Ever. Since their existence. As far as we know. They were believed to be a gate to the outside world for a long time. But then we weren't sure," he began. "There are creatures that have lived here for centuries, and others that were born here and don't understand the difference between outside the village and the outside world. To them it's all the same. He paused, and there was something sad in his face. "But some of us remember living much different lives." He stared at her in a way that felt familiar again and she squirmed in her seat. "We're all creatures of the gods," he continued. "Their *pets*. But they didn't like our strength and knowing things we weren't supposed to know, so they wanted us destroyed." He spoke as if she understood everything he meant, but Samantha was more confused and tried to listen without interrupting with questions.

"We didn't know what was coming for us. We were all existing as men did when the wind came. We didn't harm anyone who didn't attack us first. None of us acted outside our instincts that were carefully chosen by our creators." Kuma gripped the arm of his chair and Phoebe moved uncomfortably in hers. "For days the Anemoi blew in every direction, coming and going. They took us from our homes without warning. We had no time to prepare or to fight for ourselves. Others who felt threatened by men threw themselves into the wind when it passed. Some were left behind. They dumped us here, within these walls, hiding us away from the rest of the world. And now, over a thousand years later," he sat at the edge of his seat and fixed his expression on Samantha, "here *you* are. Something needs explaining, and I don't think we're the ones needing to do it."

Kuma stared at Samantha and she suddenly felt afraid. She didn't understand his story, or what happened to them. She thought of a dream she used to have, how familiar it all sounded.

In her dream there was a bear reaching to her in the wind tunnel. She looked at Kuma. *How can that be*, she thought. Kuma looked at her impatiently but Samantha had no answers for him, for any of them. She knew nothing about this place or why she was here. She was just a fool who could instead be wearing her beautiful clothes, sitting on a large stone porch sipping tea while her husband built their fortune. But she was here, within strange walls getting stared down by a hairy man-bear.

She looked at the aggravated beast and said, "Tell me about the walls."

He leaned back and Samantha relaxed.

"The walls are made of branches created by the gods," he explained. "Many have tried breaking them down or climbing over them and under them, but the gods are set on keeping us here. They go for days, we believe in a perfect circumference, nearly two months of travel."

Samantha was surprised. She had never heard of this place, and it was right there all along. How could a place so big be hidden from the outside world? That was impossible. "How can that be?" she asked.

"The gods. It's their doing." Kuma grumbled and shrugged.

"Where is the sun?" Samantha pressed.

"Some of the winged creatures have gone as far as they can. Those who can go beyond the clouds say the walls meet high above at a center." Phoebe said.

Samantha thought of the leaf that fell on her when there were no trees around. It made sense now.

"What gods do you mean?" Samantha finally asked. Phoebe stared at her as if she were asking a question she already knew the answer to.

"The goddess Athena brought us here," she explained, and when she said Athena, the way she stared at Samantha, it gave her chills. "The Anemoi told us she had given them instructions for our safety. It was all the explanation we've ever been given. We thought they might bring all of Greece when they kept returning for several days, but then they just stopped."

"Athena. The gods," Samantha said out loud, trying to figure it all out. She thought about books she had read then asked, "Are you talking about Greek mythology. You're all creations of the Greek gods?"

Kuma huffed at the idea of mythology, "We're no myth."

Phoebe had a grin on her face that slowly grew as she looked at Samantha. She stood up from her seat and slowly approached her. She pressed against the back of her chair, unsure what Phoebe was doing, and wishing the large creature would quit looking at her like that. Had she suddenly decided to eat her? Phoebe stood at Samantha's feet and looked down at her. She grinned and panted and Samantha could see something had excited her, but she wasn't saying anything and it was making her feel very uneasy. She squirmed in her chair again, looking for a possible escape if she needed to run. Perhaps she could jump out the window the small boy had peeked through earlier. If she was able to make it that far.

"Phoebe, what is it?" Samantha cried out. Phoebe suddenly fell to her knees, tears ran down one cheek and she cupped her hands to her heart. She laughed, then quietly wept and reached for Samantha's feet. Samantha looked to Kuma for an explanation but the bear looked just as surprised as she was. She felt Phoebe's hands on her feet and she gently touched her shoulders and pushed her away. She suddenly wanted as much distance between her and the ogre as was possible.

"Phoebe, what are you doing?" Samantha asked again, hoping she wouldn't become the nights main course. She felt a little guilty for having such thoughts about a creature who had been so good to her, but she wasn't sure anyone else would feel any differently in her situation.

"Why did it take so long?" Phoebe sobbed.

"What?" Samantha looked to Kuma again, who was looking irritated now as he pushed himself out of his chair. He walked over to the ogre and pulled her from the ground, throwing her back in her seat. She landed with a thud, the chair scraping along the floor a few feet before stopping.

"That is enough of that." He growled at her. His voice shook the walls and Phoebe jumped, wiping her face and quieting herself.

"Kuma," Phoebe sniffled, "don't you see it?" She pointed to Samantha and Kuma looked. Then he looked back at Phoebe.

"I don't know what you're talking about," he thundered back. Phoebe gaped at him as she watched Kuma stomp out of the room. She stared at the floor and Samantha sat frozen, unsure what to do. Everything they told her was unbelievable. But sitting in a room with a talking bear and a story creature was just as unbelievable and yet there she was. She wanted to know more about this place, but she also needed to get out of this place.

Afraid to move, Samantha watched the shadows slowly creep across the floor until Kuma returned. He approached Phoebe, telling her, "I'm sorry. I don't mean to diminish your hope." He reached out his hand. She peered at it and reluctantly returned the gesture. They grabbed each others forearms and shook.

Kuma turned to Samantha and gave her a hard stare. "There might be other creatures here that are going to see you as something you're not. Do not let them. Letting them believe and leaving them to learn you can't save them will get you killed. There are enough broken spirits here and you are no goddess." His voice grew louder and angrier.

Samantha didn't understand his words or how to take them in. She felt as though her brain had suddenly stopped working. What was he talking about? Save who? Of course she wasn't a goddess, who would think that? It was clear she had to focus on getting outside the walls of this strange, and perhaps forbidden, place as soon as she was able.

Heavy footsteps trailed across the floor and out the door. It closed with a heavy bang and both Phoebe and Samantha jumped. They looked at each other, then at the door. Kuma was gone.

"I'm sorry," Phoebe said as she got up and started gathering their bags and her scabbard. "I don't know what I was thinking."

Samantha felt sorry for her. She understood what it was like to want something so bad, to feel it at your fingertips, and be told *no*. She wanted to comfort Phoebe.

"It's okay, Phoebe. I don't want to cause any trouble. Maybe I should go my own way, find my own way out." she offered.

Phoebe straightened herself with all the bags draped over her shoulders and stared at Samantha. A weak smile displayed on her face for a moment before she walked out of the hut.

She called over her shoulder, "I told you, that's not how things work here."

It was dark now, torches were lit and few creatures were out. Samantha considered her options. Realizing how few those were, she grabbed her things and followed Phoebe.

"Where are we going?" she asked.

"To the lodge."

They walked down a few different streets before coming to a two story building with a sign hanging over the door. There were no words, just a strange symbol.

Samantha followed Phoebe inside and she immediately spotted Kuma sitting at a table with a large cup of ale. He was probably the first creature anyone noticed when they walked in. He towered over the other creatures, even sitting down. He looked at Samantha but didn't get up. Phoebe asked for a room and they were led up the stairs. Samantha looked down at the eating area below as she followed. Besides Kuma, there were three satyrs laughing loudly together in a corner, knocking their cups around, splashing their drinks on each other. A large bird-like creature lay in a pile of hay in a corner close to a large fireplace, pulling apart a carcass with her beak and dropping the pieces into the mouths of two small identical creatures peeking out from under her. That explained the funny smell. Their squawking was just as loud as the satyrs laughing. She heard something rustling above her and looked up. On a high crossbeam a large white owl popped berries into his mouth with his large talons. His large blue eyes stared at her, each blinking one at a time. He was beautiful with white feathers that had just a touch of gray on the tips. She turned to make sure she wasn't going to walk into Phoebe's backside, then looked back to the owl. His head poked forward, his eyes frozen wide open. He slowly reached out one of his talons, stretching out his beautiful wings, displaying his snow white feathers. She stopped and watched him. He never blinked as he stretched gracefully on the beam. Samantha hoped he might take flight so she could watch him fly away. In one swift movement his talon stabbed another berry and tossed it in his mouth as he folded in his feathers and let out a long hoot. An odd red creature below threw bread at him and the owl looked down and squawked.

Samantha laughed then finished up the staircase after Phoebe. They entered the room and Phoebe dropped the bags in the corner. Turning back to the door she mumbled, "I need a drink."

"I could use one, too, if it's okay." She realized she had spoken too quickly. She forgot the money her uncle had given her was somewhere in her bag of clothes.

"Come on," Phoebe said as she exited the room.

The owl continued watching from the beam, and Samantha noticed the group of satyrs had quickly left. The bird creature still fed her babies, and Kuma sat at his table, staring into his cup. He looked up when he heard their footsteps on the stairs. Samantha thought she saw Phoebe blush, though it was hard to tell through her green complexion.

Phoebe pointed at the table and Samantha sat down next to Kuma while she got two large cups and a pitcher full of ale. No one spoke, they only stole glances at each other as they drank.

Kuma finally broke the silence and asked, "What are you doing in this part of Arguris?"

Samantha looked up from her drink and saw him studying her.

"What do you mean," she asked, "Was I supposed to stumble upon a different door in the dark?"

Kuma looked at her quietly.

"Humans don't often travel outside the big city," he said, "Many creatures here have never seen the city, or a human." She assumed he was referring to Chraimyth. It was beginning to make sense the strange way she was looked at on the street. She hoped it wouldn't cause any problem. But she was glad to here him talk about a big city. Maybe it wasn't Chraimyth, maybe it was where she was supposed to find Jesup.

"I assure you, it's nothing to fear," he said softly.

"I'm not afraid, I'm lost and I need to get back to where I was." she took a sip of her drink and her face crinkled like she had tasted a sour lemon. She had an idea and hoped Kuma and Phoebe would be willing to help her. "What if we return to the doors, together? Maybe they'll open again. If they opened for me once, why wouldn't they do it a second time?" She watched Kuma and Phoebe give each other a long stare, like they knew something she didn't.

Then they looked at her and both nodded in agreement.

7

Samantha walked alongside Phoebe and Kuma, thinking about what Kuma had said about Arguris, and wondering if she should tell them about her dreams. After Kuma's reaction to Phoebe, Samantha decided it was best to keep it to herself. She wasn't sure what use the information would be anyway. It certainly wouldn't help open a door. Still, she couldn't stop thinking about the dream and the similarities to the story Kuma had told her.

In her dream she was in ancient Greece, standing in the middle of the Parthenon with a little wooden ship in her hands. Children, women, and men all dressed in simple white garments, were gathered around her as she showed them how each part would work. They looked on in amazement, as though they had never seen such a large boat. She pointed passed them and suddenly they were all standing on a beach, looking out over the sea. In the water was a large ship, a perfect replica of the wooden toy she had just held in her hands. The people shouted with joy and gathered around to hug her, the children all asking for a toy ship of their own. As if pulling them out of thin air, she handed each child their ship. Once they took it in their hands, they transformed into creatures Samantha had never seen before. They growled and roared and a strong wind blew around her until a tornado formed, lifting the creatures high over her head. Her fear of them turned to sympathy and she reached out to them. They fought against the wind tunnel and reached out to Samantha. The others who were nearby watching screamed and scattered, some disappearing into the waters of the sea, others burying themselves into the sand. Samantha reached as much as she could toward the creatures, the wind howling in her ears as she stood in the center. A large hand brushed her fingers and she stared into the face of a large bear. He showed no fear, but fought against the current tearing around him and tried to grab her hand. Samantha yelled out and the tornado retreated into the sky, all the creatures disappearing with it. She stood on the beach alone, in the calm of the clear sky and cool winds blowing through her hair. She looked around for any signs of life, human or creature, but she saw no one. She heard shuffling in the sand behind her and spun around. Her jaw dropped as she stood face to face with her reflection. Though this woman looked like a goddess in her flowing gown and golden jewels. She held a long golden spear and a shield. Her long flowing hair was decorated with a beautiful golden crown. "Who are you?" she spoke, and as she did so, her reflection spoke too, in unison. The woman looking at her seemed unphased, but Samantha was confused.

The woman said, "I am you." And Samantha felt her lips move and her voice speak at the same time.

She put her hand to her throat in fear and noticed the garment flowing from her arm. She looked down and saw herself wearing the same flowing gown as the other woman.

"How can this be?" they said together. The woman suddenly became afraid and pointed passed Samantha. She spun around to see what was behind her. Samantha would always wake up afraid.

She pushed the thought aside and adjusted the cord wrapped around her waist. She was thankful for the change of clothes. Her old dress was too hot and she couldn't breathe in it. She hadn't even asked about it when they left Cyrene. In her new dress she could breath freely and she kept cool. She had found a small pair of pants patched together among the other clothes they had packed for her and she put them on. The entire outfit was far from fashionable but it was liberating to walk so freely. She let her hair blow in the soft breeze and enjoyed not having pins poking at hear head and pulling her hair at the roots. She felt free.

She looked at her companions, covered in bags and weapons. They hadn't complained but it didn't seem right to be a part of the group and not share in the work. Samantha reached out to Phoebe and asked if she could carry a bag for her. The ogre gave her a funny look but took one of the smaller sacks off her shoulder and tossed it to her.

Samantha smiled and looked at Kuma as she hung it on her shoulder. He was looking off into the trees and brush, focused on something Samantha couldn't see. They continued to walk, but they slowed as Kuma sniffed at the air. They were a few days into their journey and Samantha remembered the area. It had been raining before, but the grassy fields and scattered trees told her they weren't far from Phoebe's home. No one else seemed to live out here. Samantha guessed he may be hunting since they were running low on deer meat. He kept looking behind him and to both sides of the road, as if something were approaching. Sensing the trouble, Phoebe began to do the same. They both stood guard as Kuma listened, and Samantha watched them and tried to listen as well. She only heard birds chirping and the grass swaying, nothing that seemed abnormal to her. Still, she could tell they sensed something that wasn't obvious to her.

"Why don't we hide, instead of standing out here like sheep?" Samantha said quietly. She headed to the brush and Phoebe began to follow. Kuma let out a loud growl, dropping his bag and the large halberd he had brought with him and sprinted into the brush on the other side of the road. Samantha saw a figure emerge from the tall grass and try to run away but it was not quick enough. Kuma threw himself on the skulker. There was hollering and complaining, then a painful scream as Kuma dragged it behind him back to the road. He threw the creature in front of them as he stepped out of the brush.

At was a satyr. His back was covered in scratches from being dragged, and he had sticks and leaves stuck in his dirty brown hair and beard. He groaned in pain.

"Why have you been following us?" Kuma demanded, hovering over him. The satyr was afraid and Samantha stared at his shaking legs. She remembered seeing other satyrs in Cyrene, but she hadn't been able to examine any so closely. His hooves were covered in dirt and the fur that went all the way up to his waist was matted and dusty. A small tail pressed against his back end, twitching. He had strong muscular arms, and Samantha tried to look at his face, but his back was to her.

She walked around to stand by Kuma and get a better look. Phoebe stayed close beside her, like a bodyguard.

"I wanted to see the goddess." his voice trembled, and Samantha thought there was something familiar about it. She wasn't sure how that could be since she had never met a satyr before. He was here to see the goddess. He had been wasting his time.

Kuma growled and glared at Samantha a moment, then picked up his bag and weapon and walked on.

His glare made her uncomfortable and she didn't like feeling guilty for something she didn't do. Why was he mad at her? She wanted to see more of the satyr, but Phoebe motioned for her to follow and she obeyed, leaving the satyr behind. They caught up with Kuma and Samantha looked back to see the satyr had gotten up and was still following them. He was too far away to see his face clearly.

He didn't have anything with him. Unlike the bear and ogre who were prepared with food and weapons and blankets, the satyr walked empty handed. Samantha felt sorry for him. She turned around and slowly walked up to the satyr. She knew if he attacked her that the bear and ogre would be there to defend her. The satyr stood frozen, looking like an animal left out in the cold. He lowered his head and stared at the ground as Samantha came up to him. She dared to touch him and lifted his chin so she could see his face. Dark green twinkling eyes stared at her. There was something familiar about them, but she couldn't figure out what it was.

"Are you hungry?"

He nodded and Samantha looked at Phoebe. Phoebe groaned and walked over, grabbing a chunk of meat from her bag and tossing it to him. He ate quickly, his head lowered, and every time Samantha moved to see his face better he would turn away.

"Your grace, please, I only want to serve you." the satyr said when he had finished. He cleaned his hands on his fur and grabbed her hand and knelt in front of her. He looked frightened and she wondered what else, other than Kuma, scared him.

Kuma groaned and marched over, standing between them, towering over the satyr with his weapon held in front of him.

"I don't think I require a knight in shining armor right now," Samantha said as she stepped in front of him and motioned for the satyr to stand up.

"What's your name?" she asked him.

"Nnnii...um," he stammered, "it's Pan."

"Pan, I'm Samantha. I think I'm beginning to understand this thing about the goddess, and apparently that I look like her. But I'm not her. I'm just Samantha. Nothing special, I assure you," she watched the expression on his face drain away. "I'm sorry, Pan."

"Your grace, I'm sorry but I have to insist on offering you my service." he looked at Kuma, then reluctantly back to Samantha. "I *know* you're the goddess Athena," his certainty disturbed her, "And if I have to hide in the grass to follow you everywhere you go, then I will. But either way, I'm coming with you."

He bowed, just like the satyr in Cyrene, and Samantha blushed. She was used to being greeted formally by gentlemen, but being bowed to as though she were royalty made her feel ridiculous.

Phoebe pulled the bags from her shoulder and dropped them at Pan's hooves.

"If you're coming, you're carrying."

She walked away, rubbing her shoulder.

Kuma glared at Phoebe as they continued down the trail. Samantha grabbed the satyrs arms as he picked up the pile of bags. "For your own good and mine, don't call me 'goddess'. Believe what you want, but I'm just an ordinary girl. Not a goddess, not a savior. I have nothing to do with this place, I'm just Samantha and I'm going home."

"Your grace, you are beautiful." Pan walked towards the others, his hooves pounding softly on the road. Samantha watched him. Something was so familiar about his face. She felt like she had known him for a long time. She didn't like that feeling, like she knew these monsters. She had read a lot of books that mentioned beasts like them, except Kuma. Maybe it made more sense than she thought.

"Samantha!" Phoebe called. Samantha gave the Satyr one more glance then ran to join the ogre and bear.

It was two days more journey to the doors, and Samantha tried to pay more attention to the scenery around her. She wanted to be sure she could bring her uncle back here. She tried to imagine the look on his face when he realized she had already made a discovery and she hadn't even reached the next town. It was still hard to grasp that they were trapped here. There were no walls surrounding them from any point she could see. Instead there were tall pines and beautiful elm trees and low mountains. The only evidence that something was different here, aside from the residents, was the hidden sun. Instead the sky was always covered in a soft haze that the daylight crept through, and at night it became pitch black. There was no moon or stars to guide their way. It was impossible to travel by night so they always made a camp just off the road before it got dark. Most days they only traveled a few hours, giving themselves time to hunt if they needed.

The air was fresh and smelled like pine and lavender. It was a beautiful place, and it was quiet. Nobody seemed to live between Cyrene and Phoebe's home. At least not near the road. They never passed other travelers.

Sometimes the road became steep and Kuma or Phoebe would give her their hand when she slipped on her sandals. She had asked them again about a carriage but they looked at her funny. They gave her funny looks to almost all of her questions, and Pan hardly lifted his head when he spoke to her. She wondered if he had done something to Athena that he was ashamed of. Kuma had made it clear they wouldn't discuss Athena, especially anyone referring to Samantha as the goddess. Most of their journey was in silence, with Samantha asking questions about Arguris with little to no answers in return. It was as fantastic as it was frustrating traveling with her three odd companions.

Each night Pan pulled out a flute and played for them as they ate by the fire. They were beautiful tunes, and Samantha liked how they seemed to put Kuma at ease the most, though he did his best to pretend he didn't care.

On the last night, they sat around a fire eating the last bit of deer meat. Samantha filled Pan in on how she came to Arguris and why they were headed to the doors. He didn't seem surprised by her story. In fact, he gave no reaction to it at all.

"It's been a long time since I've been to Speranta," he said.

"Speranta?" Samantha hadn't heard that name before.

Pan looked at the others. They continued eating.

"The doors. It's what we call them," he explained.

"What does it mean?"

"Well, it used to mean hope," he threw a bone into the grass behind him. "But now it mostly just means *Aha, jokes on you!*" He huffed as he wiped his hands on blades of grass between his hooves. "Who puts a huge door out in the open that no one can use?"

"We'll see what tomorrow brings," Kuma said deeply and quietly.

They reached Speranta the following day and Samantha looked for any sign of the anacondas or Chimera, though she wasn't sure she'd recognize the creature since she had only seen it in the dark. They were all gone.

She remembered the snakes slithering off behind her before she saw Chimera leap at her and wondered if they were far away. Speranta stood taller than she remembered. But it had been dark, and now, with the daylight pouring through the trees, she could see just how majestic the entrance really was. The two dark oak doors stood several feet high, at least twice as high as Kuma, and they were wide enough to fit the school house she thought. White ivy covered the walls around them and Samantha was sure she had never seen a vine so beautiful. The ground had been flattened where the doors had opened before, and a few small trees leaned away with their roots partially sticking out of the ground. Pan ran over to them and began pulling them up straight and burying the roots. He spoke to them as if they were children coming home with scraped knees.

"What is he doing," Phoebe asked Kuma. She looked at the satyr irritably.

"Leave him. It's keeping him busy and out of our hair," Kuma watched as Pan pressed the dirt around a small tree whose branches were almost bare.

Samantha continued studying the doors, looking for any symbols she had seen after the snakes had vanished into them. The surface was perfectly smooth, no door knob or knocker, just like the other side.

"What now?" Phoebe stared up at the wall that climbed as far as their eyes could see.

Kuma looked at Samantha and she realized they were waiting for her to answer.

"I don't know. I was on the other side and there were snakes. They did something and the door opened." She was embarrassed by her own uncertainty but she didn't have any answers. She stared up at the wall in astonishment. "Wow, you weren't kidding. And this stretches around the entire place?" As far as she could see, branches, entangled together, formed a wall in any direction. It went up for miles, disappearing in the distance; and it was hard to tell through the brush how far it stretched around them.

"Yes it does," Pan said walking up behind them.

"What snakes? What did they do?" Phoebe demanded.

"I don't know. I mean, I'm not sure. They were on the door, they snaked around, then they were gone and the door opened." Samantha motioned with her hands as she spoke, then she threw them up in defeat. "I did nothing but stand there."

They looked at her as though they were waiting for more. She wished they would leave her alone. She couldn't see anything here that might help. There were no statues on this side. Nothing to come to life. She just wanted the doors to open so she could leave.

Just then there was a slow, soft crunching sound and they all looked in its direction. A dark figure stayed low in the tall grass it crept toward them. Kuma stepped in front of Samantha, guarding her, and Phoebe stood next to him. Pan stood between them and whatever was approaching and slowly walked back until he was standing next to Kuma. Kuma shoved him back next to Samantha. The satyr looked frustrated but stayed in place.

A large black lion with a beautiful full mane emerged, blue eyes glaring at them, moving from one to the next. She paused when she saw Samantha. Her tail lingered over her head and Samantha noticed it was covered in scales, and the tip had bright yellow eyes with a tongue flicking about. It peered at Samantha, and she felt as though it were looking deep into her soul. She gasped as she watched the snake sway over the lions head. The creature's hind legs didn't match her front, but instead looked more like Pan's goat legs. Her back was bare, no coat of fur covered it, but a wide stump sat just behind her shoulder blades, the skin scarred and wrinkled.

Chimera.

Samantha remembered the large animal from the night she had arrived. This was the creature she saw staring at her, that had caused her to faint. It looked even more intimidating up close in the light.

Kuma held out his halberd and Chimera smirked.

"Do I threaten you, bear?" She asked slyly. Her voice was raspy and aged. She kept her head low as she stared at them, moving slowly.

"What do you want?"

"I want to see those doors open. I want to see what she can do.

  Just like you," she sneered.

Samantha looked at Pan, then squeezed passed Kuma and the ogre. If this creature was only curious about the door, a simple explanation should be enough for her.

"I didn't open the doors. I'm sorry I can't help you. It was the snakes. But they're not here." Samantha pointed to Speranta. The lion beast growled a low, rumbling growl and only then did Samantha realize how careless she was.

Kuma put his hand on Samantha's shoulder, ready to push her back, but she pulled away, stepping closer to Chimera. She wasn't sure where the courage was coming from, but something about the way the creature tried to intimidate her was getting under her skin.

"I don't know why I was let in, and I don't have any answers about these doors." Samantha told Chimera. "I never knew they existed until just a couple weeks ago," she had lost track of the days but guessed it was about right.

"But you're here now." It was clear Chimera didn't believe her.

Samantha lowered her head. She had a feeling she wouldn't be able to comfort this animal with words. Only actions would make her content. She would have to prove how useless she was. Samantha looked at the doors and studied them. She walked to them and felt the surface of the wood. They all watched her intently. When Chimera stepped toward Samantha, Phoebe stretched her sword out. The creature just glared at her and continued.

"Open it." Chimera commanded, standing just inches away from Samantha.

Samantha looked at her, unsure what to do. The lion creature was as tall as she, and there would be no time for her to run if she chose to attack. What was wrong with her. She was safer hiding behind Kuma. Instead she had foolishly put herself at the mercy of this strange talking lion. She could die at any moment. Over a door.

"I can't," she said.

The two stared at each other. Samantha could see the anger and desperation in Chimera's eyes. Like a wild animal caged for the circus. Samantha wondered what the beast would do if she didn't open the door for her. She had to think of something quickly, something that would put distance between them.

"As it is that the doors only opened for me, any inkling of killing me should be put out of that vexatious mind of yours," she said boldly. The others stared at her, surprised. Phoebe's jaw dropped open and Pan was smiling, while Kuma stood ready with his weapon should he need it if Samantha pressed the wrong buttons.

But then Chimera laughed and turned away.

"I won't kill you, yet," she scoffed. "I know who you are. I know why you're here."

She slinked behind Kuma and Phoebe as she spoke.

"We all know who you are, don't we," she snarled at Pan, who stumbled and fell over.

"A-a--a-athena." Pan stammered, staring at the large lion inches above his face. Kuma rolled his eyes as he turned slowly with his weapon, watching the beast circle them.

"That's right," Chimera said, "Athena, our captor and savior. How nice of you to finally pay us outsiders a visit." She was mocking her, but she didn't need to. She wasn't Athena. Samantha let her head thud against one of the doors. She understood their desperation for someone to come along and be their hero, but she wasn't it. The doors opening for her, and not this Athena, was just a coincidence. It didn't mean anything.

"You had no right to take us from our homes and I demand to be released. Open these doors, or you will pay with your life." Chimera opened her jaw wide as if she were going to sink her teeth into Samantha right there. Instead she let out a loud roar, lifting her head so she stood tall and proud.

Samantha covered her ears and turned her head away. She realized if she couldn't open the doors, she'd be stuck here with this creature. She didn't see any reason to feel confident that she'd be able to hide from her or that her companions would protect her for the rest of her life. What if she met other creatures that mistook her for Athena and made the same demands?

Samantha looked at Kuma. As if understanding, he went to her side. Chimera watched him, challenging him with a low rumbling growl.

"Stay back, Chimera," Kuma warned. "She is no goddess. She is a mere mortal. Weak in her flesh and nothing to Arguris."

"You lie," Chimera shouted and leapt into the air. Kuma raised his halberd and swung at her.

Her tail reached forward and wrapped itself around the handle, pulling it away from the lions head. Kuma didn't let go as the lion beast knocked him to the ground. He yanked his weapon until the snake unwound herself. Chimera bared her long fangs and wide jaws were ready to close on him. The bear rammed the handle into her head, causing her to fall back whimpering.

Phoebe ran forward with her sword raised, ready to bring it down on the lions head, but she drew back as the snake lashed forward, snapping at the air, ready to bite anything that came too close. The tail swung in all directions, biting at each of them, daring them to come closer as Chimera stood up and glared at them. Kuma and Phoebe circled around her while Pan held Samantha away.

"Chimera," Samantha called, but Kuma stopped her.

"Hush, woman." he said. Samantha was annoyed by that, but obeyed.

"Be on your way, Chimera. Life moves on for everyone today." Kuma grumbled at Chimera.

Chimera panted and looked between him and Samantha. Then she looked over her shoulder at Phoebe.

"Protect her for as long as you can. Hide her away. But she opens that door, or she's mine." Chimera threatened with one last glare at Samantha before leaping into the tall grass and running toward a dark forest that could be seen miles away. The four of them watched her go, then looked at each other. "She's going to kill me, isn't she," the words sounded foreign as she said them. It was a strange feeling to consider she might be killed by that beast and no one would ever find her. She could be left to rot somewhere in the forest.

"Chimera isn't a creature you provoke," Pan cautioned. He was shaking, staring off in the direction Chimera had disappeared. "She believes, as I do, that you are the goddess, Athena, who brought us here to save us."

He looked at the ground then continued, "But you never returned. You never came back to set us free. No one did. So there are some who harbor ill feelings towards you and all the gods, but especially you, since this place was your doing."

"But I'm not Athena!" Samantha insisted. Pan looked at her sadly, and Phoebe stared, her expression hard to read.

"You are," the ogre said gently. "You're different, and you act weak, but you're a god. And I will help you remember."

"She's not a god. Let her be," Kuma began gathering bags and throwing them over his shoulder. "She'll need to be trained either way. Learn how to defend herself. We'll return to Cyrene for supplies, then I'll take her east to train."

"Wait, what? But I don't want to stay here. I want to leave. We need to get these doors open or find another way,"

Samantha insisted as she pushed and pulled at the door anywhere she could get a grip on. The others stared, each one filling pity for her. They had all been through this before. They knew how this ended.

"Am I really stuck here," Samantha could the knot dropping from her heart to her stomach. She felt sick. "I left my home so I could be the person I want to be and I find myself here with everyone, once again, telling me who I am and what I need to do! I want to decide what to do with myself." She could barely hear herself talk. Her heart was racing and she could feel the panic grow.

She wrapped her arms around her stomach and stared at Kuma, trying to slow her heavy breathing.

Phoebe stabbed the ground with her sword and left it there. She stomped toward Samantha and scoured at her, squinting her eyes and said, "Welcome to Arguris."

Samantha was taken aback by the ogre's sarcasm, but she quickly understood the irony of what she had just said. But she wasn't Athena and they couldn't blame her for whatever sort of captivity they thought they were in.

"I'm sorry, I didn't mean to be insensitive," she said.

"You'll have plenty of time to decide what you want to do. You can be whoever you want to be while you learn to defend yourself." Kuma responded, heading back to the road.

"It might help you remember. Athena was a good fighter," Phoebe patted her shoulder, a grim expression still on her face, then pulled her sword from the dirt and followed the bear.

Samantha watched them go up the path, Pan following behind, glancing back at her every few steps.

She looked around, debating for a moment if she should go the other direction, look for another way out. She looked back at the trio getting farther away.

She considered for a moment, *I did want adventure.* But was this what she really signed up for? Then she thought of Chimera finding her alone in the woods with no means to defend herself and realized she needed these creatures.

Her eyes were wet and she wiped them dry then took in a deep breath. She called out, "Wait, I'm coming!"

8

"We go there." Phoebe pointed to the cave they had slept in before. The group followed her. There was nothing living inside this time, but a stench of blood hung in the air. They dropped their bags on the floor. Samantha spread her blanket out and sat down. She pulled her golden trinket from her bag and fidgeted with it as she watched the others. Kuma and Phoebe gathered their hunting weapons while Pan arranged their sleeping areas.

He had become some sort of servant along the way, not so much at anyone's insistence as it was his way of contributing something other than his flute. Samantha wondered how he knew where to find them. How long had he been waiting for Athena and how did he know where to look? What made him so confident about who she was? She didn't how he and the ogre had assumed this role for her just because she showed up. What if a man had stumbled through the doors? Who would they assume he was? She decided to push the thoughts away for now. She wanted answers, but she didn't want to encourage any of them into dwelling on things that simply weren't true.

Kuma left with Phoebe to hunt for their dinner and Samantha helped Pan gather sticks for firewood after the blankets were laid out. He still seemed nervous around her and didn't talk much.

Within the hour four small rabbits and a deer were hanging over their shoulders when the bear and ogre returned.

"Come." Phoebe motioned to Samantha, holding the rabbits in front of her. Kuma called for Pan. They all walked outside the cave and sat in the grass along the wall. It was still some time in the afternoon. Samantha had begun to learn how to tell the time of day by the temperature. Since there was no direct sunlight, the shadows never moved. But the temperature changed. The afternoons were always the warmest, and it began to cool down again in the evening. That was always when the light began to disappear.

Phoebe took a rabbit and showed Samantha where to cut along the fur, then she tugged at it until it was loose and pulled the skin off with one good yank. Samantha cringed at the sight of blood dripping down the rabbit's now fur-less body. Phoebe gave her a playful shove.

"You can't eat if you're afraid of the dead," she laughed. She threw a dead rabbit in Samantha's lap and held the knife out to her. "Go. You don't eat unless you prepare it."

Samantha stared at her, assuming she was joking. But the ogre grunted as she pushed the knife at her until she took it. She reluctantly picked the dead rabbit up by its feet as Phoebe had done and held it in front of her. She glanced at Kuma, but he was busy showing Pan how to do the same with the deer. At least she had the smaller animal. Samantha considered at some point in the adventures she had hoped to be on that she would learn this skill. She just never imagined the details, in particular the blood. It had a smell that made her stomach turn.

"Well, what are you waiting for?" Phoebe watched, waiting for her to do something. Samantha cringed as she held the knife to the rabbit. She pierced it and dragged it along the fur line, just as Phoebe had shown her. Then she grabbed the fur, ripping it off with ease. Phoebe nodded in approval. Samantha held the rabbit over the grass so the blood didn't drip on her dress. She was surprised she wasn't puking by now. Doing it herself kept her focused on the purpose, she needed to eat. She wondered what other skills they could teach her. Then she could leave them and work on finding her own way out of Arguris with at least a small fighting chance if Chimera found her.

"Now you stick it," Phoebe threw a stick at Samantha, her face full of amusement.

"You like laughing at people don't you?" Samantha teased as she watched Phoebe stick her own rabbit and place it over the fire.

"Is laughter a bad thing where you're from?" she asked, sounding concerned.

This time Samantha laughed. "No, but it might be considered poor manners to laugh at someone."

Phoebe thought for a minute then said, "But if it makes you laugh, you should laugh."

It was agreeable enough, but Samantha found herself wondering what Sylvia would say to that. She'd most likely throw her shoulders back and give Phoebe a dirty look. The look the Samantha had come to know meant *do not communicate with*. She was glad she wasn't here to do that to Phoebe. She kind of liked the ogre.

"Yes, you should," she smiled in agreement.

They prepared the rest of the rabbits while Kuma and Pan finished preparing the deer. When they were finished Pan darted away to find water to clean off the blood. He was not as easy a student as Samantha and he didn't enjoy piercing the animals flesh.

Samantha watched him run down the sloping hill towards a stream. She wondered what it felt like to run so fast and free, to stretch her legs and bound over the grass with such ease and grace.

Pan fell, but picked himself up quickly and looked around. He was too far away to notice Samantha watching. He pat down his fur then dashed away.

Samantha laughed at the sight and Phoebe looked in the direction she was staring.

"You're the one with bad manners now I see?" she nodded towards Pan then looked at Samantha, disappointed.

Samantha couldn't help laughing harder. It felt good. Even though she was in more danger than she had ever been in her life, in that moment she suddenly felt free.

Kuma sat quietly, as he always did. He seemed to never speak unless it was necessary. Samantha wanted to hear him laugh, though she wasn't sure he knew how.

Pan returned and they shared the rabbits and cooked some of the deer for the rest of the journey back to Cyrene. As they sat around the fire Samantha told them, "I never meant to end up here and cause you all this trouble. I know Chimera said she would kill me, and you guys are being really generous to help me. But you have to go home. You're not obligated to me." Kuma put his rabbit down and folded his arms, glaring at her across the fire. The reflection of the flames danced in his dark eyes, making him look more infuriated than she hoped he really felt.

"You don't know what kind of creature Chimera is. If you're still convinced you can just walk out of this place you need to get that notion out of your head because it's not happening. And Chimera has spent over a thousand years doing nothing but following the road that runs along the walls of Arguris. She knows it probably better than anyone else. If there was another way out, she'd know about it and she'd be gone long before any of the rest of us learned about it," he leaned forward and went on. "We know that you have no idea what you're doing, and *you* better start knowing that real quick. It'll make it easier on us to help you."

He picked up his rabbit and continued eating as he looked at her. She looked to Phoebe and she was staring at the flames as if hoping she wouldn't be asked to share her opinion. When she looked at Pan he shoved a large strip of meat in his mouth so it was too full to speak.

She pulled a blade of grass and twirled it in her fingers, thinking. She was hoping another solution would come but soon realized Kuma was right. She had no idea what she was doing.

--

Hissing and flapping wings came from the branches overhead as Chimera made her way through the Haken. It was a dark place, where fog always hovered just above the ground. The trees carried no leaves, and the bark was black from centuries of mucky water seeping through the trunks. Puddles spotted the dead woods, surrounded by mud and large rocks covered in a brownish-gray moss.

There were large spider webs up ahead, and as she came closer to them she could see how thick they were. Whatever got trapped in them wasn't coming out. The webs grew and grew the further she walked, until they covered most of the ground and she had to step carefully to avoid getting tangled in them herself.   She came to a cluster of trees wrapped together in webbing so thick you couldn't see into them. It looked like a cave. Chimera stood outside a large dark opening in the front and called out, "Arachne!"

After a moment, sounds of something striking the ground in a fast rhythm of heavy thuds was heard as it approached. Chimera raised her head high and waited for the creature to appear. She smirked when she saw the large legs of a spider emerge in the doorway. The top of the spider was the upper body of a woman. Her hair was covered in a net of webbing. She wore deer skin around her chest and a necklace made of hairs and teeth woven together. She was neither ugly nor beautiful, but she was to be respected. Chimera knew not even a creature as intimidating as herself could escape the wrath of Arachne if she ever rubbed her the wrong way. The spider was no taller than any of the other average creatures in Arguris, and she smiled at Chimera when she saw her.

"Chimera, it's been some time." she reached out her palm and Paphene laid her head on it. Arachne pet the snakes head then looked at Nova. "Something's bothering you. Is it the usual?"

"Something's happened," Chimera spoke carefully.

"Obviously. Spit it out."

"Speranta. It opened," Chimera said.

"What do you mean, *opened*," Arachne asked as she crawled around Chimera.

"I mean I was standing right in front of the doors when they opened," she paused then added, "and a girl was standing on the other side."

Arachne leaned down so she was eye to eye with the lion creature. "What are you talking about?" She looked between Paphene and Nova.

Chimera stared back, holding her ground. She hadn't come to waste anyone's time, and she would be heard.

"The doors opened, and I tried to get through, but the trees closed in. I was forced to return. When I did, the girl had fainted and a large snake was carrying her off. I didn't see where they took her." Chimera looked upset and Arachne could see she was telling the truth.

"Speranta opened? Are you sure?" Arachne asked anyway. She didn't seem moved and Chimera wondered why she wasn't more excited.

"Yes, I saw it with my own eyes. I walked through them and to the other side." Chimera told her.

Arachne paced a moment, then asked, "And the girl, where is she?"

"I don't know."

Arachne tried to put the pieces together.

Chimera had nothing else to share about what had happened so she went on. "She looks just like her."

Arachne spun around and studied Chimera. Then she walked close and crossed her arms

"Like who," she asked, but they both knew she already knew the answer.

"Athena has returned." Paphene leaned forward.

Arachne looked around the Haken, up toward the rustle of wings, out to all the trees and her woven webs. She looked at

Paphene, then to Nova. She snickered, then began laughing long and loud.

"Chimera, you aged fool," she bellowed, "If our goddess had returned, the walls would be down. She may be our captor, but it was the good intentions of a protector that brought us here. I share your harbored feelings, but I believe you've begun to see visions that aren't there."

She patted Chimera's mane, which the lion hated and she growled at the spider.

"Oh, come creature," Arachne motioned toward her webbed home, "let's sit and talk like the old friends we are."

Chimera didn't feel like a chat. She didn't want to go inside the spider's dark webbed cave. She had been laughed at and mocked. She wanted to rip Arachne's head off and feed it to the creatures above. Speranta had opened, she was sure of it. The girl had been there, and she had seen her again in the same spot with the other creatures. She hadn't imagined them. She growled at Arachne, "The bear was with her. Just the other day. The girl was trying to open Speranta again."

Arachne looked annoyed as she asked, "And did she?"

"No."

The spider let out a simple *hmph* and shrugged her shoulders, then disappeared into her cave. Chimera followed. It was dark and she had to wait for her eyes to adjust. The floor was bare, but on the walls she could see creatures of all sorts wrapped in webs, kept warm to become Arachne's meals within the fortnight.

She knew how easily she could be caught in that web. Just one shot and she'd be tangled, stuck to the spider's thread.

"I know it sounds mad," she went on, "but I saw her, twice. She is Athena. I know it. She will open the doors, or I will have her head, I've already promised that."

Arachne settled herself into a large nest of webbing and motioned for Chimera to come closer. She approached reluctantly and sat a few feet away from the edge of the web.

"Why kill her? She gave you the opportunity to live a life safe from those who would destroy you. Yes, she abandoned you, and all of us. But she did save you." Arachne questioned.

"She is not just responsible for dropping us from the wind into this place. She is responsible for Chartis." Nova growled and Paphene ran her head along the bare stump on Chimera's back. She lowered her lion head and bared her teeth as she thought about the events that led to Chartis' destruction.

"Tell me about it." Arachne instructed.

Chimera looked at a small knife dropped on the floor under one of the creatures caught in the webs. Then she closed her eyes as she recalled the events that led to her sister's death.

"It was a long time ago, in Caria, my home. I hunted as men hunted, and they called *me* a torturer. They think we put ourselves into the wombs of our mothers to be born what we are. I am the creature that I am, and I became his quest. Bellerophon. He ate and drank at the tables of men whose women he would take for himself, and they were too afraid to punish him. So they sent him after me, thinking they'd be rid of him by my wrath. I would have been glad to take care of the vile beast, but even simple men can have the cleverness of a god. Bellerophon told a story for his better welfare. He claimed he had poured lead down my throat. That would have been clever, but the beast that he was, he lied. He rode a Pegasus, staying out of reach, and I was helpless but tried what I could to defend myself as he shot arrows at me. Bellerophon must have thought he had already won. He was cocky, laughing, riding in circle's on his golden saddle above me. The horse was ascending and he hadn't noticed, he was laughing so much. He almost fell off the saddle and his sword fell from his waist when he grabbed the reigns. I was too slow to move out of the way. I jumped to avoid the blade, and doing so provided a clean cut for the sword to run itself across. It took Chartis's head, giving me my scar. Bellerophon saw the head, and I was weak from all the blood lost. I fainted, so I appeared dead. He assumed his victory. When I woke he was gone and my scar had already formed, a gift from being the daughter of monsters, I'm sure. I haven't been able to make fire since." Chimera said.

"But what does that have to do with Athena?" Arachne asked.

"It was Athena who gave him the golden saddle. She encouraged him to come and kill me when the men sent him. She wanted me dead." Chimera said.

"Or maybe there was another destiny for Bellerophon greater than your own." Arachne offered.

Chimera glared at the spider. She had had enough. She got up and walked to the entrance of the cave then looked back at Arachne. "Athena will pay for what she's done to me. I came to ask your help but I see that was a fool's errand. She will die if she doesn't release us."

Arachne quietly watched from her nest as Chimera walked away.

Chimera prowled through the trees, eager for a hunt, something to distract her from the annoying spider woman. As she tried to listen and smell for prey, she heard wings following her overhead, landing from tree to tree.

"Come down," she demanded. "What do you want?"

A feathered creature landed in front of her. She looked much like a human, with long dark hair and eyes. Where are arms would be, she had large wings that fell to her side from shoulder to floor. Her feet were like large eagle talons. Every inch of her body was covered in dark feathers, aside from the hair and tiny white feathers that covered her face. Her expression playful, daring. Chimera wasn't in the mood for games. The harpy walked back and forth in front of her.

Chimera thought about attacking, saving herself the trouble of a hunt, but the bird finally spoke.

"I heard your conversation with Arachne," she screeched. Her voice made Chimera's ears hurt, and she didn't care what the harpy had to say, she didn't want to hear that sound again. She walked passed her and moved toward the road leading out of the Haken. The harpy flew to her side and stared at Paphene. "If the goddess is here, and she does not free us, we will help you destroy her," the harpy said.

Chimera took a moment to let the ringing in her ears stop. "Why do you think I need your help? It's one girl. She doesn't even know who she is."

"But she will," the harpy assured her, "and when she does, you'll need help. Athena is the goddess of war, remember? She'll destroy you."

"And what do you get out of it?" Chimera studied the bird.

"That is our concern. When the time comes, you know where to find us." the harpy looked over Chimera, a smirk appearing on her face, then she flew off, disappearing into the trees.

9

Phoebe and Samantha stayed at the tavern when they arrived in Cyrene. Kuma took Pan home with him, unwilling to let him wonder alone, in fear he might share his assumptions about Samantha with other gullible creatures. Phoebe had agreed it was best to keep Samantha's identity hidden whether she was a goddess or not, so Samantha pulled her shawl over her head and wrapped it over her face so only her eyes peered through. The stares didn't last as long now, and she admitted to herself she felt safer under her cover.

Later in the afternoon, Kuma and Pan joined them for dinner and they huddled around a table outside the tavern. Samantha had changed her clothes and Phoebe paid a girl to wash all of their dirtied clothes for them.

They all seemed happy to have a decent chair to sit in, and eat at a decent table, a meal they didn't have to find for themselves this time. Samantha chewed the meat slowly, savoring the taste of herbs and spices. While she didn't favor the ale, she drank anyway, grateful for the flavors dancing on her taste buds. She looked at the others, they had already finished their food and were watching her.

Then someone spoke from somewhere above them.

"Well, I suppose centuries later is better than never, but you could drop a sign of promise every now and then, you think," a white owl flew down, surrounded by a cloud of dust, landing on the table next to them. It pecked at some of its dirty feathers then blinked his large blue eyes at Samantha, studying her with expectation. She recognized the owl from the beam the last time they were at the tavern, and though she didn't quite understand him, she guessed the bird was talking to her the way he stared at her impatiently. He seemed to be waiting for her to explain herself, she supposed, his feathers twitching here and there making little clouds of filth that surrounded him before settling on him once again. Phoebe reached over and swatted at his back. He jumped before she could hit him and dirt filled in the air around them as he flapped his wings. Everyone coughed and waved at the air. "Filthy bird!" Phoebe turned her face away as the bird came back down, flapping his wings at her with a loud, "Aha!" Phoebe got up from her seat and stood behind Samantha.

The owl settled his feathers and looked at her. She said, "I'm sorry, I don't think I am who you think I am. There seems to be a common misunderstanding here." The owl looked at the others. Phoebe shrugged her shoulders, Kuma just stared, daring the bird to press him on the matter. Pan was about to speak but Kuma stopped him, saying, "Sit. Whoever she is, there's things to do and it's none of your business, owl."

Samantha thought of Chimera and her threats. She wondered how any creature could hold anything against anyone for so long. Why hadn't she moved on by now, and found her happiness? But Samantha knew the answer to that. She herself couldn't accept the circumstances of her own life, no matter how safe and providing they were. She shouldn't expect a creature come straight from the gods to have lower expectations than herself.

Her thoughts were interrupted when she felt the rustle of feathers in front of her and dust filled her nostrils. She coughed and leaned away.

"I am sorry for that," the owl looked at her apologetically, "I had a run in with a mouse who was set on *not* becoming my dinner. Unfortunately for the rodent, his fate was already sealed."

Samantha looked unamused and sipped her drink.

"Name's Rudy," the owl said.

"Samantha," Samantha replied. The owl gave her an awkward stare, then puffed his chest out and she wondered if she had offended him.

"You are who you say you are, but I tell you, you're not," he was about to say more when Phoebe smacked the table behind him, scaring him away.

Samantha watched his large wings as he flew above the street and disappeared into the night.

"Well, he's odd," she said, relieved to see him go. "Who is he?"

No one seemed to be familiar with the owl. Samantha hoped he wasn't like Chimera. At least so far he didn't seem to be.

"I'm glad you found better clothes," Kuma looked at the garments covering her, "it would have been harder to teach you how to use a sword in the other thing you had on."

"A sword?" Samantha hadn't even thought about it until now. He said he would train her. Why did she assume that meant learning how to use a shot gun? Then it dawned on her all their weapons were very old-fashioned. She hadn't seen a single fire arm. But she imagined many of the residents of Arguris wouldn't need any weapons anyway. What did they have to fear here, except perhaps angry beasts like Chimera.

"We'll discuss it tomorrow," Kuma grumbled. "She'll choose her weapon, then she won't rest until she's ready." He slammed his cup down, tossed a couple wooden chips on the table and left without another word. Pan smiled at them, winking at Samantha, then followed Kuma who gave him a low growl when he reached his side. Pan just laughed a cheerful laugh, patted his back and continued to walk at his side. Samantha pointed to the chips, "I'm sorry, I don't think I have the right coins." She reached into her skirt pocket but Phoebe held up her hand.

"Briggets." Phoebe took a few more out of the satchel hanging on her waist and explained the currency to Samantha, showing her how to tell the difference between each.

"Is this the same currency you had before this place?" Samantha asked, flipping a brigget around in her hand. It was larger than any of her coins, but light and she wondered what sort of wood it came from.

"No, we're all from different places and many of us didn't have any on us at all when we arrived, so we had to make our own for everyone to use. Though some still barter, and that is just fine."

Samantha flipped the coin around in her hands a few more times, impressed with the creatures ability to adapt and persevere. It seemed peaceful here. She wondered what life was like for them before Athena brought them here.

They returned to their room and fell asleep quickly, Samantha dreamed again of toy ships and wind tunnels.

The next morning Samantha woke up to Phoebe separating their things into two different bags, throwing one over her shoulder and grabbing her weapons. She looked over at Samantha.

"You'll meet Kuma downstairs, and I have to go," she said as she grabbed the last few of her things. Samantha wished she would come with them, but she knew Phoebe had to get back to her own business. Who knew what Kuma was putting on hold. Samantha had seen no signs that he had family, nor had she seen any other creatures like him. As she thought about it, she wondered if Kuma was the only one of his kind. He never spoke of any others. Not that he ever spoke much at all. At least not to her.

"Will we see you later?" Samantha asked.

"We'll see," Phoebe smiled at the doorway, "Destiny loves its surprises." She disappeared into the hallway and Samantha could hear her thud down the stairs.

There was nothing for her to do now but wait. She sat on the bed and let out a heavy sigh. She thought a moment of Sylvia and Marcus, Edward, Celeste, Uncle Nicolas. She wondered what they were doing, if any of them would accidentally stumble upon the doors and come find her. If she had, it was possible they could, too. She reminded herself that she had left for a reason. She might be here by accident, but she wasn't captive. She had left home of her own free will and she shouldn't want for anyone to ache for her. She scolded herself for being selfish then wrapped one shawl around her shoulders, and another over her head. She grabbed her bag and made her way down the stairs, choosing to sit near the door so she could see Kuma coming down the road. When he did finally appear, the owl was riding on his shoulder.

Samantha watched them for a moment before she went out to meet them. *The stories I'll have to tell one day*, she thought to herself. She walked out of the tavern and smiled at the pair as she approached. Kuma took a large bag from his shoulders and dropped it in front of her. Metal clanged inside.

"You'll carry this for the duration of the journey," he said. "We'll stop only when I say stop, and we'll sleep when I say sleep. Drink when you have the opportunity. If Chimera finds us, you hide and leave the fighting to me."

Samantha frowned and bent down to pick up the bag. It was heavy and she had trouble lifting it off the ground. She looked at Kuma for help. He folded his arms and he and Rudy stared down at her. She wondered why the owl was there at all.

She knelt down and stuck her head under the strap. Leaving one side on her shoulder, she pulled the other side down and stuck her arm through the loop. Grabbing the sides of the bag with her hands, she lifted herself up with her knees and stood straight. She adjusted the bag so it hung behind her and the strap laid over her chest. She looked up at the bear and smiled. "Okay, anything else?"

Kuma reached into a bag and pulled out a canteen and fixed it over her shoulder. Samantha could see water drip from the cover. He tied a small pan around her waist, then hung the bag over her shoulder. She felt the weight, but thought it bearable. "Couldn't we just keep everything in the bag?" she looked at everything hanging on her.

"No." Kuma grunted. He began walking and Samantha followed behind, the canteen and pan knocking her knees and her side. The sun wasn't too high yet and they walked perfectly east. For the first few hours they walked through gentle countryside. She could see the hills to the south that they had come through before, and mountains appeared ahead, guarded by a thick forest. To the north was more forest. She was happy when they reached the edge and could get into shade. She expected to feel more exhausted from carrying the heavy load for so long, but when Kuma told her they were stopping near a stream, she didn't collapse. She lowered herself to the ground and pulled the bags over her head. She walked to the stream and filled her canteen then drank. After she had refilled it she splashed some cool water on her face and looked up just in time to see Rudy swoop over the water and pull out a fish. He disappeared into the trees to eat. Kuma sat on a root protruding from the ground and polished his halberd. When Samantha came close he tossed her a chunk of bread from a cloth. She ate it and observed her surroundings. It wasn't much different from what she had seen already. To look at the woods anyone would think it was like any other area of forest surrounding Chraimyth. Only in this part of the forest, mythological creatures lived in it. She wondered herself what creatures might live nearby. She looked for homes or caves, but there was none.

When they had rested a good hour, Kuma started them on the road again. Samantha carried her bags, canteen and pan banging along. She impressed herself with her stamina. She was sure she'd be complaining about her feet, or the weight of the bags by now. She could tell by the glances Kuma was giving her that he expected her to be complaining by now, too. He turned and whispered something to Rudy. The owl nodded then disappeared into the forest.

"Where is he going?" Samantha asked.

In response, a gust of wind blew at her neck as Rudy lowered himself onto the bags and peered over her shoulder.

"You looked a little unbalanced. Thought I could help." Rudy sneered.

Samantha looked at Kuma who kept walking without a word. She rolled her eyes and thought about knocking the bird off as she had seen Phoebe do at the tavern. She punched at him with her elbow and he fell backward with a squawk.

"Hey! I was only following orders!" he yelled as he shook the dirt off his feathers.

"And I thought you needed to stretch your wings." Samantha retorted. The owl flew away and Samantha watched him disappear above the trees.

The road curved and as they came around Samantha saw a large bridge crossing the stream. Her jaw dropped as she admired its beauty. It was wide and looked as though the elm trees on either side had intertwined their roots to make railings. The roots were covered in moss and lady bugs crawled everywhere. Thin vines hung from the trees above with white buds growing on them. Samantha felt as though she were crossing into some enchanted land, but she remembered she already had. Though she hadn't seen much enchantment yet.

"Wait." Kuma suddenly said. He sniffed the air and looked around. Samantha looked around, too. She thought maybe Pan was sneaking behind them again. She didn't hear or see anything though. She wondered what Kuma was smelling. He approached the bridge and peered underneath, sniffing and watching. After a few minutes he waved her forward. As they crossed the bridge, Samantha put her hands on one of the roots and she thought she heard a woman laugh. But when she looked around no one was there. She felt a tingle in her hand and she looked to see it was covered in ladybugs..

"Kuma, look!" she laughed as she reached out her arm. He looked at her hand, then at the railing where she had touched it. It was bare. None of the other bugs moved into the empty spot.

"Put your hand back." He pointed.

Samantha pouted but obeyed. She put her hand where she had before. The ladybugs immediately began crawling away, back onto the roots. She heard the laughter again, but still saw no one.

She took her hand off the railing and the lady bugs spread out again.

"Who was that?" she asked Kuma.

"The wind." he mumbled as they pressed on.

When they had crossed the bridge Samantha looked back to take in its beauty one more time. A red cloud hovered at the end and she thought it looked like a figure waving at her, but she couldn't be sure. It dispersed and she could see that it had just been the ladybugs flying in a swarm.

They traveled a few more hours before they reached the edge of the forest on the other side, right at the foot of the mountains. Samantha gazed up and wondered if Kuma planned for them to climb it. Instead they veered off the road and walked along the edge of the mountain. There was no trail to follow this way. Samantha realized there was no need for a trail when they quickly came to one that cut through the mountains. It was a steep dirt path with stones placed as steps every few feet. Kuma had no trouble climbing the hill, but Samantha struggled with bags falling off her shoulder and the canteen and pan falling poorly against her as she tried to keep her balance. There was no rail to hold onto and she didn't want to roll down the hill. Whenever she came to a low hanging branch, she lifted herself up with it. Kuma was several yards away in no time and Samantha was afraid she'd lose sight of him.

"Kuma," she called out. But he didn't hear her. He kept climbing and she struggled to move any faster. When she came to a large step she stopped to adjust her bags. Kuma was gone. She needed to find him before she got lost, but she couldn't do it with all this stuff on her. She took the canteen and pan and threw them in the bag. Then she took the smaller bag and pushed it in with the large bag Kuma had given her. She was amazed at the number of swords and daggers. When she had only the large bag and her own bag, she looked at the trail climbing above her and she began to run. It was much easier to move without everything pressing against her. She called out for Kuma a few more times but he didn't answer. When she reached the top of the hill, he was resting against a tree, Rudy sitting on his shoulder.

"Good, you figured that one out." Kuma said as he looked her over. Samantha was about to protest but he climbed on. The trail leveled out at the top and the air was wet but cool. A floral scent filled the air but there were no flowers.

Kuma led them off the trail once more and they came to a small wooden house in the middle of two small mountain peaks. Trees and beautiful green foliage surrounded it. It looked exotic and completely out of place. As if they had just walked into a jungle.

"You can prepare the beds while I get our dinner." Kuma said as he disappeared behind the house.

Samantha went inside and dropped the bags. It was as she expected, simple, with few furnishings, only the necessities. She wondered if anyone decorated their homes here. It seemed they lived only for the essentials and no pleasures. There was a table with four chairs, a few cushioned seats on the opposite side, and a separate room with four cots. She decided pushing a couple together would work for Kuma's size. She went out and carried Kuma's bags in, pulling out blankets and making the beds for them. Kuma returned shortly after with a few birds.

Samantha watched him pluck the feathers and decided this evening might be a good opportunity to get to know Kuma better, maybe find out why he seemed annoyed by everything, especially her.

Later when they were eating she decided to ask him, "Why don't you think I'm Athena?"

It was the first time she had seen such a smile on the bears face.

10

"Gods are too proud to forget who they are." Kuma snickered. "You don't remember an entire lifetime, let alone an eternity of existence. You're no god."

Samantha thought about that a minute. It did make sense. No god she had ever read about just *forgot* who they were. At least there was no record about it. Gods were strong, invincible, immortal, all-knowing. Twice in her life already she had been carried off after becoming unconscious. Hardly the behavior of a god. Gods had powers, special abilities. All she could do was carry heavy bags up a mountain of stairs.

"Why bring me here to train then?" she asked.

"Right now you have no return home, making you one of us. Those who live in Arguris know how to fight, it's part of the culture, our history, though we rarely find reason to put our skills to use," Kuma ripped into the the small piece of meat on the table. Samantha thought maybe three birds weren't enough for such a massive bear.

"Arguris is your home for now, and you have to learn to live in it. You've already made an enemy promising to take your life. You must learn the skills to defend yourself. Anyone deserves that much of a chance," he went on, tossing bones on the table.

Samantha picked up the bones and laid them on his plate.

"Well, I appreciate it, but what about your family, your work. I shouldn't be any reason for you to put your life on hold." She leaned back in her chair and folded her arms. Seeing Kuma eye her uneaten food, she pushed the plate away from her. He pushed it back, growling.

"Eat. Only a foolish warrior refuses his meals. You need your strength." he said.

"And I need answers." Samantha argued as she pushed the bird aside and picked up a potato.

Kuma folded his hands on the table and looked at her.

"I have seen what this place does to the lost, to those who have lost their purpose. My affairs are none of your business, only what I am offering you." He got up and walked to the doorway and stared out into the woods. Samantha wondered what he meant by *the lost.*

"I am thankful for it, Kuma, really," she walked to his side and stared out the door with him. "I just don't know why you'd help a stranger, that's all."

He gave her his usual grim expression before saying, "Sleep. You'll need to be rested before tomorrow." He opened the bag of weapons and began laying them on the table.

"Good night then." Samantha said.

Kuma grunted over his shoulder as he examined each piece and arranged them neatly on the table.

Samantha climbed into her cot and pulled the blanket over her. She wanted to stay awake long enough to ask Kuma more questions when he came to sleep, but she was exhausted and drifted off quickly.

When she awoke the next morning, Kuma was nowhere to be seen. The table was still covered in weapons and some long swords sat against the wall near the door. There was a knocking sound coming from behind the house and Samantha quietly went to investigate. Kuma was chopping firewood over a stump, each time tossing one piece into an already large pile, and the other into the woods.

"Why are you throwing those away?" Samantha walked to the tree line to see several pieces of wood scattered on the forest floor.

"I'm not throwing anything away. They'll be put to use." he said.

Samantha wondered what use they were scattered in the woods.

"Anything I can do to help?" she asked.

Kuma paused, looking at her. Then he tossed the axe at her and she jumped back, letting it land at her feet, shooting a glare of disapproval at the bear. Kuma snorted as he walked over and picked it up.

"Watch the handle." he said as he backed away and tossed it again. Samantha kept her eye on the handle, reaching out her arm and grabbing it. She squeezed her eyes closed as she felt the weight bare down on her hand, fearing she would drop it and chop her foot off. But she held it steady, then smiled at Kuma, who just grunted.

"Good, you can catch. Now put it down and go pick up the wood," he pointed to the woods. Samantha opened her mouth to protest but Kuma just grunted again and pointed to the scattered firewood. Samantha strolled across the forest floor, piling the wood in her arms then tossing them in the pile Kuma had started. Occasionally he would yell, "More than that," if she came back with only one or two pieces. They were on a slight slope, and she lost her balance coming back up the hill with her arms loaded. It took her a few trips back and forth to get the hang of carrying five and six pieces of chopped wood. When she had picked up every piece, Kuma handed her the axe again.

"Every piece, half as small as they are now," then he disappeared into the house.

She looked at the doorway, expecting him to come back with another axe. He wanted her to do all this by herself? Samantha had never held an axe before. Her uncle had let her hold the weapon's in his weapon room, but he didn't have any axes and he never actually taught her how to use any of them anyway. She placed a piece of wood down on the stump as she had seen Kuma do, then lifted the axe over her head and brought it down as hard as she could onto the wood. It cut only an inch into the surface and she had to hold the wood under her feet to pull the axe out. She looked over at the pile of wood waiting to be chopped, then at the house. She let out a groan then tried again.

One hour later she had ten pieces of wood chopped into half the size they were. She couldn't feel her arms and could barely lift the axe. Kuma had come to watch, but didn't say anything. They heard someone approach and turned to see Phoebe with two large sacks on her back.

Phoebe walked into the cabin briefly then returned, hands on her hips. "Well, let's go," she stared at Samantha, who looked to Kuma. He nodded and she followed Phoebe inside.

Kuma sat on a tree stump and rubbed his fur. He stared through the trees, remembering the woods of his homeland. Arguris was nice, and served its purpose, but he missed the smells, and the streams. Here he could always smell the faint stench of centaurs, or the sweat of the ogres. He remembered the sunset on top of the mountains. There was no sunset here, nor a sunrise. Rain would fall through the branches far above them, and sunlight beamed between the branches so that sometimes he forgot he was living in a large dome. He thought of the stars, and he wondered how beautiful the sky would look if the dome ever opened above them.

He was pulled from his thoughts when he heard a scream from the cabin, then Phoebe's voice, "We're okay!" he listened to a bit of commotion and grabbed his halberd, ready to defend, not happy that he may have to pick between either of the women. As he slowly approached the cabin, Samantha appeared at the door, thin white linen draped over her shoulders, crossed over her chest and around her waist, falling to her knees. A tattered gold rope tied around her waist, gladiator sandals laced up her calves. She now wore a light colored pair of pants with some sort of detail stitched into them but he wasn't sure what it was. Her dark hair fell around her shoulders, just touching a gold armband on her left arm. The diadem the ogre had given her still decorated her forehead. She was without her spear and shield, and it had been over a thousand years, but Kuma knew exactly who she was the spitting of. He watched Samantha adjust the ornament on her head and Phoebe slapped her hand away, growling at her. Phoebe spotted Kuma staring and smiled, proud of her work. "Believe it now?" she called. Kuma didn't realize his mouth had fallen open as he closed it and made his way to them. He circled Samantha and groaned, "What did you do to her?" She was beautiful, the most beautiful creature he had seen in centuries. Phoebe pouted and shoved Kuma. "I made her look like the goddess she is. I thought maybe if she wore something more like what Athena would put on, it may help her memory," Phoebe shrugged as she played with the layers of material on Samantha's shoulders. Samantha looked uncomfortable at the realization of Phoebe's purpose.

"I could have returned with her old dress. We could watch her and see if she melted or not. If she didn't, then she's a god," Phoebe teased Kuma and Samantha laughed.

She looked down at herself and ran her hands over the light material. She had only ever seen anything like it used as trim along the neckline. Not as an entire dress, or at least half a dress. She loved how smooth it felt under her hands, and how light it hung, as if she were wearing nothing. She felt weightless and had the urge to start running through the trees just to feel the breeze around her legs. She looked at the armband, at the two snake heads hissing at each other and their scales wrapped around her arm. They reminded her of the anacondas and Samantha wondered if Phoebe had picked them out for the purpose. She closed her eyes a moment, searching for her earliest memory, hoping something had changed. But still the only thing she could remember was the house mother's bony arms under her shoulders and the girl holding her waist as they brought her to her feet and took her inside the orphanage. There was nothing before that.

She looked at Phoebe and shook her head, "I don't remember anything."

"It's okay, it might take some time," Phoebe patted her on the shoulder.

Kuma huffed and peeked inside. There were piles of garments on the floor, all colors and materials. He wondered how often the ogre planned to play dress up with the girl.

"Okay, we need to get to work," he pouted at Phoebe, who was still beaming as she stared at Samantha. Samantha looked pleased herself, though she kept trying to pull off the head piece and Phoebe kept smacking her hand away.

"Oh, one more thing," Phoebe said. She ran inside and returned with a brown wooden stick only a couple feet long. She pulled on each end and it extended several more feet instantly. It was taller than either Phoebe or Samantha. Phoebe handed the pole arm to to Kuma.

"I thought you might like to use it," she said.

"Thank you," Kuma took it from her and looked Samantha over. Samantha looked down at her dress and understood. These were not the garments to train in. She returned inside and found more suitable clothes. Phoebe had brought enough for her to wear something different every day for at least a month. When she had found something more comfortable she met Kuma and Phoebe in the yard.

Phoebe shared she'd decided to stay while Samantha trained and offer any assistance, even if it was just to hunt. "I see you're set on wood," she teased as she looked toward the back of the house.

Suddenly Samantha found herself falling to the ground, a burning pain on the back of her legs. She cried out as she hit the ground.

"Always be on guard," Kuma instructed.

"What kind of a teacher are you," Samantha yelled as she stood up, rubbing her legs and wiping dirt off her arms. She looked at Kuma who just grinned, aggravating her. She reached out for the pole arm, intending to take it from him and hit him with it. She assumed it wouldn't hurt him much since he was so big. But before she could touch it she was picking herself off the ground again.

"Be ready," he commanded.

He spent the next hour showing her defensive moves, then he sat her down on the stump, instructing her to sit quietly with her eyes closed and listen until he came for her.

At first she listened for any sound of a large bear approaching and a large stick cutting the air so she could duck, but all she heard was the rustling of leaves and the occasional chirping of birds. She couldn't remember hearing those sounds in Chraimyth. All the sounds she could remember hearing was the clanking of teacups on plates, boots on marble floors, and wagon wheels rolling down the street. Sylvia's voice going on about marrying Edward. She didn't miss Edward, even if he was rich and kind. She worried that he and everyone else would be concerned for her, but she didn't yearn for his company. For anyone's really. Perhaps it was because she knew she wasn't far from home. Not as far as she hoped to be. Though, in all the world, she doubted she would ever find such a place as this. What would explorers and scientists say if they ever found out that mythological creatures passed down through stories, and some never even heard of, existed right under their noses all along. In fact, they had been here long before any of them. She wondered how all these creatures would react to the outside world. To them everything was as it was before. Nothing had changed, nothing had progressed. Through centuries, they had remained the same. How could that be? Man, humans, were always moving forward. Always inventing and changing things. But these creatures had come from gods. They were intelligent, they knew how to survive. They were clothed and fed, they lived in houses and carried weapons. How could there not be even a thing as a wagon?

"Haah!" someone hollered in her ear and she fell off the stump. Phoebe was bent over laughing and Rudy sat on top of the pile of wood, chuckling. She realized she hadn't seen him since yesterday and hadn't even thought of him once.

"Would have heard me coming if you were listening," Phoebe chimed.

Kuma walked out of the woods with two large boars and Pan behind him. When had he arrived? Samantha hadn't been focused at all. Had she been, she would have heard the tap of Pan's hooves when he walked, the leaves that fell from Kuma's feet when he picked them up, the flapping of Rudy's wings as he landed on the wood, and Phoebe's heavy breathing. Anyone could have noticed those sounds. She felt embarrassed that she had failed such a simple task, but Kuma didn't lecture her. Instead he handed the boars over to Pan and instructed him to help Samantha prepare them for the week. They looked at each other, wondering if he was serious. They had skinned one creature each, at least Samantha had. Kuma thought they'd be able to properly butcher these pigs and have meat safely prepared to feed to them for a week? She thought perhaps that meant they'd be moving on. To the training grounds perhaps. This was just a resting spot. There wasn't much land for training, at least not what she had imagined. The yard was only a few yards wide in any direction before running into trees.

"So we're moving on then? Further east?" she asked. She admitted to herself she was curious to see more of Arguris.

"No, you'll train here. We'll save time if we don't have to hunt every day." Kuma replied.

"Are you staying, too?" she looked at Pan as he untied the pigs and dropped them on the ground.

"Yes, I told you I want to serve you," he looked hurt for a moment, as if he thought Samantha was asking him to go away, then went after Kuma to get the knife. He tossed him one and the satyr caught it with ease. Pan turned to Samantha and threw the knife at her. It flew at her fast and despite wanting to dart out of the way, she found herself frozen with surprise. Suddenly she couldn't think, the knife twisted in the air as it came toward her chest and all she could do was surrender. Then she felt her arm shoot out in front of her, grabbing the knife at the handle just inches from her shoulder. Pan was smiling at her and Kuma was racing at him. The satyr held up his hands to stop the bear, yelling, "I knew she would catch it!"

Kuma dragged him back to the boars and pushed him on the ground next to them. "Just do your job," he growled at him.

He came over and took the knife from Samantha and threw it so it stuck into the ground next to Pan's hand. He disappeared inside and Samantha glared at Pan. Pan was glaring at the door.

"What were you thinking? You could have killed me," she said as she sat down in front of one of the boars.

Before he could answer Phoebe rushed over, motioning for Samantha to get up. "You're not skinning any animal in those clothes."

Samantha followed her inside and wondered just how often Phoebe was going to make her change.

11

Chimera threw herself against the doors again and again. She kicked with her hind legs, and the wood didn't scratch or dent. She tried tunneling under them, but she already knew it was a fools errand. Thick roots were woven deep into the ground and no amount of biting or clawing would break them. It infuriated her that this was the only thing in Arguris that dared to defeat her. Every living thing there feared her. She did not pretend to be anyone's friend, nor did she desire them. She had fallen into the routine of roaming the cage for any way out, and now that Athena had returned, she was more determined than ever to make sure she was there when the doors opened. But they hadn't. And Athena hadn't returned despite her threats to the girl. It had been two months since Chimera had seen the girl and her companions. It had been a week since she combed Cyrene for any clues to their whereabouts. They had gone east, the innkeeper thought he overheard them say. But he wasn't sure. It didn't matter. Chimera would cover every inch of Arguris if she had to. She would drag the girl to Speranta with her teeth if she thought she didn't need to return. Chimera was angered that Athena could show her face and take so long to let them free. The walls should have been down by now. Everyone who wished for it should have been days into their journey home already. How could Athena show her face without any explanation. Chimera remembered her saying she was someone else. How dare she take her for a fool.

"Let's go, we're going to give them good reason to think we're fools if you don't stop throwing us around," Paphene said into Nova's ear. "We'll go east, and we'll find her."

Nova looked around once more, tired of feeling defeated and ignored. "She better hope we don't."

Chimera traveled back to Cyrene, then followed the road east. She came to the root bridge decorated with vines and white buds. There were no lady bugs, and no one laughed as she crossed. It was quiet, not even the wind whispered through her mane. She had crossed the bridge before and was always greeted with the eerie silence. She thought it humorous that not even the trees would like her.

A scent filled the air and she looked around her. When she saw no one, she looked to the trees. A large owl flew from branch to branch, watching her. She had seen the owl now and then, but it had never bothered her, let alone shown any curiosity about her. What did the bird want now? She studied the owl a moment. None of the birds would waste time following a beast. She was neither food nor friend. The bird was up to something. *Athena.*

The owl was with Athena, Chimera assumed.

"How smart for the girl to think she can keep track of our whereabouts," Paphene sneered. She thought if she followed the owl, it would lead her to Athena. Chimera waited for the owl to fly away then followed it back over the bridge and off the path. It traveled north for several miles, then veered west. When they had come to a clearing in the woods, the owl flew in large circles, Chimera following below, watching the owl, not minding the trees. The owl ascended and was soon too high to see. When Chimera looked around her, she realized she didn't know which direction she had come from. With no ability to see the sun, it was easy to lose ones sense of direction. She knew she had been tricked. She roared and hissed at the sky, then began following her scent back to the bridge.

Surely the owl leading her away meant she had been near. They'd be gone by the time she arrived. The owl would warn them and they would leave, but she'd pick up their trail and follow them. She'd catch up with Athena eventually.

When she reached the foot of the mountains, Chimera was alert of every scent, but all she could pick up were prey and the clan of minotaurs that lived nearby. It was possible they had gone there. But she also knew there was a cabin in the other direction. It would take longer to find them if she went the wrong way, but it wasn't like she was running out of time. She turned and pressed forward. The minotaurs were a days journey away. It'd be daring for them to go there. No one bothered the minotaurs. If they weren't there, she'd cut through the higher ranges to the cabin.

She thought back to the Haken and the harpies offer. They would be useful right now. The harpies could travel faster and their aerial view could see more. They'd have been able to tell her where the girl was. They could have brought her back hanging from their talons.

But it was in Chimera's nature to hunt. She enjoyed it. It kept her senses sharp and alert. Her new prey gave her a great reward to look forward to. She thought nothing of the taste of her flesh, but letting her body rot where ever it went down.

--

Though the sword served well for a quick death, Samantha found she preferred the pole arm Phoebe had provided. She felt as though she glided and danced with the long stick as she moved and twirled it around her. Phoebe said she moved effortlessly, as though she already knew how to use it. She was a natural. Of course Phoebe argued with Kuma that it was more proof that Samantha was Athena, and her ability to use the pole arm was a sign that her memory was returning. Samantha had to admire Phoebe's faith. She was just sorry it was buried in a false hope. She could learn to fight, but she would never be a goddess.

Kuma had insisted Samantha spend equal time learning how to use the sword so she was adequate in both skills. She had used swords with varying blades. Some curved to a point, some just shy of being called a dagger, and others long and heavy. He taught her how to find her balance with each weapon in her hand. And every day she sat quietly listening, until her thoughts came to cloud her mind and she drifted away in her daydreams. That was typically followed by Phoebe or Pan startling her from her trance, making her fall over in frustration.

She had gotten to know Kuma no better in the months that had passed, but she had observed his leadership. Had he been human, he would surely have led an army, and maybe been the greatest general of that time. Perhaps he had led an army, and that was why he was here all alone. She pictured him with an army greater than the gods, making them jealous, and that was why they wanted him destroyed. It was a fitting story, and one she would love to hear him tell. But there must be a sad ending to it since there was no army with him now, nor did he mention the use of one when Chimera made her threats. He was determined to teach her how to fight her own battles, and every day she felt more prepared for the day Chimera might come for her. She had a feeling she should feel lucky to have Kuma aiding her, protecting her, teaching her. He had a greatness about him she had never known in any man. She respected him and wanted to please him.

She thought less and less of those she had left behind in Chraimyth. While she had known them for a few short years, these months in Arguris felt more like home than there. Here she wasn't waiting to be led around and told when to sit and stand, who to marry and how to feel about it. Here she was pushed and encouraged to look deep within herself and create a self that conquered, that braved...that was free. Still there were many unanswered questions, and she couldn't forget that everything she was doing was wrapped around the one fact that there was a creature she had never before seen or heard of outside of Arguris, and it wanted to kill her for not setting her free, for not being the person it wanted to believe she was.

After the first few weeks had passed, she had suggested Chimera had given up, maybe even forgotten about her and moved on. Pan was the one to correct her.

"Chimera does not forget. Speranta remains closed, the walls still tower over us," the satyr said pointing above him. "She has not forgotten. She's looking for you right now."

And so she continued training. The house had become their home and she came to enjoy the quiet of it. The woods behind it were filled with berries and they lived off that and rabbit and birds. Occasionally a deer would roam by and Kuma would have Pan or Samantha skin it. They spent most evenings sharpening swords and Phoebe taught Samantha how to clean her own clothes. Pan would take her with him to a stream he had found about half a mile away and they'd carry back water. Rudy came and went as he pleased, having quiet conversations with Kuma, then disappearing for days at a time. They were in the yard practicing with the long swords when Rudy had returned from one of his lookouts. He informed them that Chimera was only hours away and they quickly packed their things and headed further up the mountain.

"Why can't we face her now? All of us against one animal," Samantha watched Kuma toss weapons in bags and Phoebe carelessly crumple up the dresses and shove them in another bag. They stopped and looked at her, then at each other.

"She's right," Phoebe said and stopped packing.

"Chimera is very strong, and you're not ready for her yet, but we can fight for you," Kuma suggested and pulled some of the swords back out. Pan walked over and Kuma handed him a sword.

"Actually, I'd be better off with that one," he pointed to a short dagger and Kuma handed it to him. He walked a few steps away than swung the sword around with one hand while holding the dagger in position in the other. He looked at everyone watching him. "I know how to fight. I'm not just the imbecile you treat me as."

They looked away, and Samantha felt ashamed. She was the only imbecile there, but she had to admit even she treated Pan like he was a thorn in her side.

They took some time to go over their strategy and discuss what they knew of Chimera and how she fought. No one knew much except she fought like a lion and her tail was full of venom.

"So we kill a lion and avoid the snake?" Samantha asked.

"You're going to stay inside with Rudy." Kuma instructed. Rudy didn't seem to mind. There wasn't much an owl could do against a lion anyway. But Samantha hoped to confront Chimera, to at least try get her to believe Samantha wasn't who she thought she was. It wouldn't help having Pan and Phoebe there. Pan had already shared Chimera's assumption at Speranta.

The three soldiers waited in front of the hut while Samantha and Rudy waited inside. She pulled a chair over to the window and sat down, peering out at the path leading to the trail ahead.

It wasn't long before Chimera's figure could be seen passing behind the trees and tall grass. When she came into view the others raised their weapons and Samantha leaned back so she could still watch them but not be seen. Rudy flew to the window and perched himself on the edge.

"So she's moved in, is that it?" Chimera grumbled and stopped in front of them. They didn't say anything. She looked at the house, then at Rudy. "Why don't you tell her to come out, so we can have a chat."

Rudy looked back to Samantha, who was already heading to the door. She walked out and stood between Kuma and Phoebe.

"Chimera, we weren't expecting you," Samantha taunted. Kuma and Phoebe looked at her and Chimera bared her teeth, the snake flicking its tongue.

"I'll escort you back to the door," the beast hissed, "Let's go, so you can do your job."

Samantha sighed and stepped forward. "Chimera, I understand who you think I am, but no matter how insistent you are, I can't just become her. You can escort me where ever you want and those doors are not going to open for me or anyone else. You've already seen me try."

Phoebe stepped up next to her and gave her an apologetic look before speaking to Chimera, "The doors will open when they are meant to be open. Not on your command."

They both seemed to irritate Chimera only more and she bared her teeth and growled, lowering herself and they could see she was going to jump at them. Samantha felt Kuma pull her back. She turned to look at him and his expression was firm. He nodded to the house and Samantha ran as Kuma rushed forward with his halberd and Phoebe raised her sword. Pan held his sword and dagger in each hand, ready to fight. She felt more prepared to help them, but she agreed this was not the fight to test her strength and ability.

Chimera leapt at them and Kuma swung his weapon. With one hit the animal fell to the ground, unconscious. They all looked at the creature laying motionless, weapons ready, until they were satisfied she was out, at least for the time being. Samantha hadn't even had time to make it to the window to see what happened. She wondered if Kuma had killed the beast. She felt ashamed of the part of her that hoped he did.

Phoebe was the first inside the door and she hurried to the bag she had been packing, "Now we need to go. It won't be easy getting her to listen again." Samantha gathered all the food and Pan helped Kuma with the weapons.

"He didn't kill her?" Samantha asked quietly has she threw the bag over her shoulder.

"No, he knows you don't want that," Phoebe said as she fussed with a sword that wouldn't fit in the bag. She wondered why anything she wanted to stop the bear from doing what needed to be done.

They watched Chimera as they quietly made their way down the path.

They veered far away from any trail and scaled walls up to tall cliffs that stood deeper in the woods, further east than the house. Samantha wanted to argue for any other way to go, but when she looked around, they were surrounded by tall, steep peaks. No lion could climb these. She wasn't sure they could. Pan climbed swiftly up the walls, his narrow hooves perfectly balanced on the smallest of ledges, jumping from one to the other with ease. He helped them when there was room for it, and told them where to put their hands and feet to make the climb easier.

Samantha was tempted to look down, but she knew better and kept her eyes on the cliffs above. The air was growing cold but the bags on her back gave her some warmth and she clung close to the side of the mountain. Rudy was already waiting at the top, staring down at them as they climbed. Kuma's large paw slipped and dirt fell into Phoebe's eyes below him. She instinctively went to rub them and lost her grip. As she began to fall Samantha reached out just in time and grabbed her wrist. The large ogre was heavy and her wrist was thick. Pan quickly climbed down as Phoebe's arm began slipping through Samantha's hand. She held on as tight as she could, but as the ogre's large hand slowly slipped through her fingers, she began to lose her own grip. They were too far above the ground for her to let go. She had to hold on if Phoebe was going to have any chance. She squeezed her hand as tightly as she could and Phoebe cried out. Suddenly Pan was next to her and she looked at him desperately. He gave her a quick smile and wink, then dropped down once more, throwing his leg out, knocking Phoebe into the wall and holding her there until she found her footing and was able to grasp the wall again.

"I'm good!" Phoebe called out after a moment, still catching her breath, and began to climb. Pan stayed next to her the rest of the climb. Phoebe looked up only when she had to. When they reached the top Phoebe fell to the ground and Samantha joined her. The ogre grabbed her neck and looked at her. She said nothing, just stared at Samantha, inches from her face, both of them panting like dogs. Then Phoebe let out a cry and began laughing. At first Samantha was surprised, but found herself laughing, too.

It had been the closest she had even been to seeing someone she cared about die, and she was glad fate had more plans for Phoebe. When they had collected themselves and joined the bear and satyr, Phoebe bowed to Samantha, then locked arms with Pan, and surprising everyone, kissed his cheek.

"You saved my life," she explained. "It's appropriate." Then she rolled her eyes and punched him playfully in his shoulder. Kuma walked over to her and put his left arm on her left shoulder, she did the same and they looked at each other quietly for a moment, then bowed their heads with their eyes closed. Samantha watched, impressed with their ability to say so much without a single word. It was a display of sorrow and forgiveness, honor and respect. She felt the urge to run over and throw her arms around them in a group hug, but that would have been childish, though Phoebe might have gotten a good laugh out of it.

They scouted the top of the cliff, peering over the edges, and when they agreed there would be no plausible route for Chimera to find them there, they decided to set up for the night. Pan pulled out his flute and began playing a romantic tune.

"Put that away. Let's not make it any easier for her," Kuma instructed, speaking about Chimera.

Later that night Samantha sat by Phoebe at the fire. She looked distant and Samantha knew she must have been thinking about her brush with death.

"You would have done the same. I know you would have. We're a family out here, we look out for each other."

Samantha said. The words surprised her, the way it made her feel to call the odd bunch a family. She saw Phoebe watching her and they looked at each other a moment. Phoebe *was* like a sister, and she knew now that she would do whatever it took to help her, whenever she needed it.

As the night grew they became quieter, listening to the sounds of night. Samantha had moved over to Kuma and leaned against his arm to stay warm. He didn't seem to mind. She took her golden trinket from a bag she had tied to her waist. She didn't play with it as much as she used to. But tonight she wanted to look at it.

"Can I see it?" Pan stood over her shoulder, reaching out his hand. Samantha handed the object to him and he began studying it as though it were something familiar.

"Do you know what this is?" he asked her.

"Just some trinket I had on me when they found me at the orphanage." she shrugged. "I don't even know why I keep it. I guess it inspired my desire to see the world."

Pan smiled as he circled them, looking it over again and again. When he returned to Samantha he handed it back to her saying, "Wait til morning. I'll show you in the light."

He looked excited, like he had just made a great discovery. She looked at the gold piece again but didn't see anything particularly interesting about it that should have him smiling from ear to ear. She thought maybe he had planned to tease her with it tomorrow. She would put it away in her satchel and refuse to take it out if that was the case.

That night they laid a little closer together, partly to keep warm since they hadn't grabbed enough blankets, but partly because they wanted to be close to each other, to feel the presence of each one around them.

Samantha began drifting off when she heard Pan grunt like he had just been punched in the gut, then quietly say, "Okay, okay."

12

A fog surrounded the camp when they woke the next morning. They could barely see each other when they stood side by side. Samantha waved her hands in the mist and it swirled like the milk she blended into her coffee back in Chraimyth. The air was still cool and she pulled out her shawl, wrapping it around her shoulders. Kuma grabbed the pole arm and tossed it to her. The shawl fell to the ground as she caught the weapon. She reached down to pick it up but changed her mind when she saw Kuma's figure running through the fog at her with a sword raised over his head. Apparently no type of weather, hot nor cold, sight nor blind, would stop him from training her. She jumped out of the way as he brought his blade down and ran at her again.

They battled through the mist for an hour. Samantha fell again and again, Kuma yelling at her to get up as he swung the blade at her. She tried to keep her eye on Kuma's shoulders as he had taught her, but it was hard to see and she also had to watch for the cliff. She dodged his sword and managed to keep them moving in a circle. Eventually she would have to attack, knock him on his backside or the sword from his hands. None was an easy task against such a massive creature. Pan and Phoebe stood off in the distance, barely visible in the fog.

Kuma attacked again and Samantha blocked his blade with the pole arm. He grabbed the end of it and she held on firmly. She jumped, then let all her weight fall as she slid her legs between Kuma's. Her body followed and she yanked on the pole arm as her arms straightened over her head. She collided to the ground and looked up to see the bear flip over, landing on his back, groaning. She felt the victory of knocking the beast on his back, but his groans worried her. She hadn't thought about the sword in his hand. Was he groaning because he was injured? She got up and stood over him to examine his body. The sword lay at his side and the pole arm at his head. He pushed himself up, glaring at her. She could tell he was okay, but he clearly didn't enjoy her move. She couldn't help smiling.

"Are you okay?" she ask Kuma, brushing dirt from his fur. He shrugged her off and she stepped back.

"I'm fine," he grunted. Then he softened and said, "That was a good move. It was creative and effective. Remember it and use it when you need to. But always remember to keep an eye on your surroundings. There may be others attacking at the same time. You'll have defeated one, but you need to be ready to defeat more."

She listened and nodded. Though she didn't think she'd ever fight anyone, not with Phoebe and Kuma and Pan always guarding her.

The fog slowly lifted in the following hours, and they sat, just waiting, looking over the horizon as it came into view. Far off to the south they could see a swarm of harpies circling. Samantha squinted to try and see them more clearly. It was horrifying and fascinating to watch them.

"The fog has lifted, but it will still be slippery," Pan announced. "We'll need to be careful going down." He tried not to make it obvious that he was speaking more to Phoebe than any of them, but red stained her green cheeks anyway. They moved to the opposite end of the cliff. There were more peaks ahead, but the climb down wasn't as steep as the other side. Phoebe laughed with relief, and Kuma closed his eyes and bowed his head in thanks. Pan and Samantha smiled at each other and Samantha wondered if Pan found it just as amusing that the two strongest creatures among them would appear the most afraid. But she was relieved, too. She didn't want yesterday's events to occur again. If any of them were to die in the following days or months, it should be more honorable than a slip on a rock or dirt in an eye.

They made their way down the peak and pushed forward. Chimera could have woken up by now and they weren't sure how far behind she was this time. Kuma didn't seem to have any certain plans for where they were going. He only knew he wanted to make the path difficult, if not impossible, for Chimera to follow. They wound around peaks and through more forest. They came to a tall wall of thick moss. Phoebe pulled back a layer and they looked at the tangled branches behind it. They had reached another portion of the wall. The ogre, bear, and satyr looked at each other a moment. Samantha ran her hands along one of the branches, not sure what she was looking for, perhaps just trying to appear useful. Then she heard the laughter. Just as it was on the bridge, it was here at the wall. She looked to the others, Phoebe and Pan were smiling at her, Kuma stood expressionless.

"I've never heard that come from the walls before," Pan said, running up to touch the branches himself. He frowned when there was no laughter. Instead, he cried, "Ow!" and pulled back his hand, blood trickled down and a long thorn sat on the branch that they were all sure wasn't there a second ago. Pan sucked on his wound, giving the wall a dirty look. Phoebe and Samantha laughed.

"What do the trees have on you, Pan?" Phoebe teased.

"They got jealous." Pan winked at Phoebe, who rolled her eyes in return.

"Let's keep moving, we'll stay close to the wall," Kuma instructed.

Samantha touched the branch once more, smiling when she heard the gentle laugh. She wondered who it belonged to. They traveled north along the wall, mindful of keeping to stones and logs when they could to cover their tracks. Birds flying nearby provided food, though they didn't stop to eat. As the forest disappeared, large boulders took its place and they had to travel further away from the wall to get around them. The smell of trees disappeared and the air became dry. Nothing flew in the sky above them and more forest waited a few miles ahead. A large rabbit bounded from between two boulders and Kuma handed Samantha the bow and arrow. She aimed and drew back the bow but was too slow. The rabbit darted back into the boulders. She quietly followed it as it continued weaving through the large rocks. It was quiet and she knew she was alone, the others hadn't followed. They would let her do this on her own. The rabbit found a dead bush to hide under, but it was not well concealed and Samantha lifted the bow and pulled back.

The rabbit fell dead, an arrow stuck in its neck. But Samantha still held hers back, aiming. She hadn't shot her arrow yet. It had come from someplace else. She looked around for Kuma or Phoebe, but she was there alone. She approached the rabbit to examine it, but another creature emerged from behind a boulder.

A young boy stopped in his tracks when he saw Samantha. They stared at each other, neither sure what to do. When she looked at him further, she saw he wasn't just a boy, he also had the full body of a horse. She tried to remember what she had read about such creatures in her books. Centaurs, they were called, right? A quiver hung on his back and he reached for another arrow. Samantha quickly lifted her bow and they stood aiming at each other. She didn't want to shoot the boy, but she also didn't want to die over a rabbit.

"I can leave. The rabbit is yours," she offered, slowly lowering her bow and backing away. The boy panted in fear and pulled further back on the bow. Then he looked behind him and Samantha could hear the hurried clack of hooves. Another centaur, she assumed his father, slowly approached and looked to see what was frightening his son.

When he saw Samantha he raised his own bow at her. She listened for sounds of her companions but it was quiet, she was alone with the two centaurs.

"I'm sorry," she tried to explain. "I was hunting the rabbit. I didn't mean to scare your boy. The rabbit is yours. I'll just go."

"Who are you?" the centaur asked.

"Samantha. Just Samantha. There is no other name I go by," she rambled nervously. That puzzled the creature and he lowered his bow.

"What are you doing here?"

"I'm just passing through with my friends," she pointed behind her, but of course no one was there.

"Da, can I get the rabbit? I shot it." the boy lowered his bow and stared at the rabbit with his arrow sticking through its neck.

"Yes, go." his father replied. He approached Samantha and circled her. She stood straight, frozen, fearing what his hooves might feel like if he decided to trample her.

Aside from being made half man, half horse, he looked like he was filled with nothing but muscle. He wore only a leather vest, and leather was woven through small braids in his long brown hair. There were scars on the body of the horse part of him and she noticed one of his hooves was cracked. She thought of horseshoes, but she didn't know how they worked, let alone if she'd be alive much longer to explain it to him anyway.

Kuma finally appeared with the other two, stopping when they saw the two centaurs with Samantha.

The man horse looked at them, ready to aim his arrow. "Are they your party?" he asked Samantha.

"Yes."

"We didn't mean any trouble. We were only passing through." Kuma explained.

"Yes, I heard." the centaur replied, still studying Samantha. "Just Samantha, and all of you, you'll come with us."

Kuma was ready to argue but Phoebe stopped him. "Its likely a safe place for the night, accept the offer."

They followed the centaurs out of the rocks and into the forest on the other side. The trees didn't sit as close together here and there was no brush covering the ground. As they traveled further in, going west, they spotted more centaur grazing, young ones running freely through the woods, laughing and playing. They stopped when they saw the party coming with the two centaur. A circle of tents was gathered in a clearing ahead. There appeared to be a herd of thirty or so centaur, young and old alike, living there. They all stopped what they were doing and stared at them. There gaze falling mostly on Samantha.

The centaur led them to a large tent at the far side of the circle, instructing them to wait while he went inside. Samantha looked around at the tents. Each one had dried herbs and flowers hanging over the entries. Long logs were piled in the center of the encampment for a fire. There were smaller fires burning in front of some of the tents with large pots hanging over them. Female centaurides stood in front of them, pretending to mix whatever stew was inside, though they mostly stared at Samantha. She imagined this being how her uncle lived on his journeys around the world.

The centaur returned and motioned them inside. The tent was even larger inside, a platform standing on the far end with two centaurs standing in the center, waiting for them. Baskets of vegetables and flowers lined the walls, mixed with bows and swords.

They stood at the foot of the platform, none of them speaking, just watching.

"Leave your weapons here, and you are welcome to stay for the night." the bigger of the two centaur spoke. He had a leather vest similar to the one the other was wearing, and his neck was covered with layers of beaded necklaces falling to his chest. Leather braces wrapped his upper arms and cuffs on his wrists. Part of a scar was on his right shoulder, disappearing under the vest, and another under his left eye.

"Thank you," Kuma said graciously.

"I am Raftik," the centaur said, putting his hand on his heart and bowing slightly. He motioned to the centaur next to him, the female. "This is my wife, Lorna." She was only slightly shorter than he was, with her dark hair fixed atop her head. Her skin was as black as her horse hair and her eyes were as dark as the night. She was beautiful.

Then he pointed to the centaur who had brought them. "The one who led you here is Milothe. His son, who is sorry he aimed his arrow at you, is Boro."

They all bowed as their names were spoken, even Boro, who shyly smiled at Samantha, holding his arrow far back at his side, as if he were ashamed to still have it.

"I am Kuma," Kuma said, then he motioned to each of them as he introduced Phoebe, Pan, Rudy, and finally Samantha. Raftik and Lorna gave her a curious look but kept their thoughts to themselves. Samantha recognized their expressions, the same she had gotten from everyone else she had met. She didn't belong, something was different about her, possibly familiar. But they were not making accusations, yet. Instead they called for beds to be brought to the large tent for them to sleep and invited them to eat at their fire that night.

Raftik motioned they were free to go, but Kuma stood in his place. The centaur looked at him, wondering what more he wanted.

"I'm sorry, but you need to be fully aware of our circumstances." Kuma said. Raftik glanced at Samantha, as if he already knew she was likely the center of any dilemma. Without mentioning Speranta, Kuma explained they were being followed by Chimera, that she had ideas about Samantha and had threatened her. He let him know where she was last seen and explained the route they had taken to the point they met Milothe.

Raftik didn't respond right away. Instead he looked to his wife. She looked over them, stopping longer on Samantha, giving her a stern look. She stepped off the platform and walked to the human. Looking down at her she asked, "Do you believe yourself to be the one who gave us this sanctuary?"

Samantha was relieved at her term, *sanctuary*. If she had used words like prison, cage, or even hell, she would have became afraid. But sanctuary was a word used by someone who wouldn't threaten to kill her.

"No, ma'am, I don't." Samantha shook her head. The others stood quiet, though Phoebe and Pan exchanged looks. Lorna saw the exchange and questioned them the same, "Do either of you assume her to be the goddess?"

They stood quietly, unsure how to best respond. Phoebe lifted her chin and said directly, "Yes, I do." Pan reluctantly nodded in agreement. Lorna smiled then looked to Kuma. They stood eye level and Kuma stared directly at her.

169

"And you?" she asked him.

"No. She is human." he said confidently.

Lorna rejoined her husband and he waited for her answer.
"It is interesting that of all of her kind within Arguris, you
should choose this one to suddenly put such a great faith in.
And to even stir the hopes of your Chimera. But it seems god
or not, she's not a threat and you have our protection from
anything that should enter our camp." Lorna said. Raftik gave
his approval with a simple nod, and they all bowed to show
their thanks. They left the centaurs in the tent and retrieved
their bags. Kuma took Samantha outside the encampment to
train more while Phoebe and Pan offered to hunt for dinner.
The young centaurs had gathered to watch Kuma and
Samantha fight, every so often yelling, "Whoa!" or "Ooo,"
whenever Samantha lost her balance or got knocked over by
Kuma. Samantha found it hard to concentrate with the
children yelling, then she saw Lorna standing with them,
observing her. The children held her hands and wrapped their
arms around her legs. She watched as Samantha tried to hit
Kuma, but instead was defeated again and again. She joined
the children when they laughed, and that angered Samantha.
Lorna saw this and brushed the children off and galloped to
where they were fighting.

"Please, allow me a few lessons while you're here." Lorna offered. Samantha shook her head at Kuma but he backed away.

Lorna had her own pole arm and held it at her side. She motioned to the children, saying, "Do you see them there? They are not laughing and going on because they want to know how you'll respond to them. They are watching how you respond to the moment you are in. But you forget where you are." She surprised Samantha with a whack on the leg. "The moment you are in right now is a fight. There is nothing else to concern yourself with." She whacked again. Samantha tried to block it with her pole arm but was too slow. "Your objective is to put me in defense. You only try to stop the blows coming to you, but you are not sending any back. I have nothing to fear from you. I know I can defeat you." Samantha fell on her backside as the pole arm lifted her feet off the ground. She tried getting up, but Lorna held the pole inches from her face. "If you're only going to wait for the attack, you may as well surrender before you've begun. Attack your enemy and show them you're not afraid." she lowered her weapon and began making her way back to the camp. She stopped and turned back to Samantha.

"I agree, you are no god. We will make sure you are not harmed here if that creature shows her face. But you will need to become a warrior quickly if you are going to have enemies."

she trotted off, joining the children who encircled her, praising her skill and strength.

Samantha threw the pole arm down and turned away from the camp. She stared at the trees, huffing, fists at her side. Kuma joined her, not saying anything, just putting his hand on her shoulder, staring out into the same trees.

13

They ate with the centaurs that night, Phoebe and Pan having caught two wild boars each, and twelve birds. The tribe seemed impressed with their work and gave them beaded necklaces like Raftik wore. Pan wore his proudly, but Phoebe tried to tuck hers in her satchel. Samantha happily helped the centaurides smack her hands away. She noticed Phoebe didn't seem quite herself since returning from the hunt, but brushed it off. The amount of food they caught looked like their hunt was a lot of work. She would be exhausted.

They were all gathered around a large bonfire. The logs in the center of camp lighting the night. Kuma sat at Raftik's side and they seemed lost in their own conversation. Samantha watched them and assumed they were talking about Chimera. She was sitting with Lorna on the other side of the fire and decided to move closer to hear better. Lorna called her back and waved for her to come to her side. She was sitting behind her with young centaurs and their mother's surrounding her. She smiled at Samantha as the children made room for her and she sat down. She looked back to Kuma, but the bonfire was between them and she couldn't see him or Raftik anymore. After further observation, she realized all the male creatures were gathered at one end of the fire, and the females at the other. She realized Lorna had probably just saved her from embarrassing herself. She was curious about it and asked, "Why don't you eat together?"

Lorna laughed as she tousled a young child's hair, "What do you mean? We are together."

"No, I mean, why aren't you next to your husband, and your husbands next to you?"

"Men learn from men, women learn from women, as well as nurture the children," she said smiling at the girl next to her. The centaurides behind her smiled in agreement. Samantha understood, but thought it still silly that they didn't eat their meals together. She had been impressed with how civilized the centaurs were. By how calm they all were in fact. History made them out to be monsters, villains. They were to be feared and killed on the spot. They were conquests for heroes. Samantha wondered if it was Arguris that made them so peaceful. There was no one to threaten them here, she assumed. They had nothing to fear, no one they needed to hide from. She wondered what sort of hero Athena was to them. She had given them a second chance. If the gods wanted to destroy them, Samantha wondered if the creatures knew how lucky they were to be here. Her thoughts were interrupted by Lorna's fingertips gently touching her arm.

"I'm sorry if I upset you earlier. You're not familiar with my tactics and I hope I did not hurt you," Lorna said sincerely.

"It's okay. Women teach women, right?" Samantha smiled and felt her cheeks grow warm.

She combed the crowd for Phoebe, but she was nowhere in site. She hadn't even noticed she had left. Pan sat with young centaurs across the fire and waved when he saw her watching him. She excused herself from Lorna and looked in the tent but it was empty.

"Lorna, do you know where Phoebe is?" Samantha asked when she returned.

"No, do you need help looking for her?" Lorna offered as she glanced around the bonfire.

"I'm not sure, I'll go ask the others first." she walked over to Pan and Kuma, but neither of them had seen her since she helped light the fire. They both joined her, combing the camp, but Phoebe was nowhere.

"There aren't any cliffs nearby, are there?" Samantha asked, trying not to worry about the strong ogre. Pan let out a short huff of a laugh and peered towards the woods. Kuma looked as well.

"The woods here are safe," Raftik said, watching their gaze. "If she wondered off into the woods, I'm sure she will be fine. The fire is bright enough to see from quite a distance, and there is seldom a threat from any of these trees." He slapped Kuma's back and gave him a reassuring glance before returning to his place by the fire. Samantha went back to Lorna.

"Do you mind if I look in the other tents? Just in case?" she asked.

Lorna looked to the centaurides and they nodded their approval. "Sure, go ahead."

She watched them pull back flaps and peek inside. All the tents were small and there were no separate rooms, so there was no reason they had to go inside. Samantha figured it gave the centaurs some reassurance they weren't rummaging through their things or stealing from them.

Samantha pulled back the next flap. Phoebe was laying on the ground, out cold with beads of sweat covering her face and arms. Samantha looked around the room for anyone else, but there was no one.

She ran over and checked to see if she was breathing. She was, but barely, and her skin was hot.

"Kuma!" Samantha cried out, taking Phoebe's head and laying it on her lap.

The bear arrived immediately, followed by Pan, Raftik, and Lorna. A few of the child centaurs peeked their heads in but their mothers pulled them away.

Raftik took one look at Phoebe and called out, "Cairon! Come quick!"

Samantha knew immediately who was coming. She had seen him sitting with the men at the fire. While a centaur like all the others, he had a unique dress none of the others shared. His leather vest had dried herbs hanging from the front, a leather headband around his forehead with small vials going across. Each was filled with a different color liquid, some with gray and brown powders. His hair and beard were white with age and he looked like he knew the greatest secrets of Arguris, and perhaps even the old Greek world.

Cairon examined Phoebe, demanding everyone leave the room, allowing Lorna and Samantha to remain. They helped him remove her clothing so he could fully examine her. They covered her with a blanket and Cairon began carefully looking at her skin.

On the back of her thigh a small insect was burrowed head first into her leg. The skin around it was red and swollen, pus oozed out around it. Samantha felt her stomach turn and looked at Lorna. Her dark face was paling as she watched the doctor work.

"Is it a tick?" Samantha asked, trying to hold herself together. Cairon quickly looked for more but that was the only one. "If that's what you call them, yes," he responded as he pulled a tool from a pocket in his vest. "Here we call them *nightmares.*"

He carefully grabbed the insect and Phoebe let out a quiet groan. Cairon twisted and pulled and the head of the nightmare was out. Samantha fell back when she saw the long face and tentacles flailing around, looking for something else to attach to. It was no tick. It was horrifying to look at and she couldn't imagine the pain it was causing Phoebe.

"I thought the woods here were safe?" Samantha cried as she dried Phoebes forehead and held a cool, wet cloth on it.

"They must have traveled too far west. There is marshland over there and that is where these insects make their home. They feed on the frogs and any other wild thing that dares to venture there," Lorna explained.

Cairon cleaned the wound then took a vial with gray powder from his headband and emptied it over the area. Phoebe moaned again and Samantha held her hand to offer some comfort.

"Will she be alright?" Samantha asked.

Cairon explained, "Not many survive a nightmare. They bite and release their venom, their tentacles attach to the vein and continue to release their poison until they die. This one was still alive, but it's clear the poison has begun its effect. She will begin to have nightmares, and she will scream. She will beg for death, and in two days time it will most likely find her. If she is still alive on the third day, there is hope she will return, but there is nothing else we can do."

Tears fell down Samantha's face. She thought of all the medical knowledge she had, only realizing it was far too little and she had no idea how to help her friend.

"We must keep her cool," was all she could offer. Lorna nodded and went to collect more water and rags.

Kuma and Pan walked in and seeing Phoebe ill on the floor, Pan cried out and ran to her. He grabbed her hand and laid his head on hers.

"Can't you help her?" Pan stared at Samantha, much the same way she had stared at him when she clung to Phoebe as she was slipping from her hands on the mountain wall. Pan had been able to save the ogre then, but Samantha was helpless now. She knew the hope Pan had, but she could not satisfy the faith he put in her.

Lorna squeezed his arm, "Everyone's power is limited, remember?" Pan nodded sadly. Even if Samantha was Athena, there'd be only so much she could do. Gods each had their own set of skills, and Samantha didn't know if healing was one of Athena's.

"Pan, I'm sorry, I..." she couldn't finish. She couldn't bare disappointing him or thinking of Phoebe spending her last days tortured by dreams that made her beg for death. She looked away as the knot grew in her throat, telling herself to keep it together.

She tried to think of something from her books or her uncle's stories, but anything she came up with seemed too silly. She figured trying something would be better than sitting aside just waiting.

"I read somewhere that the human touch can have healing powers. I don't know that there is any truth to it but I suppose we could try." She put her hands on each of Phoebe's shoulders, unsure what to do next. She looked at Kuma and Pan to join her, but they just watched her.

Pan said, "You're the only human here, Samantha." Samantha blushed and closed her eyes, massaging Phoebe's shoulders and began humming a lullaby. She knew she had no idea what she was doing but she it felt better to do something productive, and she didn't want anyone mourning Phoebe while she was still breathing.

Kuma cleared his throat from the doorway, staring at the floor. He pretended to kick at something at his feet then looked at Samantha.

"We have to leave her here. We'll need to move on in the morning," he said quietly. He didn't want to say it, but he wanted to make sure they kept a fair distance from Chimera. Staying at the camp had already lost them time and he feared Chimera was already closer than he'd like. They didn't want her showing up at the camp, but the longer they stayed, the greater the chances grew. Still, leaving one of their companions behind was simply out of the question. Phoebe had taken care of her from the first day she set foot in Arguris. She never complained. The last thing Samantha was going to do was abandon her.

Samantha looked at Kuma with disbelief and his eyes were filled with pain. She could tell he struggled with the idea.

"We're staying here," Samantha argued. "The centaurs already told us we have their protection. Chimera is one creature, I think any one of us could handle her, let alone an entire tribe."

Kuma grunted and kicked the floor again then left the tent.

Phoebe was moved to the large tent and rested in a cot. She continued to sweat with fever. Her moans growing more frequent and Lorna informed them it was a sign the nightmares had set in. All they could do now was wait. Pan stayed at her side while Samantha asked Cairon more about the nightmares, telling him she had never seen one before, or heard of it. He told her they were native to Greece and had come there on one of the original creatures brought to Arguris and that was all he could tell her aside from what he already had.

They all tried their best to sleep that night, but even Kuma tossed in his cot, eventually deciding to sit at the tents entry as a guard. Pan had pulled his cot against Phoebe's and laid with his hand resting on her arm. He seemed to sleep the best, being given comfort feeling her warmth perhaps. Samantha continued to put her hands on her shoulders, massaging and humming for long periods of time until her throat became dry and she had to stop for water.

She went out for a second time that night, to a trough sitting outside the tent, filled with water. She filled her canteen and looked around the camp. She was surprised to see centaurs standing guard at the far end, staring out into the woods. Raftik stood at the front with ten centaurs behind him. They were armored and held swords and bows, quivers hanging from their backs full of arrows. She looked around for Lorna and saw her standing at the entrance of a nearby tent. She began walking to her until Lorna held her hand up, motioning for her to stop. Then she put her forefinger to her lips and quietly made her way to Samantha.

"Come," she whispered and led Samantha back inside.

"What's going on?" Samantha asked.

"Chimera is here. She was spotted half a mile out. She is lurking, waiting." Lorna examined Phoebe as she spoke, wiping a cool cloth down each of her arms, glancing at the door flap every few seconds.

Samantha didn't see Kuma. She hadn't seen him outside either.

"Kuma," Samantha inquired.

"I haven't seen him," Lorna said.

Samantha looked for their bags, the one with their weapons, and found it open. Two swords were missing and she didn't see them anywhere in the tent. She grabbed her pole arm. Lorna galloped to her quickly and took her arm.

"No. You must stay here. You are not ready and they can handle this. Please, stay with your friend." She held out her hand toward Phoebe, inviting Samantha to turn around. Samantha stared at the centaur standing guard, then at Phoebe moaning and sweating, Pan hovered over her with worry written all over his face.

"No," she said looking back to the centaur, "Phoebe would fight, and so will I."

She marched over to the centaurs, her pole arm at her side. Lorna's face was angry as she disappeared inside her tent then came rushing out. Samantha was ready to argue, but instead the centaur held out a beautifully engraved metal chest piece to her.

"I think you were meant to have this," Lorna said, "I hope it protects you well."

She helped Samantha put it on and she was surprised how well it fit her. She thanked Lorna and made her way next to Raftik. There was still no sign of Kuma and she thought maybe he was hiding in the woods, preparing for a surprise attack.

They stood watching the dark, listening. Finally a low rumbling growl could be heard to their left. They all turned to see Chimera slowly making her way out of the trees. The snake snapped at the air and the lion bore her teeth. She found Samantha quickly and glared at her.

Raftik pointed and yelled at Samantha, "Go!" And she hesitantly obeyed. She ran to Lorna's tent, where she and the other centaurides were putting on their own armor and grabbing weapons. She was relieved. They filed out of the tent and made their way around to where Phoebe and Pan were safe inside. Each centauride positioned themselves evenly apart, guarding the tent. Samantha stood at the entry watching as Chimera eyed her and growled at the centaurs blocking his path. She paced back and forth testing them and looking for her way around. She turned back and walked a few paces toward the forest. For a moment Samantha thought Chimera had given up too quickly but then she turned around and came back. She crouched down and prepared to jump. Raftik pointed at her and let out a loud cry. All the centaur leapt forward, swords raised and ready to come down on the creature. Chimera flew over them, roaring as she landed. She looked at Samantha and ran toward her. Arrows flew through the air in both directions as the centaurs aimed, but Chimera was swift and they pierced the dirt behind her. Samantha felt herself shaking, knowing this was no training, this was real and this creature would kill her. She knew why Kuma had told her she wasn't ready. Chimera was directly in front of her only seconds away. Suddenly her pole arm didn't seem enough to fight either the lion or the snake. She stood ready, twirling the pole arm over her head, trying to decide her move, unable to predict Chimera doing anything but sinking her teeth into her throat.

The centaurides were gathered at her side and aimed their arrows. When Chimera was only yards away, they let them loose, piercing Chimera's shoulders, paws, and the stump on her back. The creature, both lion and snake, let out cries as they pulled on the arrows and stumbled back. All the centaurs gathered around her, more arrows aimed. Chimera roared and swung her heavy paws at them. The snake reached out and bit one of the centaur. He cried out in pain and fell to the ground. The snake continued to snap, daring any of them to come close. Samantha watched as the fallen centaur began to shake and foam at the mouth. His veins turned black and his skin blue and in the same moment his body lay still. One of the centaurides cried out, "No!"

Chimera gathered what strength she had and leapt over the centaur, landing on one of the tents. It crashed around her and she stumbled over it, trying to make her way out. The centaurs followed, shooting their arrows. Chimera continued to cry out, but refused to fall. She collided into tents, ripping them apart with her teeth until she found herself outside the camp. Raftik and several other centaurs chased her into the woods, swords raised.

Samantha stood frozen, staring at the poisoned centaur. Others came and carried him away. Lorna and the centaurides lit torches and walked around the camp, assessing the damage putting what they could back in place. The cries grew faint as the centaur chased Chimera further into the woods. They would likely not return until the morning, when they were sure Chimera was far enough away, if not dead. Samantha couldn't make herself move, she could only stare at the ruined camp. Lorna touched her shoulders and she hit her with her pole arm, gasping and pulling back when she realized what she had done.

"Lorna, I'm so sorry!" she exclaimed.

Lorna rubbed her arm, but smiled at her and led her into the tent. Pan was standing in front of Phoebe's cot, two swords in his hands, ready to fight. Lorna shook her head and he lowered his arms, letting out a sigh of relief and returned to his seat next to Phoebe.

"Lorna, I'm so sorry," Samantha said, this time saying it for the camp, and the centaur. She wanted to tell Phoebe she was sorry, and Kuma, wherever he was. If she had not come, none of this would have happened. If she had simply married Edward, Chimera would still be on her usual journey around Arguris and none of their lives would have been interrupted. They would have no need to come here and every person in her life would be content. Never in the years of memories that she had, did she feel as selfish as she did right now. She knew she had hurt the people in Chraimyth who loved her, especially poor Sylvia and Marcus. And here in Arguris she was responsible for the death of a beautiful creature who didn't even know her. Yet he gave his life to protect her.

"You didn't do this," Lorna tried to comfort her. Samantha didn't understand how she could be so calm, collected. Suddenly a blood curdling scream filled the room as Phoebe threw her head back on the bed, making them all jump and stare. Phoebe lashed out as if she were trying to keep something away. Lorna grabbed a long strip of leather and instructed Pan and Samantha to hold her arms down. Phoebe was strong and they struggled to hold her still. Her screams hurt their ears and they held their heads between their arms to muffle the sound. Lorna quickly tied the strap around Phoebe's chest and under the cot, holding her down, safe. Samantha began massaging her shoulder and humming, hoping the touch and soothing sounds would calm her. Phoebe's screams continued. She looked at Lorna and Lorna looked back at her. They didn't say anything, but Samantha knew Lorna was telling her to be prepared.

14

With every step, piercing pain raged through Chimera's body. Her feet, legs, and scar carried the arrows the centaurs had shot at her. She kept running through the trees, aimlessly through the dark. The centaurs stayed close behind, their swords ready and she knew if she stopped they'd be on her. She didn't want to go far. The girl would likely already be making her way out of the camp and Chimera didn't want to waste time tracking her again. The centaur weren't giving her much choice, however. They were spread out in a wide line, ready in case she decided to try and circle around. That was exactly what she wanted to do.

She came to a clearing and could hear the water in front of her. She let her eyes adjust, seeing the lake and running to it until she reached the edge. The centaurs were coming at her fast and she had no choice but to swim. At least she'd be safe there. The centaurs weren't fond of the creatures in these waters and they wouldn't risk following her.

Sure enough, they stood beside the lake and watched her disappear across the water.

The lake was large and she could feel the creatures below tug at the arrows stuck in her feet. She cried out as they toyed with her, but she feared nothing more of them because they desired creatures that were easily tempted, and she wasn't. She swam slowly, as the water stung her wounds and her muscles ached. They'd heal quickly once she could pull the rest of the arrows out. As she made her way across the water, she thought of the girl standing in front of the tent, ready with her pole arm. She thought it was curious that the girl claiming she wasn't Athena would be armed with such a similar weapon. Why not a sword, as is the most common choice among amateurs, she wondered.

It was several minutes before she dragged herself over the grass on the other side. She collapsed, exhausted and sore. Paphene began wrapping herself around the arrows, pulling them out and throwing them into the water. Each time, she and Nova both would wince. Nova licked the wounds and when Paphene was done she reached out and bit a rabbit hiding in a bush next to them and dropped it in front of Nova. She ate it, then closed her eyes.

Chimera woke up the next morning energetic, refreshed. She looked over her wounds and they were healed. Not even a scar remained. Her muscles didn't ache and she could walk without pain shooting through her body. There was a time when she suffered her wounds and bore her scars like any other creature. She never knew how she obtained the gift, but she learned to use it to her advantage.

"We need to go back and follow her," Paphene suggested after their morning hunt.

They walked along the waters edge, looking to the other side, but it was too wide.

"We need an army," Nova thought out loud.

"For one girl?"

"Yes, for one girl and everyone who protects her." Nova said through gritted teeth.

"If we find her while she's still convinced she's nobody, she'll be an easy victory." Paphene argued.

"Like she was last night?" Nova retorted back.

They were both quiet for a moment.

"The harpies then?" Paphene assumed.

"Yes."

Chimera ran south along the lakes border until she had reached the mountains. The harpies were at the other end and she crept up to their perch slowly so they could see her coming. She hung her heads low to show them she was not on the hunt. It didn't take them long to spot her and they swooped down, squawking at her and flapping their wings. She was forced to move back, away from the cave.

"I have business!" she finally roared, growing irritated at their persistence and the pain their obnoxious sounds caused her ears.

They looked at one another, then up at a harpy sitting on a branch above them. She nodded her head and they flew off, allowing Chimera to pass. The harpy flew to the cave and stood at the entrance, waiting for Chimera.

"Why do you waste our time?" she hissed at her. Chimera cringed as she spoke.

"I've come to ask your aid," she said.

"Explain."

Chimera told her the same story she had told Arachne, including the fight at the camp with the centaurs.

Other harpies had flown down to listen as she told the story and she was happy they seemed interested.

"You idiot," the harpy snapped when she was done, "kill the one who will set us free."

"If she refuses to open Speranta, yes," Chimera insisted, "Perhaps her death will break the spell over this place." The harpies squawked to each other at this suggestion, then the one said, "What do you want from us?"

"One of your own at the Haken has already offered her help. I only ask that you send a harpy out to find her and give her word that I am here and need an army."

The harpies screeched with laughter and Chimera became impatient. She roared, silencing the flock.

"Okay beast, you can have your way, but you'll stay out of ours while you wait, if they do come at all," the harpy said with a glare. She nodded to another, who flew off toward the Haken. It would be a few days before any word came back, and Chimera planned to keep her distance in the mountain so she'd be out of their way and could think of where to look for Athena next.

"You'll come inside," the harpy demanded, stepping aside. She went in, and the sounds of the squawking and screeching echoed off the wall, making her ears ring until she felt deaf. She saw large nests with young harpies calling out and mothers feeding them raw meat. She was led past them down a winding tunnel. Harpies guarded her on either side, as though she were a prisoner. They towered over her, their wings rubbing against her side down the narrow path. She didn't like being this close to them, with that horrible sound surrounding her.

As if they were doing it on purpose. She couldn't think. It was even hard to focus on where she was going. Something was wrong, she sensed it as the tunnel narrowed and the air grew thick. She tried to get control of her senses. She suddenly felt herself being pushed and she fell into a deep pit. She groaned as she picked herself up. The pain in the ribs that had just broken slowly easing as they mended themselves. The pit was only a few steps wide in either direction and when she jumped to escape, there was still several feet above her to the top. She jumped again and again, trying to dig her claws into the stone wall, but only scratching the surface and colliding with the floor below. She let out a roar that echoed around her, drowning out the harpies sounds briefly.

She had been captured. There was no shelter in the pit and no where for her to hide.

"You fools," she screamed, "Let me out!" A harpy peeked over the edge and Chimera watched her. It squawked and laughed when Chimera cringed, then it threw a dead pig down to her and disappeared. Chimera sniffed the pig. It was fresh, it's body still warm. She ate reluctantly, throwing the rest of the carcass out of the pit. She studied the walls carefully, looking for any ledge or cracks she might use for footing. The walls were perfectly smooth. She tested the ground below her, but other than a layer of dust, it was as solid as the walls. There seemed to be nothing left to do but wait for one of the screeching birds to come and tell her what they intended to do with her. She laid down and buried her head under her paws, Paphene slithered under the lions mane. There was not much they could do to muffle the sound and Chimera thought she might die of insanity.

She laid for several hours, falling asleep when she could no longer bear the sounds echoing off the walls. When she woke up, harpies were circled around the edges above her, staring down at her, taunting her. She didn't give them the satisfaction of even a roar, but circled slowly, studying each of them. They become quiet and she heard something being dragged across the floor. Two harpies pulled a large stone pot to the edge and tipped it over. Chimera had nowhere to move, leaving burning hot rocks to hit her body. Paphene hid her head between the hind legs and Nova pressed hers against the far wall. The rocks singed her fur and she cried out. The harpies above cackled in amusement. Paphene took two rocks in her mouth, one at a time, and shoved them in Nova's ears then hid herself under her mane. The rocks had cooled, and they helped muffle the sound.

When the harpies saw they could no longer aggravate the beast, they left her. Chimera closed her eyes, taking in the beautiful sound of quiet. Nova whispered a "thanks" to Paphene and she began piling the rocks.

The sky darkened as the large flock blocked the sunlight above. Creatures below gazed up to see what cast the shadow. Hundreds of harpies flew in tight formation toward the mountains to the east. Feathers dropped every now and then, and the young creatures on the ground chased after them. They spread out among the perch when they reached the lair, and one went directly to the cave.

"Typhora!" she called.

"Linaphese," Typhora flew down from her perch and greeted her.

"So we'll have our freedom after all, it seems," she said as they fluttered their wings together in greeting.

"It seems a waste of vengeance to fight for a beasts sore feelings," Typhora offered, leading Linaphese toward the pit.

"Yes, but she seems certain this being is Athena. And if she's right, then we have just cause to fight."

"You'll understand if we don't join you," Typhora stopped in the tunnel and looked at Linaphese. "Athena owes us much, but we have lived content and have bothered no one. No one has bothered us in return. These walls have been a safe house, and provided more comfort than our kind was ever given out in the world. Defeat the goddess and all the rest if you must, but if the walls come down, our flock will remain here."

Linaphese eyed her sister. She knew she was toying with her. There was no peace for their kind as long as they needed men. And they would never stop needing men. Which meant they would always hunt, and kill. That was why the humans stayed so far away. They knew they weren't safe in Arguris. They were never supposed to be there anyway. Yet some had cast themselves into the wind to escape something. Typhora wasn't worried about peace. She wanted to remain one of the great predators. They had been told the stories of men who hunted their kind long before Arguris ever existed. Typhora was right, they were safe here, but Linaphese wasn't worried about who would be pointing arrows or throwing swords at them.

Linaphese decided to say nothing. If her sister didn't fight, then she'd take the flock.

Typhora showed her to Chimera and Linaphese gasped. Chimera leapt from a small pile of rocks, falling on her back when she saw them peering down at her. "What have you done?" she demanded.

"Just safe keeping is all. I told you, no one has bothered us, and we've bothered no one. I wanted to make sure it stayed that way," and she motioned for the harpies to help Chimera out of the pit.

Some things hadn't changed. Typhora was always something of a sadist.

Chimera stood, raising her head to glare at Typhora, but they could all see she was weak and hungry. Typhora called for food to be brought to her. The beast roared in anger and lashed out her paw at Typhora. "How dare you keep me in a pit like a prisoner," she yelled.

The harpy laughed and Linaphese looked at her, aggravated. "Oh beast, be quiet before I put you back in there," she taunted.

"Typhora," Linaphese stepped in. "This is business, you'll leave her to me."

Typhora bowed to them, mocking them with her smile, then made her way out of the cave.

A harpy flew in and dropped several fresh kills of rabbits, birds, and boars. Chimera wasted no time in feeding and the harpies watched, one in amusement, the other pity.

When she had regained her strength, Linaphese took her out of the cave and they walked about the perch. It was short in the front, facing the mountains, but it stretched around and behind the cave, providing the harpies plenty of trees and ground to nest.

The mountains provided protection, though in Arguris harpies had little to worry about in way of predators.

"Rocks?" Linaphese asked when she observed the rocks in Chimera's ears.

"Yes, it helps," Chimera said smugly.

"Where is Athena?"

Chimera filled her in on the events, and they planned to send a few harpies to search for her.

"I'm going to look from the ground,"Chimera said, wanting to get as far away from the lair as she could. Typhora watched from her usual branch, squawking occasionally just to taunt her. Linaphese gave a her a disapproving look but she ignored her.

Chimera sprinted off a few yards, but then stopped and turned back to Linaphese.

"They have a look out of their own. If you see the owl, kill it, they won't be far from there" she instructed. Then she made her way through the mountains once more. She came to the bridge but didn't cross, instead she followed the creek until she came to a thick wall of brush. She knew it wasn't the edge of Arguris though. She followed the wall west, passing large totems with skulls of the half human creatures that lived there fixed on top. She rounded the corner and met two giant minotaurs standing guard at the entrance. When they saw her they snorted and huffed, holding large axes and halberds in front of them. They were threatening her.

"Open the gate, minotaurs, I need to speak to your king," she commanded.

They looked at each other and laughed, then back to Chimera.

"Be on your way, unless you want us to dine on your flesh tonight," one sneered. His voice was deep and sounded dry, like he hadn't had a drink in days.

Chimera ignored his threat.

"I'm looking for a goddess," she stepped forward, daring them to test her.

"If there's a goddess in there, she's dead by now," the other one said as he pushed the heavy gate open. He bent down and sniffed at her fur as Chimera slowly made her way past them. Other giant beasts like them grabbed clubs, halberds, and whips, ready to beat her down if she flinched the wrong way. She looked only to the minotaur ahead. The king. He stood taller than the rest.

That was their way. The largest bull was king. There was no fight for it, no politics, pure breeding. Any daughters born of the previous king would become the new kings bride. If the king had no daughter, the minotaura would fight and the strongest would wed the new king. Other creatures in Arguris stayed far away from them. They were known for their hunger for the half humans flesh. Visitors were rare and Chimera's appearance alarmed them.

She bowed before the king. He may have been the largest creature in Arguris, even bigger than the bear, she thought. He had a wide human frame, thick with muscle, covered in leather armor with metal fringe that was cut to sharp points at the end. His head was of a bull's. A gold ring pierced his snout and large horns curled out of his head. He had gray hair, like a lions mane, and it descended down his back until it disappeared at a small point.

"Hello, Chimera." his voice was deep, like it came from the far depths of the earth.

"King Korauk," she bowed once more.

"What has happened that you'd dare come see us?" he asked playfully, and the other minotaur joined in his chuckling.

"Korauk, there is a girl in Arguris, but I think she is more than that," she said quickly, afraid he'd cut her off and send her away. "I believe she is Athena."

Korauk stepped forward and looked at his tribe, then to Chimera. He circled her, sniffing at her like the other minotaur had done. Paphene raised her head and he huffed at her. She glared back and flicked her tongue.

"No one has ever tasted the flesh of your kind," he snorted. He lowered his axe so the blade grazed Chimera's face as he passed. "You're the only one," he scoffed, "what a rare treat you'd be, and we didn't even have to hunt you." Chimera felt her fur standing. Her jaw clenched. She stared straight ahead as the king circled her, threatening her, taunting her. She would kill a repugnant king today if she had to.

He lifted his weapon into the air and Chimera crouched, growling and Paphene held her head back, hissing, ready to fight. The king glared at them, then turned to the minotaurs. "It was our ancestors who decided to join the Anemoi that brought us here. The gods had no quarrel with them, but still they ran. We have remained hidden from the world all these years and now the goddess Athena may be on our doorstep," he lowered his sword and looked at Chimera a moment, then he went on, "We will demand our freedom or, when the time comes, we will feast on god flesh." He raised his sword to the sky and the tribe cheered, shaking their weapons over their heads.

Chimera sat next to Korauk at the dinner fire that evening, eating the flesh of a satyr. She wasn't particular to the taste, finding it fatty and salty, but she wouldn't complain. She looked around at the other minotaur and many of them stared at her. She wondered how many of them were craving for her flesh. She looked at Korauk. He was staring at her, too. What stopped any of them from trying to kill her? Why did it take so little to make him an ally?

Curious, she asked him, "Why did you agree so quickly to fight?"

The minotaur smiled as he ripped meat from a rib with his teeth. He chuckled, "No one wastes time coming here without there being a purpose that requires them to risk their life." He pointed a bone at Chimera. "You included."

She told him about the harpies and the scouts, and he agreed to prepare more weapons and have his tribe ready when she sent for them.

Neither of them were aware of the large owl perched on top of the kings hut, listening and observing. He quietly walked to the far edge of the rooftop before spreading his wings and flying to the centaur camp.

"She's collected harpies and minotaurs," Rudy informed Samantha, who was sitting on Phoebe's legs as Lorna tied them down. The ogre screamed as the venom continued to work its way through her body. Rudy waited for her to quiet down, then he repeated,

"She's building an army."

Samantha looked at Pan and asked, "Where's Kuma?"

15

Centaurides threw their arms up in joy when they saw the two centaurs approach. Kuma walked not far behind, carrying his halberd and usual grim expression. Two swords hung at his sides. Samantha walked out to see what the commotion was, and upon seeing the bear, she disappeared back inside the tent, reappearing with her pole arm and charged at him. As if understanding, Kuma dropped his halberd and raised his arms in front of him. Samantha swung and kicked, hitting his arms and legs, crying out painfully as tears came down her face. Kuma blocked every hit, every kick, then finally took the pole arm and yanked it from her hands, tossing it to the ground. He grabbed Samantha and bent down so he was face to face with her.

"She came and I couldn't find you!" Samantha yelled.

Kuma yelled back, "You think I teach you so you can depend on me to save you?"

Samantha was quiet. She didn't think she wanted Kuma to save her, or maybe she did. She wasn't sure. It was suddenly clear to her that despite the bears attempt at remaining detached, she had grown an emotional attachment to him anyway. She thought of him as something more than a teacher, she wasn't sure what, and that could kill them both.

"Where were you?" she demanded after he let her go. She picked up her pole arm and glared at him.

"Did you not see the children were gone?" he looked toward the camp. It was still in ruins, but the centaurides had managed to get the tents standing again and were working on mending the ripped materials.

Samantha hadn't noticed. She had been so wrapped in caring for Phoebe and helping the centaurides clean up that she hadn't noticed the absence of laughter and play. She looked around the camp, all the young were gone. Samantha thought of the centaur that had died and wondered if Chimera was that cruel that she would have attacked the children had they been here. If she was, Kuma had saved their lives. He was a hero.

"I thought you had left us," Samantha admitted, lowering her head.

"You still have a lot to learn." Kuma said, offering no comfort. He walked to the tent Phoebe was laying in and went to her side.

Her complexion had become red and her breathing was shallow. It had been nearly two days, and they were prepared to hear her last breath before the next show of light. Centaurides continuously laid cool rags on her, but her burning skin warmed them quickly and they had to drop them in water again and again to keep them cool. It seemed impossible to bring her temperature down.

"Submerge her," Kuma commanded. The centuarides looked at him and Samantha smiled.

"Yes," she agreed. "Hurry, the nearest pool of water, we need to take her there."

Kuma stood and grabbed Phoebe. They untied her and Kuma gently laid her over his shoulder and carried her to the trough. She was too large to lay in properly like a bath, but they did their best to get her under water, using cups to pour water over parts they couldn't submerge. Phoebe began to shiver as the water cooled her skin. Slowly her complexion returned to its ashy gray and her breathing sounded normal. Pan looked at Samantha and Kuma, as if waiting for approval to hope. They couldn't help but share the same feeling. Lorna seemed to look surprised, too, and she called for Cairon.

He lifted her leg out of the water and checked the wound. It looked mostly healed, aside from a small welt where the nightmare had entered and a bit of redness. He laid the leg back down and took a liquid filled vial from his headband. He slowly emptied it into Phoebe's mouth then held her jaw closed as she choked it down. He looked at them with only a sullen expression.

"She may live, but I don't want to give any assurances. I told you it is rare. But you have done well," he said. He shook Samantha's hand, as if that was the only thing he could think to do, then left.

Lorna had centaurs bring fresh pails of water to keep the trough cool. Phoebe seemed to relax and Samantha and Pan took turns holding her head up. A centaur finally brought a board and carefully pushed it into the trough so Phoebe could rest against it without her head hanging over. Samantha rubbed her shoulders, humming her lullaby, and watched Kuma talk to Raftik. She hoped Raftik was filling him in on what Rudy had seen.

If Chimera was building an army, they would need to do the same. She knew the centaurs would help them, but that wouldn't be enough. They would need to find more creatures to fight with them. But that meant she would have to make herself known, and let the creatures of Arguris decide for themselves what they believed her to be. If they believed her to be a god, she'd have to be prepared for whatever wrath they wanted to throw upon her like Chimera had already promised. She hadn't seen what else lived in Arguris. She had no idea who they could ask for help. She would have to train harder and become stronger. Samantha would have to be prepared to fight an army with only a handful of creatures willing to help her.

"Samantha!" Pan snapped as he held her wrist.

She hadn't even noticed him approach as she thought of everything that needed to be done, nor did she notice her fingers digging into Phoebe's shoulders. She let go and apologized to Phoebe, unsure if she could hear her.

"Do you still have that golden stick you always play with, the one I looked at?" Pan asked. He looked a little impatient.

"Yes, why?" Samantha said, thinking of it sitting in her bag inside the tent.

"I think it's time to show you how it works." Pan didn't look as excited as he had the first time he saw her with it. In fact, this time he looked as though he regretted having to show her. It was just a trinket. It had pretty engravings on it, but that was about the only thing she ever considered remotely interesting about it.

She fetched the cylinder from her bag and took it to Pan. He had moved outside of camp and waited for her by the trees where Chimera had come in. She handed it to him and waited.

He looked it over, then at Samantha.

"Take it like this," he instructed, putting it back in her hand and placing her fingers strategically around it. She wondered why he didn't do it himself. If he was playing a trick on her she'd make him sore, she promised to herself. As if reading her mind, he said, "This will only work at your hands. No one else."

He pulled her arm so it was stretched out in front of her, then he stepped back.

"Remember where your fingers are now. You'll use the same position every time," he said. "When you're ready, just squeeze."

Samantha looked back and forth between Pan and the object in her hand. She wasn't sure what she should expect to happen, or why she would want to do this again. Was it a magic trick? She had seen a magic show once with Celeste. Her favorite part was the levitating woman. Maybe a curtain of colorful ribbon would fly out when she squeezed.

She smiled at Pan, sure she had figured it out, then squeezed. The sound of metal scraping again metal rang through her ears and long golden poles shot out on either side. Sharp blades popped out at one end. It happened so fast and Samantha was so surprised she fell over. Pan stared at her as though she were one of the great wonders of the world. He helped her up then fell to his knees.

"This again? Pan, get up." Samantha ordered. He kept his head low and stood.

"Your highness, you must allow me to explain."

She grabbed the spear and held it in front of her and looked it over. It was perfectly balanced at the cylinder, and had the same engravings along the pole from top to bottom. She noticed toward the end there was another engraving. A snake wrapped around with its head at the top, the mouth open with the hissing tongue hanging out. She thought of the anacondas at the gate and her arm band. She looked at it and compared it to the engraving on the spear. They were identical. Her heart skipped a bit and she looked at Pan sternly.

"Okay, explain." she said.

Pan invited her to walk with him. They strolled along the outside of the camp, Samantha carrying her new spear, and Pan began.

"The spear you hold is the spear of Athena," he held up his hands before she could stop him. "Let me go on," he insisted. "It was forged by Hesphaestus. He was god of this stuff," he waved to the spear. "Each weapon was designed and assigned to each god and only those gods could yield it. Athena has three weapons. The aegis, the sword, and the spear."

"What is the aegis?" Samantha asked.

Pan pointed to her breastplate. "You're wearing it. Funny coincidence, don't you think?" He couldn't hide the smile and she could see he had it already pieced together in his mind. Samantha felt her heart palpitating. Her legs were becoming numb. She wanted Pan to stop talking. She wanted to return to the tent.

He continued, "I myself stole the aegis, and I do apologize." He stared off into the woods, lost in a memory and Samantha wondered what it was.

"I was in love with a nymph, but she refused to be taken with me. I was once very persistent with the nymphs I loved. Of course, I'm not the same satyr I was before. I thought I could win her over with a gift. Athena had been traveling near my home and when she went to visit the nymphs, I took the aegis she left at her tent."

He paused again, standing still, staring at the armor.

"I never got the chance to give it to my love. I stayed hidden with the shield while she had her men search for it. When she had gone, I came out and the nymphs were gone. The Anemoi was all I met."

"A shield?" Samantha looked at Pan and knocked on the breastplate. He laughed and explained, "When we first arrived in Arguris, it was a bit of chaos. There wasn't just some magical order where we all peacefully decided where we'd live and who would leave who alone. I held onto the shield for years, traveling Arguris, as many of us did, understanding its boundaries and looking for any way out. Of course, I also looked for my nymphs." He stared off again.

Samantha tried to picture what it must have been like to be carried off by the wind and dropped in unfamiliar territory. It wasn't hard to relate. She remembered the day she woke up in the orphanage. The old woman sitting next to her cleaning dirt from her arm and one of the girls scrubbing mud from her shoes. She had run through the house, demanding they let her go, and it took four girls her size to hold her down.

They started walking into camp, Pan still telling his story, "I decided it was time to settle into a home, begin my life and not lay too much expectation on finding freedom. I sold the aegis to a centaur in exchange for a decent house built. I lost track of it, until here. Her face is recognizable anywhere." He pointed to the face at the center of the breastplate. A female's face with snakes coming out of her head, the perfect resemblance of Medusa.

"You have had the spear all along, the aegis has found its way back to you, you've lived right outside these walls for years and you were found even closer than that when they found you in the woods," he went on excitedly.

Samantha shot him a curious look, "How do you know where they found me?"

He stopped, his face went pale and he stared at Samantha. "You told us, before, remember?" his voice shook and he took a few steps back.

"I don't even know where they found me. 'In the woods'? I never said that." Samantha studied him. She had let go of her initial reaction to him, that there was something familiar about him. Suddenly those feelings came rushing back. She studied his face, his hair, his body. She circled around him as she tried to piece it together. Kuma saw them and approached, concerned Pan was causing mischief.

"What is it?" he grumbled and stared at the spear in Samantha's hand.

Samantha shook her head at him, "I'll figure it out." she gave Pan a disgusted look and pointed back to the camp, "Go." He ran off and made his way back to Phoebe.

"Nice spear." Kuma said.

"I've had it all along. I had no idea what it was," she handed it to him to admire. "Pan showed me how to use it."

Kuma took it from her hands and it instantly closed, becoming the same gold trinket it was before. Kuma jumped and looked at her. Samantha shared his surprise.

"Here, try placing your fingers like this," she positioned his hands the same way Pan had shown her. "Now squeeze."

Kuma squeezed, but nothing happened.

"He said it only works for Athena. But how can that be?" Samantha looked over at Pan, who was watching them as he rubbed a cloth over Phoebe's arm.

"Do it." Kuma demanded.

"No." Samantha threw it to the ground and turned away so she stared into the trees.

Kuma picked it up and shoved it against her chest. "Do it." She took it from him and positioned her fingers, then stepped back and squeezed. The spear shot open just as it had done before.

Lorna and Raftik came out of their tent just in time to see her do it.

"You are well equipped," Lorna offered when they reached them. She said nothing else, but moved on to join Pan and Phoebe.

Raftik looked at them, then at the spear. "That is the spear of Athena, correct?" he asked.

"Yes," Kuma said, surprising Samantha. If he believed that was the spear of Athena, did that mean he believed she was Athena? She studied him but he gave her no signs.

"And you wear her aegis I see?" Raftik continued.

Samantha knew where he was going and sighed. "Yes, but..." She was cut off by Lorna calling for them. "Come! Come quick!" she yelled.

Samantha began to fear the worst. She held the spear vertically at her side and ran to the trough.

Phoebe was moaning and her eyes fluttered as she tried to open them. She began mumbling and Samantha tried to listen to what she was saying. She put her hand on Phoebe's forehead to stroke it and noticed the fever was gone. She felt her arms and legs, they were cool.

As Phoebe woke up, she continued to try to talk. Slowly she managed, "Get...me...out of this...thing." Pan and Samantha put her arms around their shoulders and lifted her up. The trough began to fall and Kuma caught it, holding it in place. Phoebe was still weak and they had to hold her carefully so she wouldn't fall to the ground. They carried her inside quickly and sat her on one of the cots.

She leaned forward and hugged herself, shivering. Pan grabbed a blanket and draped it over her shoulders.

"Phoebe, you did it!" Samantha cried out. The room was soon filled several centaurs. Everyone wanted to see the miraculous recovery. Phoebe looked at them, not quite sure what was going on.

"You sang to me. I heard your lullaby." she held Samantha's arm as she spoke. "I saw you singing to me. I followed you. You protected me."

Samantha smiled at her and covered her hand, "I helped with the cool cloth is all." she said, too happy to see her friend alive to think about anything else. But her joy was short lived when Pan, lost in the moment, said, "I thought I'd have to get my Rhama to bring you back."

Samantha had only ever heard one person use the phrase 'my Rhama' to refer to his doctor. It wasn't a Greek word. It didn't make sense for the satyr to be using it. She rubbed her forehead as the pieces began fitting together and her heart began to palpitate again. She felt the rage welling up as the answer became clear. *It couldn't be true*, she thought. She stood up and towered over Pan, her cheeks and ears burning. When Pan saw the expression on her face he stood and began backing away. She followed him until he was stumbling over baskets along the wall. She looked at his face, especially his eyes. Raftik walked in, followed by Lorna and Kuma. They saw Pan cowering and Samantha glaring at him. Samantha held out her hand toward them and Kuma tossed her the golden trinket. She had left it outside to help bring Phoebe in. She caught it and in an instant had her fingers positioned and the spear was open. She lifted it so the blade was at Pan's throat.

"What are you doing here?" she demanded through gritted teeth.

Phoebe tried to call out behind her but she was still weak. Lorna carried a plate of food and brought it to her, still watching Samantha and Pan intently.

"I'm here to serve you, goddess," Pan begged.

"Liar!" Samantha thrust the spear forward, stopping inches from his skin.

"I beg you, please, I don't understand." Pan lowered his head and raised his arms in surrender.

Samantha tried to understand. How was it possible? The stories didn't make sense, but his eyes. His voice was a little different but she could see which was the disguise. She looked at his legs. They were always covered before. He had always come out in curious costumes, claiming they were from far away lands. She had always thought he walked funny, but he looked older then. How did he do it?

She looked at the satyr and a cry escaped her.

"I don't know if I can trust you!" she cried, slowly lowering her spear and falling against his chest.

Everyone stared, not understanding what was happening. All they could do was watch.

"Who are you, Uncle." she asked as Pan wrapped his arms around her and she wept.

16

Pan sat inside the guarded tent. He looked at the hooves of
the centaur under the door flap, thinking how he could easily
run past them and be deep into the woods before they could
reach him with their arrows. He heard Samantha's voice a few
tents down, speaking to Lorna, and he cringed thinking of the
anguish he had caused her, and the betrayal they all felt
because of the secrets he kept. He pulled his flute from his
pocket and ran his hand over the smooth reeds then softly
played its last tune. He dropped the flute to the ground and
crushed it under his hoof, tears falling from his eyes.

"Syrinx, you deserved so much more," he whispered quietly and mournfully as he stared at the pieces on the floor. Of all the possessions he had ever owned, he had carried that flute the longest. It was a joy for him when he first made it, but over time it had become a burden. A reminder of what sort of satyr he used to be. Then it had become a key. His passage between two worlds. He had lied to everyone. He had no choice.

The door flap blew in a gust of wind and he looked out above the trees, as far as he could see into the sky. The wall was much further, but he felt his gaze fall upon it anyway. And then a memory filled his head.

The nymph was beautiful, with long earthy hair that flowed in the wind, flowers and vines growing through it, always scented with the most divine aromas. Her skin was a smooth, pale green complexion. She ran with grace, like a deer, and he loved to chase her. The woven leaves and vines around her waist flowed behind her like a waterfall, and he always came close to grabbing it but, like water, it would run through his fingers and she'd be gone, waiting for him to find her again. She loved to tease him, allowing her face to emerge from the trees as he searched for her. Her eyes were the lightest of blues, like clear waters. And her lips were curled into a provoking grin, and he tried to kiss them. She would vanish then, her spirited laughter carrying off into the woods as his lips touched bark. She looked as though all the best parts of the world had come together to form this beautiful creature. He loved her, his Eudora.

He had always loved the nymphs. Several of them. He couldn't help himself. They were beautiful and mysterious. Their swiftness and cunning attracted him even more and he spent much of his youth trying to outwit them.

Most of them hated him, and it took him a long time to realize that. They didn't laugh with him or tease him as Eudora did. She was the only one to ever let him touch her.

She stood there in the trees, a beautiful smile on her face, her hair flowing and her skirt running like a stream behind her. Pan crept slowly, expecting her to disappear, or dash away, or become a bush of roses or a tall oak. But she remained, and his heart beat more rapidly than it had in all the times he had chased a nymph. He slowly reached out his arm and she stared at it, then looked at Pan and reached hers up as well. He felt her fingertips run slowly down his arm, and he touched her skin. It was soft, even softer than rabbits fur and he felt himself begin to lose control. He gently grabbed her arm and leaned forward to kiss her, but in an instant he found himself tumbling over a thorn bush, his fur getting caught and pulled. Laughter filled the woods there and he smiled at the bush, picking off his fur and letting it drop to the ground.

"You love me, Eudora," he said to it, "I will find you a great gift, something deserving of you, and I will hope for your lips as thanks."

Pan watched the door flap fall and the trees out of view behind it. He smiled. She was out there somewhere, right now.

Just then Samantha barged in with a plate of food and cup of water. She scoured at him as she shoved them at him.

"Are you really that proud of yourself?" she asked as she sat down in front of him. Kuma entered behind her and stood quietly, folding his large arms in front of him. He could feel the tension and knew they had come for answers. He wasn't sure what he had to say would help them feel any better, or bring comfort to Samantha.

Raftik and Lorna walked in with long spears and stood on either side of the exit. Pan fidgeted with his plate.

"Why?" Samantha looked at him like a mother asking her child why they stole from someone else's harvest. She folded her arms and they all sat and stood in silence, waiting.

He took a deep breath and exhaled with a loud huff. He set the plate and cup behind him and looked at the group, ready to tell them everything.

"We're guarded by dryads of the Arcadian forest. You asked them here yourself, your highness," he looked at Samantha.

She glared back at him and through gritted teeth said, "Don't call me your highness, or Athena, or anything other than Samantha."

Pan looked at her sadly and nodded.

"My reputation with the nymphs is true, but for centuries I have loved especially one." his face flushed. He had never told anyone about Eudora, or the truth about the walls. It felt strange to say those things out loud.

"I've known all along what the wall was, having spent most of my life around them. But it is hard to tell one apart from the other when they are in this form, and I spent a long time searching for my Eudora, playing my flute for her, hoping she'd answer." He wanted to say her name again. It felt like honey on his lips, but he went on. "I never found her, but instead I was confronted by another nymph. She was dressed in armor that I had never seen on a nymph before and she offered me a deal. She told me she wouldn't help me find Eudora, but she'd promise to let Eudora watch me from her post if I promised to keep them informed of the world outside of Arguris." He felt the pain build up in his stomach as he thought of the betrayal the creatures in front of him were feeling. "They told me to play my flute there every time and they would open the wall for me. I was gone for months at a time, walking the forest alone, miles in every direction. I'd find human civilizations but none were close enough to be of any threat. I never made it as far as home, nor anywhere that looked like we are close." he said looking at Kuma and the centaurs apologetically. He wished he could tell them something better. "Chraimyth was the first city established so close to Arguris. I put together a disguise and hid my legs so I could blend with the humans." He looked at the floor, not wanting to see the hurt he was sure was on Samantha's face. "Over time I was able to buy my own land and I became close friends with a man who now calls me his brother. He doesn't know who I really am. Since then I've traveled back and forth between Arguris and Chraimyth, using my flute to gain entrance and leave, telling the nymph everything I've seen and every place I've been."

"And what about me?" Samantha asked impatiently. "Let's get to the part where you see me in the woods, then insert me into your life outside these walls and refuse to tell me who you are!"

"I assure you, it was never my intention to hurt you. I was returning to Arguris from a long leave to Chraimyth when I saw you in the woods. From outside of Arguris you can not see the walls. They're invisible." Pan watched as they exchanged confused glances with each other. "You wore a hood over your head and I couldn't see your face. I only knew I needed to keep the person away from the wall. I grabbed a rock and threw it at you and it hit your head, knocking you unconscious. It wasn't until I turned you over too see who you were that I realized you were Athena." He looked at her and she was sitting quietly, staring at him intently. "Part of my agreement with the nymphs was death. Should I bring anyone in, I, and they, would die. Should I be forced to tell anyone about my agreement, or try to let anyone out, I should destroy my flute or I, and they, would face death."

They looked at the broken flute scattered next to him. Kuma growled.

"I brought you to the orphanage and left you at their doorstep. I was afraid and didn't know what to do. It was not my doing that the Roeker's took you in, that was of their own. When I learned you had lost your memory, I began to collect relics that I hoped would help you remember. I was afraid to bring you before the nymphs if you weren't ready to address them as yourself. I didn't want to put you at risk.

When you ran away that night, I followed your scent and realized you had come here. I followed you to see if your memory had come back, and to protect you."

Pan sat quietly, unsure what more he could say to explain himself. He hoped it was enough to make them understand he didn't mean to hurt anyone or betray them. They were all quiet. Samantha played with her closed spear, thinking about what she had just heard. Kuma watched her, and Pan noticed the odd expression in his face. He wondered what secrets the bear had to share. Raftik and Lorna left the tent and Pan grabbed the plate behind him and began eating. Samantha scoffed at him and abruptly stood and left.

"I am sorry, Kuma. I forget the consequences and jump into action too quickly. Please help her understand I never wanted to hurt her." Pan stammered as he pushed bread into the soft carrots, mashing them over his plate. Kuma left, and Pan ate. No matter how angry the goddess was with him, he would still be ready to protect her. Chimera was coming with an army, and he had no intention of sitting in a tent while they went off to fight.

Lorna returned shortly later to collect his plate. She said nothing, but gave him a disapproving look. Before she lifted the door flap to leave she turned to him and said, "I think I understand your intentions, but it's for her and each of us to decide our own fate," she said.

"I just didn't want anyone to die," Pan responded, turning away and dropping his head to his chest.

"But why would the nymphs kill Athena?" Lorna asked.

"It was a risk I couldn't take. Just as the creatures born here would not know what she looks like, I couldn't assume every nymph had seen her. If she found the walls on her own, or if I took her, there was no certainty they'd trust she was Athena." Pan explained.

"Why was she there in the first place? Instead of coming through Speranta as she did now?"

"I don't know," was all Pan could offer.

Lorna looked around the tent as she thought, then back to Pan.

"You did well, satyr," she assured him. "You made hard decisions with the best of your heart. I hope she forgives you in time." She pulled back the flap and disappeared.

17

It was morning, and Arguris sat in a mass of gray. There was never a sunrise or sunset. Only the gradual light that illuminated the trees and the mountain tops. Some days the fog would lay heavy on the ground in the mornings, but every day a fog sat high above the trees, reminding them of the boundary that surrounded them.

Samantha and Phoebe sat outside the tent, polishing their armor, watching as the trees slowly came into view, first the outlines of the the treetops, then the branches.

Raftik and Kuma emerged from one of the tents, talking and laughing. Samantha watched as they shook hands, smiling to each other, she wondered what agreement they had just made so early in the morning. Then Raftik threw his quiver over his shoulder and galloped into the woods with several centaurs.

"Where are they headed?" Phoebe asked beside her.

"I'm not sure," she replied, "How do you feel?"

Even though it had been days since Phoebe awoke, Samantha still worried about her. They trained for hours together every day at Phoebe's insistence. Samantha knew it was for her own benefit, but she also felt reassured of Phoebe's condition when she saw her move and swing her blade. She'd watch how she handled the sword, her foot work, her breathing. Every day she appeared stronger and stronger.

"I'm fine, stop worrying about me," Phoebe insisted. "You saved my life, you know."

Samantha looked at her. They had already had this conversation. Phoebe insisted an image of Samantha came to her in her dreams and helped chase the nightmares away. She saw her standing there, humming her lullaby, and the darkness Phoebe couldn't escape would slowly fill with light, until the darkness eventually took over once again and she was trapped, attacked again and again by what lurked inside it.

Samantha hated the visions that it created for her, knowing how Phoebe suffered during those days, but she was glad it was over.

"We've been over this Phoebe,"Samantha said flatly. "You saved yourself. You fought through it and you stayed with us." Phoebe looked to the tent where Pan was held. "We'll have to leave soon. What are we going to do with him?"

Samantha followed her gaze and shook her head.

"I don't know. He can't be trusted." Samantha tried not to think about Pan. His betrayal hurt them all. Still, he had saved Phoebe's life on the mountain, and while she faced death, he never left her side. In a way he had never left hers either. Still, Samantha couldn't put the two realities together. Pan, disguised as Uncle Nicolas, then following her here and looking in her eyes again and again with no utterance of the truth. Perhaps she had thought she was walking through a dream. She had remembered a children's book, where a girl fell down a rabbit hole and met all sorts of talking animals, and a mad queen who wanted her white roses painted red. The girl had woken up from her dream. But Samantha still walked through hers. If it were a dream, she could wake herself up and they'd all be safe, away, in her imagination.

"I'm going to speak with Kuma," Phoebe said as she jogged across the camp.

Samantha closed her eyes and tried to focus, not on the sounds around her, not on Rudy flapping his wings overhead returning with his report, not on the clanking of pots three tents over as a centauride prepared to make the daily broth.

She focused on waking up. Thinking better of it, she laid herself on the ground right there, and closed her eyes again. She thought of her bedroom, of Sylvia bursting in to open the curtains and tell her what a beautiful day she thought it was going to be, Marcus downstairs by the marble fireplace with his pipe in his mouth and paper in his hands. Someone nudged her, and she prayed when she opened her eyes it would be Sylvia, or one of the maids coming to tell her she had slept in and her breakfast was getting cold.

"What are you doing?" came Kuma's voice. Samantha grunted as she stood up and brushed herself off.

"Trying to save us the trouble of a pointless war," She grumbled. Kuma gave her a puzzled looked and she waved him off, marching into their tent. Kuma followed her in and stood by the door flap. Samantha sat on her cot, reaching down for the sword she kept underneath and tapped it again and again on the floor.

"We need to pack soon. It'll be time to move on. Pan can stay here. The centaurs can guard him," Kuma said.

"Why are you here?" Samantha asked quietly, staring at the floor between her knees.

"What?"

"Why are you here?" she repeated. "You don't think I'm this Athena girl, so why are you here?" She stood, a hand on her hip, piercing his eyes with her glare as she waited for him to answer.

"I'm here to protect the better side of Arguris." he replied. He hoped she wouldn't ask him to explain. He wasn't sure he could. It was only part of the truth. She had already been given a blow that surprised them all when Pan revealed his secret. Kuma would have to wait for a better time.

"I'm no part of Arguris." Samantha rushed up to him, talking through gritted teeth. "I am no Athena, no goddess, and I don't belong here."

She paced back and forth between Kuma and the cots. She felt the anger building.

"Chimera should have to prove she knows I'm Athena. Pan needs to be looked at by Cairon. I am tired of traveling around this place, listening to everyone's claims of who I am and what I need to let them do for me." She grabbed her sword and lifted it into the air. "I will decide who I am!"

Kuma prepared to dodge out of the way, but Samantha turned and threw the sword. The blade ran straight through a bag of grain and into the basket behind it. Samantha stared at it a moment, and Kuma stared at her. She cried out in frustration and retrieved the sword, then marched past him and stormed through the door flap.

"Is there no plain horse I can ride?" She yelled out. The centaurs looked at her, bewildered, and Phoebe grabbed her sword, unsure what was going on.

Kuma held up his hand to keep her away, and he followed as Samantha made her way out of the camp and headed west into the woods. Kuma followed, leaving some distance between them, should she decide to throw her sword again.

They walked for some time, and Kuma worried they were getting too close to the marsh where Phoebe had been bitten by the nightmare.

"Samantha!" he called out. "We need to turn back. You're too close to the marsh."

Samantha ignored him and kept walking.

He ran until he was in front of her and he grabbed her shoulders, holding her in her tracks. When she gripped her sword he let out a loud roar and she turned pale, dropping her sword and stumbling back.

"Turn around!" he ordered.

"No!" Samantha argued. "This can't be real, none of this."

She spun, waving her arm around, pointing out into the trees.

"None of you are real. You're storybook characters. I'm stuck in a dream that won't end!"

She began laughing hysterically and Kuma watched helplessly. She went on, "If I get a nightmare to bite me, I'll begin dying, and I'll wake up at home." She tried to move on but Kuma stopped her again.

"You'll die. Now turn around!" He grabbed the arm she held the sword with and she used the other to hit him.

"I won't die, you idiot! You can't die in your dreams. I'll wake up at home!" she insisted as she pounded on his arm. It hurt, and he knew it'd be sore tomorrow, but he refused to let her go.

"It's not a dream, and you are Athena, and I can prove it!" Kuma roared and threw her to the ground. He regretted it the moment he realized what he said. Samantha looked at him with wide eyes, holding herself up on the ground, panting as she waited for Kuma to explain.

"What do you mean," she said, "you don't believe like everyone else. You said it yourself, I'm no goddess."

Kuma took a few steps away from her, rubbing his brow, wishing he never opened his door. But he knew he wouldn't have been able to turn her away if he tried. He never had a choice.

"Let's get away from here, then I will tell you everything I can."

Samantha nodded and he helped her up. She put her hands on his stomach and looked up at him.

"Not *what you can*," she said, "Everything."

Kuma nodded, and they silently made their way back toward the camp.

Samantha insisted they stay at the edge of the woods. She wanted some distance between her and everyone else. They found a couple stumps near enough together and Kuma pulled some brush away so they could sit.

He was quiet for a moment. He had hoped he wouldn't have to tell her anything. That her memory would return and all the pieces would fall naturally in place. She had already been through enough, and he didn't want to add to her anguish. But perhaps it was time. Perhaps he was the one that could jog her memory and bring her some peace.

"Kuma," Samantha said, breaking the silence. She looked at him impatiently, stabbing her sword into the ground between her feet.

Kuma took a deep breath, and said a quick prayer to whatever gods might still be out there listening.

"A long time ago I found myself wondering a cave. It was deep, and dark. I wasn't sure how or when I got there. I'm sure it was the same feeling for you when you woke up at the orphanage. The only sound I could hear was my breath echoing on the walls. I didn't know how I got there, or where I was. There was only my desire to move forward to something that was calling me." Kuma folded and unfolded his hands, staring at them as he spoke. Samantha listened. She wasn't used to seeing him behaving this way. Like a child trying to tell his mother had broken her favorite vase. Nothing he was saying made any sense.

"I found my way out of the cave eventually. That's when I saw the armor I was wearing, like I was ready for battle. It wasn't dented or scratched. It was new, shiny. There was nobody else, but I felt myself drawn in a direction as I made my way down a mountain. As though I already knew the way. It was a feeling I would come to recognize as part of my nature, but it had disappeared for many years. When I reached the foot of the mountain there was someone waiting for me. A god."

Kuma looked into the woods. Rays of light peeked through the leaves as the sun rose over the wall.

"She held a spear and a shield. An owl was perched on her shoulder. She spoke, and a snake came from the ground. She pulled up one side of her skirt and it wrapped around her leg and bit her. The marks it left came together like a scar, and looked like a bird in flight. Then it climbed my back and bit me, giving me the same scar."

Samantha stared at him, wide eyed. She dropped her sword and stood up, pointing at him.

"I don't want to hear anymore." She shook her head and waved a finger at him. She looked overwhelmed, scared. Kuma knew he had to finish.

"The moment I came out of that cave was the moment I was created, in secret. By the favored daughter of Zeus, Athena. She sent me here to protect me. She didn't want me destroyed, but she feared others would come after me as punishment for her actions." Kuma spoke louder, following as Samantha paced with her hands on her head.

"That feeling returned the same night you entered Arguris. When Phoebe brought you to my door, I knew it was you before I even looked at you."

"No!" Samantha cried. Some of the centaurs galloped a few yards away, but Kuma motioned them away.

"You are Athena. My creator. My mother." Kuma stood, speaking firmly and loud, making sure she heard his words. She swung her arm and her fist landed on the edge of his snout. She cried out in pain and Kuma groaned as the blow ached for only a moment. The centaurs seemed unsure what to do, so they just stood, mouths open and eyes wide.

Now Phoebe was running from the tent, sword in hand, fear across her face.

"I am not Athena!" Samantha yelled and Phoebe froze. Kuma stood, unsure how to offer her comfort now. It was why he hadn't wanted to tell her. And he wished he hadn't.

She began running in the other direction, toward the mountains. Kuma grabbed her sword and called out to Phoebe. "We need to stop her!" Phoebe ran for Lorna's help as Kuma raced after Samantha. He didn't need to see where she went, he could feel it. He could always feel where she was. That was how she had created him, to know where she was and to desire to be by her side. He loved her unconditionally, like any child would love their mother. She kept away with him for a long time before she ever sent for the Anemoi or Dryads. She had tired of mans continuous greed of power and machine. They praised her in the Parthenon until their praise became demands. She was alone and as men began to question her loyalty to them, she fled.

Kuma ran along the path, the thick of trees on either side, and followed her presence. She was running fast and it was taking him longer than he had hoped to catch her. Chimera would have harpies and minotaurs scattered, watching for them, and he didn't want her to be seen, especially not in her state of mind.

He felt his desire change course and he turned left into the trees until he came to the foot of a small mountain. He looked up to see Samantha disappear over a ledge. He climbed after her, letting her guide him as she climbed further up the mountain. Kuma climbed over the last ledge and looked around. He felt her beside him but when he looked around she wasn't there. There was a small ledge wrapped around the tip of the spire and Kuma stretched so he could see around it.

Samantha was inching her way over, her toes hanging off and her back pressed against the wall. Kuma could not get to her. He looked down and saw the fall ahead.

"Samantha, come back, it isn't safe." he said softly. He leaned against the wall and reached his hand toward her as far is he could.

"This is all a dream, Kuma." Samantha called back. "I'll wake up before I hit the ground."

Kuma felt his hand begin to shake and his stomach sank. No one else had arrived. He peered over the edge and saw a few centaurs scattered, at the foot of the mountain. They wouldn't be able to climb to them. He listened for Phoebe but couldn't hear her or smell her. Instead another familiar scent filled his nostrils.

He looked up just as Pan swung down from above them and collided into Samantha. She groaned and cried out, and Pan apologized. "I'm sorry, your highness," he said as he took the end of the rope he was holding onto and tied it around her waist, "but you're not going anywhere." When he was done he pushed himself so he laid on the wall next her. He held her against the wall as he through the other end of the rope to Kuma. He caught it, then Pan shoved Athena off the wall. She kicked and screamed as she swung toward Kuma.

Kuma pulled the rope, then grabbed her arm and pulled her into his. Pan inched his way along the ledge until he was standing next to them.

"Thank you, satyr." Kuma said as he grabbed the rope and held onto Samantha. He wasn't particularly happy that Pan was out of the tent, but the satyr was once again there when he was needed. And right now Samantha was the bigger problem. She fought to get out of his arms and he untied the rope and let her go. They all stood in a circle, staring at one another, panting, tears pouring from Samantha's eyes.

Phoebe finally pulled herself up and ran to Samantha. She tried to put her arms around her but Samantha pulled away. She looked to the others for an explanation but they stood quietly, Kuma just shook his head.

Samantha saw they weren't going to leave her side, not now. She didn't know what to say to them, if there was any point to any of it anyway. It was all a dream and none of it mattered. Up until now it had become some sort of game. She didn't believe they actually thought she was a goddess. Especially *the* goddess they had been waiting to come and set them free. Tomorrow she'd wake up, but where would she be? The cliff was only a few feet away, and as if reading her mind Kuma grabbed her arm and pushed her to the wall. She hit him, yelling, "Don't touch me!"

She threw herself down and stared over the forest stretched out in front of her. She focused on thoughts of Chraimyth, thinking if she focused enough on where she wanted to be, then she'd wake up. She just had to want it bad enough. Sylvia was probably sitting over her right now, waiting for her to wake up so she could yell at her then send her to the Hamilton's to reschedule the wedding. She'd become his wife and bare his children. This dream was all the adventure she needed to convince herself that home was the safest place in the world for her to be.

Phoebe and Pan sat on either side of her. She glared at Pan a moment, then went on looking over the trees. Kuma stood in his spot. It hurt him to know he had only furthered her pain. They sat for a long time, Samantha leaned on Phoebe and cried until she fell asleep. Her only words were, "I have to wake up."

Phoebe carried her over to Kuma and he laid down as Phoebe laid her next to him. He wrapped his arms around her as he remembered doing centuries ago. Pan laid on her other side, pressing his legs against hers and Phoebe laid at her head. The three looked at each other, not saying a word, then gazed at Samantha. They laid their heads down on the mountain floor and closed their eyes and slept.

18

It was dark when Samantha woke. She felt the stone under her, and the despair came upon her as if the whole mountain were resting on her. *Why can't I wake up*, she cried to herself. She pushed herself off the ground and looked at the fire behind her. Kuma, Phoebe, and Pan stared at her through the flames as they ate, then Pan reached out a stick of cooked rabbit.

She took it and bit into it, wondering if she'd ever eat a meal with her family again. Phoebe was talking, but she didn't hear her. She was trying to figure out why she was stuck in this dream world.

"What happened to me," she continued thinking to herself. She had heard of comas before. And it would make perfect sense. She thought of all the years that were a mystery to her. Who knew what she did before she arrived at the orphanage. Maybe that was all part of her dream, too.

She looked at Pan. He stared at the fire, chewing on his meat. "How do I wake up?" she asked him. She wanted to yell, but she didn't have the energy anymore. She didn't even want to speak. Her feet didn't want to move. She just wanted to remain there until she fell asleep again. Pan stopped chewing and looked at her. She looked to Phoebe and Kuma, they both stared back. None of them answered her.

She threw the rest of the meat into the fire and stared off into the darkness, trying to figure it all out.

It was impossible, wasn't it? Impossible to be traveling with a talking bear who claims she's his mother. Impossible to find out her admiration for a favorite relative turned out to be that of a satyr. Impossible that she'd become best friends with a ogre. She thought about all these things, and the centaurs, the nightmares, Chimera. She tried to think of what she knew about the goddess Athena. She couldn't think of anything. Phoebe knelt down beside her, holding out another stick of meat, smiling at her. Samantha didn't smile back, but took the meat and ate. Phoebe sat down, and when Samantha had cleaned the flesh from the bone, she took her hand and held it. Samantha choked back the sob, but tears escaped and ran down her cheek. Phoebe wiped them away and wrapped her arm around her.

"I know how difficult this is. We're all here for you." she said softly.

Samantha looked at her, studying her face. "Can't this all just be a dream?" she begged. "I don't know how to be what you all say I am."

"You only need to be what you say you are, we can only remember who you've been." She replied.

Samantha thought it over. She considered two possibilities. Her dream was holding her in until she learned something or this was all real and there was truth to what they told her and she had to allow herself to believe she might be their goddess. She stood and walked along the cliffs edge, Kuma stood up and started toward her but she turned and faced them.

"I don't know who I am." she admitted. "I have no memory of my life before Chraimyth."

Rudy flew down just then and walked back and forth at her feet.

"The truth of it all is we all know who you are, at least what you could be again. And you know who you were just a few months ago, and who you are now." He pecked at a feather then continued, "I think the only thing left for you to do is to choose who you're going to be here on out." He looked at her with his large eyes but Samantha was in no mood for his amusements. She moved her foot in front of him, pushing him aside. "Hey!" he squawked and flapped his feathers at her legs. Then Kuma added, "While you are here in Arguris, many will believe you are Athena, as we do. And you'll have to live prepared for that, until the day Speranta lets you out, or the satyr finds a new flute."

Pan sneered. "That flute was one-of-a-kind. It can not be replaced." Then he looked at Samantha. "I meant it when I said I am here to serve you. I know I have failed you in the past, but it was a result of what I felt were the best of my intentions. From here on, I know how to make myself more useful and you have my life." He stood and bowed to her. She wasn't ready to forgive him, but she nodded, and he smiled.

"Is there anyone in Arguris that might be able to help me with my memory?" she asked them. She was trying to be strong. All she wanted to do was fall apart, but that wouldn't get her any closer to home.

They sat and thought about it, then Pan offered, "I think there might be someone in Parthens." They all looked at him. He looked back to Kuma and Phoebe as though they should know what he was talking about.

"Where is Parthens?" Samantha asked.

"It's far west of here, further than Cyrene." Kuma grumbled. She wondered why he didn't approve.

"We can't go there?"

"Traveling isn't safe. Raftik has already left to gather the rest of the centaur tribes. We need to gather who we can as well." Kuma said.

"There's a clan of satyrs not far from Parthens. We could visit the city, and talk to the satyrs.

Phoebe nodded in agreement and Samantha looked to Kuma. He looked at Pan a minute, as if there was a reason he didn't want them going to Parthens. He finally nodded in agreement. "We'll go in the morning, but for now we sleep. It's too dark to climb down now."

Samantha found it hard to sleep that night. She had already slept through majority of the day after her breakdown. She thought of Parthens and who might be there. If they helped her, if her memory returned, who would she discover she was? She tossed and turned between Kuma and Pan until she felt Phoebe's hand on her head. The ogre stroked her hair and Samantha allowed herself to relax. Her eyes grew heavy and as she fell asleep an image of the girl from her dream appeared.

Rudy woke them up before the sun had even come over the trees. He dropped fish from his claws and beak for them to cook, then sat on a perch, cleaning his feathers. They cooked and ate quickly, then climbed down the mountain and made their way back to the centaur camp. Lorna was waiting with a few centaurides by her side, and she looked concerned as they approached. "Is everyone okay?" But Samantha knew she was asking about her.

"Yes, we're heading to Parthens." Samantha told her.

"But Raftik," she began, but Kuma cut her off.

"Raftik understands the circumstances. We had an agreement." Kuma told her. Samantha looked at him, remembering them shaking hands before Raftik rode off.

"What agreement?" she asked.

"Raftik left Kuma in charge of our tribe until he returned." Lorna said, sounding upset.

"Then you'll stay behind." Samantha stopped and looked at Kuma squarely. He looked back at her with his grim eyes and grunted.

"I already told Raftik we would stay only as long as we could, he understands."

"Then it's settled." Samantha looked to Lorna, who looked at Kuma then back to Samantha.

Lorna wanted to argue but she could feel the tension around the companions and didn't want to get involved. She nodded, "Yes, it's settled. I can handle the tribe, it is my place."

Samantha ignored the stares the centaurs gave her when they returned to camp. She went straight to the their tent and packed her things. She heard Kuma tell Lorna where they were headed, and to have Raftik send the tribes that way. Then he joined her in the tent, followed by Phoebe and Pan. "Are you sure this is what you want to do?" Kuma asked her. "Yes. I have to try, I have to know. We'll all get something out of it. If I can't wake up on my own, then I'll let someone do it for me. If I don't wake up, then I guess we'll find out where this dream takes us" she said, tossing the last sword in the bag. She felt her pocket for her spear block then pulled the door flap back and looked to the center of camp. The morning fire had already been put out, but she looked around it for any scraps that may have been left. One of the centaurides approached with a bag and opened it so she could see what was inside. Cooked meats and breads were wrapped in portions enough for the four of them to feed on for a week. She thanked the centauride and threw the bag over her shoulder. Lorna stood in front of her tent and when Samantha looked her way she held her hand to her chest and bowed her head. Samantha returned the gesture and the centaur laughed, disappearing into her tent. Phoebe came to her side and explained, "That is a gesture the centaurs give as a pledge of loyalty. It wasn't necessary for you to pledge to her." Samantha nodded.

"When we are near the water, stay to the branches." Phoebe told her.

"The branches?"

"The nightmares stay to the grass, they don't like wood. It will take too long to..." Samantha stopped her.

"Why don't we just burn them?" she asked, looking at the torch sticks surrounding the camp.

Phoebe looked too, considering the option. "Hold on." she said and disappeared into Lorna's tent.

Kuma and Pan were already walking her way when Phoebe returned with Lorna.

"Fire won't help," Lorna explained to them. "You would need to burn the whole marsh to get rid of them. You'll still be at risk. Stay to the trees until you reach the waters edge. Get in quickly and pay no mind to what you feel in the water."

"What's in the water?" Samantha assumed there were more creatures in Arguris that she hadn't seen, but the thought of diving into a body of water filled with some unseen monster seemed unnecessary.

"Don't worry, they won't have any interest in you. They are very particular of their victims, but they do enjoy exploring the visitors that cross above." Lorna told her.

"There's no other route?"

"Not one quicker than that." Phoebe said.

Lorna handed them each a torch and they said their goodbyes. It was half a days journey to the marshland and they put themselves in the trees long before. The branches were thick and didn't sway even under Kuma's weight. They wound through the branches, carefully jumping from one tree to the next. The ground below was dark from the shade of the trees and quiet. It looked lifeless, but knowing the nightmares that crawled in it made it haunting.   It was muddy and wet, with patches of tall grass, and she could see footprints where Phoebe had probably been hunting there before. No one could have guessed it was crawling with a tiny minacious insect.

They reached the last tree, as near to the water as they could get, but there was still several yards between them.

"What do we do?" Phoebe asked. She looked frightened and Samantha couldn't blame her.

They all studied the distance to the water and looked for a solution.

"We use our weapons, and cut down a tree." Kuma suggested.

"No!" Pan snapped immediately. "We can not harm the trees." They didn't understand his concern. The trees were tall enough that if they cut it down, it would fall and provide a safe path for them to cross.

"We don't have a choice," Kuma said. He leapt to the next branch and followed it up to the trunk. The rest of them followed.

"Be ready to jump and run," he instructed them. He lifted his halberd and swung it hard into the trunk. It sliced half way through the wood, as though he were cutting through butter.

Samantha hadn't realized how strong Kuma was, or how much he held back when they fought together. What else was he holding back from her? The tree shook and they shifted to keep their balance.

He looked at them then raised his halberd again and swung. Loud cracking echoed as the tree began to tip. Kuma pulled himself up the trunk so there was room for the others to climb behind. Phoebe followed and pulled Samantha behind her. Pan waited until it was halfway to the ground then he jumped. They each pulled themselves up to their feet and jumped over branches as they raced to get as far across the falling tree as they could before it hit the ground. Samantha mimicked Phoebe's every move since she couldn't' see anything in front of her. They swung around branches and pushed leaves away from their faces

"Hold on!" Kuma's voice could be heard ahead. They wrapped their arms around the nearest branches and held on as the tree crashed into the ground.

There was a blood curdling "No!" and Samantha reached out just in time to grab Phoebe's hand. The ogre pulled herself up and stared at the ground next to them. Samantha patted her back then said, "Let's go."

They rushed to the end of the tree and Kuma grabbed each of them without a word and threw them into the water, then he jumped, almost landing on Samantha's head.

The water looked calm and inviting and she couldn't imagine what could be living below, or what sort of creature it preferred. The other side of the lake was too far ahead to see and she hoped they'd be left alone, and that she would last long enough. They all carried heavy bags on their backs and Samantha cringed when she thought of the wasted food she carried.

They swam slowly and for a long time. Nothing had bothered them and Samantha wondered if maybe the creatures Lorna mentioned weren't here anymore. Maybe they had died a long time ago, or been caught and eaten. The day was bright overhead and Samantha felt herself moving along well despite the heavy bags hanging from her shoulders. She had looked several times for any signs of an island they could rest on, or something to float on, but there was none. Suddenly she heard Pan grunt as something tugged on his arm below. She could see the panic on his face as he fought whatever was under the water. Suddenly he disappeared and Kuma shoved his bags at Phoebe and dove in after him. Phoebe and Samantha waded, trying to see into the water but it was too deep and too dark. "Kuma," Samantha called down nervously, "Pan." She spun around, looking for any sign of them.

Kuma appeared a few feet ahead of them, Pan in his arms. They both gasped for air and Kuma floated on his back, lifting Pan onto his stomach.

"Swim!" he called out as he whirled his arms around, pulling Pan across the water on top of him. Pan sat there, holding his legs close to his chest, staring into the water, his eyes wide. Samantha looked around but the water was still, aside from them splashing through it. She had felt nothing, and Phoebe nor Kuma showed any indication that anything had touched them either. Why had it only gone for Pan?

When they finally reached shallow water Pan slid off of Kuma and ran across the shore. The rest dragged their bags and weapons behind them and collapsed at the waters edge. This side of the lake was open, with little trees, and the ground was dry and bare. Pan looked himself over and aside from a few scratches on his arms he was okay.

"What was it," Samantha asked.

"I don't know, I couldn't see it," Pan's voice shook. Samantha wanted to feel sorry for him, but she couldn't. Not yet.

They rested for awhile, then checked their weapons and armor and laid them out to dry. Samantha checked the bag of food and was taken aback when she unwrapped a few portions and saw they were still dry. She looked at the inside of the bag and saw it was lined with multiple layers of animal skins. She handed each of them some meat and bread, and they took their time eating. Samantha looked at the countryside ahead of them but saw only flat land.

"How far is it to Parthens?" she asked.

Phoebe looked out and pointed, "We'll travel the rest of the day, then it'll be another three days journey from there."

"Three days?" Samantha looked at the plains again. There was no cover that she could see. They'd be out in the open, easy to spot.

"We'll have to move fast." Kuma said, is if reading her mind. She looked at Pan, he was staring over the water, fear still set in his eyes.

"What's in the water?" she looked at Kuma and Phoebe, then they all looked over at Pan.

"A creature that desires man. Satyrs don't usually take to the water, and I think they were satisfied with the half of him that is human." Phoebe told her.

"Why not the rest of us?" Samantha was confused. She herself was human, and aside from Phoebe's skin, she could be considered human. While Kuma was clearly bear, he had plenty of physical human characteristics.

"The rest of us aren't *man*," she enunciated the word man, and Samantha understood. She went over to Pan and put her arm around him. She was still angry with him, but he had saved two of their lives already, and she was glad Kuma could save his.

19

They had slept out in the open, taking turns keeping watch. Other than the cries of a family of foxes nearby, and the orchestra of crickets, they heard nothing. Samantha watched her companions sleep. They each slept heavily, and she laughed at Kuma. He looked just as glum when he snored as he did throughout the day. His eyes were pinched tight, as if he were forcing himself to rest.

He knew about her birthmark.

She had only found out from one of the maids who bathed her. Another of Sylvia's silly requests. She decided it was only more reason to believe she was dreaming. Kuma rolled over on his side and Samantha looked over his fur. He was as black as the night, dirtied by their travels and leaves were stuck in the fur around his feet. She was tempted to pull them out but didn't want to wake him quite yet. There were small patches of fur missing in some spots, replaced with scars. She wondered how long he had had them, what they were from. On his back she noticed a dark spot where the fur was gone just under his vest. It didn't look like the rest of the scars and she thought it might have been a fresh wound from whatever had attacked in the water. She leaned forward and gasped when she saw it clearly. It was a birthmark in the shape of a bird, exactly like hers. If this was a dream, then this all made sense and it didn't matter. But if it wasn't...she didn't want to think about that yet. She nudged Kuma and he nodded, grabbing the halberd laying at his side and standing up. Samantha stared up at him a moment before laying down. Kuma was not the type of creature to waste time on lies, especially those that would change the course of someone's life. She thought of what it must be like for him, if she was Athena, to see his mother after so many years, and feel like he couldn't say anything. She tried to imagine what she'd do if she ever found her mother, her real mother. She wanted to imagine running into her mother's arms and feeling like her world was complete. But she knew the real experience would likely be more mundane. She let herself doze off to sleep, still hoping she'd wake up in Chraimyth.

There was still a days journey to Parthens, and the landscape hadn't changed much except a low steady climb as low green mountains stretched ahead of them. It was a beautiful sight, and Samantha thought it was just the sort of place she'd want to build a home.

"Parthens is there." Phoebe pointed to the side of the mountain. They were still too far away and it was still early enough that a haze in the distance made it hard to see clearly. Samantha was happy to have the destination in sight anyhow. Despite the disappointment of realizing she was still in Arguris, Samantha held on to the hope that whatever creature they were seeking in Parthens would be able to help her. She had decided not to think too much on what her memory might bring back. Instead she focused on enjoying the beautiful countryside. The parts of Arguris that she had seen so far had been overgrown with brush and forest. But there were no trees in sight here and the green grass lay like a blanket over everything. It was peaceful, and there was a scent of lavender in the air, but she couldn't find the plant anywhere she looked.

She thought about Kuma's and Pan's stories. Kuma said she was his mother, his creator, and he bore the same mark. She couldn't imagine creating anything as grand as Kuma. And that's what he was, grand.

Pan said he had been living outside of Arguris as her uncle, but her adoption by his 'brother' was just a coincidence. He was the reason she ended up at the orphanage. She wondered why he didn't just bring her to his mansion instead. She brushed the thought out of her mind, not wanting to irritate herself.

"Head's up!" Came Rudy's voice from a distance.

They spun around and saw Rudy racing across the sky toward them, a small flock of harpies were close behind, rushing at them from above. Samantha opened her spear, and the others stood ready with their swords and halberd. The harpies flew at them with their large talons open. They screeched loudly as they came down on them and all but Kuma cried out as they held their ears. He swung his halberd and a harpy fell to the ground, her feet rolling into the grass. She screamed and Kuma stood over her and ended her. The other harpies stabbed at Samantha and the others with their feet, and they fought back, dodging their blows and swinging their blades wildly while trying to ignore the torturous sound ringing in their ears. Samantha managed to block a harpy with her spear, but she couldn't get enough space between them to stab her. The ringing in her ears made it hard to focus, but she tried again and again to knock the bird away and gain some space.

Pan and Phoebe seemed to struggle, too. Pan tripped over his hooves as he tried to fight the harpy and her painful screeching. Phoebe cried out, trying to be louder than them, but the screeches were piercing and ached. Kuma swung his halberd above them, bringing down another harpy. He swung at more, but they flew high above them, still squawking and their talons stretched out.

Kuma pointed for them to run and they ran as quick as they could toward Parthens. It was still too far away, but if they could find cover they would go there. Rudy saw the harpies dive and he pushed against the air until he was directly in their path. Several flew right past him, and he got caught in the current they created, then he felt his wing bend where it shouldn't. It lay limp as he barreled into the ground.

Suddenly Samantha felt a sharp pain in her shoulders as a harpy dug in her claws and tried to lift her off the ground. The pain was too much and Samantha felt faint. She dropped her spear and watched it retract as Pan managed to pick it up and stuff it in his bag. The harpies didn't attack them, but screeched loudly and slapped their wings in their face, making it hard for them to fight back. Only Kuma was able to keep himself together. Samantha screamed as she felt him push her to the ground, bringing the harpy with her. Her talons ripped at her skin and she could see her blood on the grass. As she watched the blood pool she considered this wasn't a dream.

This was real, and she had to fight for her life, or lose it. But right now she couldn't get passed the pain in her ears and her arms. She felt weak and wasn't sure she could move. The harpy wouldn't let go of her, and as she fought Kuma, Samantha tried to reach up and remove her claws. She screamed as the pain radiated through her arms as she tried to move them. Pans hooves appeared near her face and she looked up just in time to see him behead the harpy. Her body fell and Pan held onto it while Kuma pulled the talons out of her shoulders. She screamed as the last one came out, and Phoebe rolled her over, holding her against her chest.

She looked up to see three harpies flying east. They were too far to hit with anything so they had to let them go. There were several more laying on the ground and Kuma walked to each of them, making sure they were dead. Pan helped Phoebe clean Samantha's wounds as she tried to stay conscious. She didn't feel she would faint from the pain, or the blood loss, but instead from the experience of it all. She had always lived in the safety of her parents walls. There was never anything to fear but not having the right material or pattern for the next occasions dress. Here, the world was real, and she had tried to ignore it, pretend it was a dream, and it had almost cost her her life, and possibly those of her companions.

"I don't think the wounds are deep, and if you'll allow me to say," Phoebe was staring down at her over her forehead, "gods heal quickly, and you should be fine before we even reach Parthens."

Samantha couldn't admit the pain was already gone. She wouldn't believe anything about herself until she had her memory back. Phoebe helped her to her feet and she was relieved the dizziness had gone away. She looked around at the dead harpies and the blood stained grass.

"Should we do something about this? Will it attract anything else *undesirable*?" Samantha asked.

"No, we don't have the time. They already know we're here. Those that escaped will report our location and there will be more after us soon," Kuma said as he wiped the blood from his halberd. "I hope Raftik is having luck with the other tribes."

Pan collected their weapons and Phoebe dug out a fresh garment for Samantha to wear.

"You don't want to go into Parthens looking like death," she stated. She shooed the other two away so Samantha could change. The fresh clothes felt nice, and Phoebe told her they would dig a hole to bury the bloodied clothes in, that it'd be bad luck to save it. She thought it would be a good idea to wear the aegis, but Phoebe told her to keep it in the bag with the weapons. It would draw too much attention if especially another immortal recognized it.

Pan handed Samantha her retracted spear and looked at her wounds, giving her a smile but not saying anything. Kuma spotted Rudy hunched over his wing, squawking in pain. "I don't think I'll be looking out anymore," the owl said as he revealed to them his broken wing. "Aren't we a bunch?" Kuma carefully picked him up. Pan and Phoebe gathered their things and staying close to Samantha, the made their way to Parthens. The rest of the journey they kept their weapons ready, and their eyes opened.

—

The sword fell through the air, slow, as if time were stopping, falling towards the earth below. She looked at it, ready to jump out of the way, but her body would move no faster. Every muscle felt frozen. She cried out, but it didn't matter. Time moved too slowly and as she pushed herself away with all the force she could muster, the swords blade suddenly raced through the air, coming down on her and welcoming itself to part of her soul. She collapsed, unsure what had happened. The pain didn't come as quickly as the feeling of being lifted into the air. As though she were lighter. Then the stinging pain radiated through her body as she stared at the decapitated creature in front of her. It looked back in frozen horror, and she recognized it, then everything went black.

Chimera woke with a jolt, hearing the sounds of large wings batting at the air as the harpies neared.

"We spotted them heading west, to Parthens," the first one said before they had landed.

"You'll make the report, and tell Linaphese to head there with the army. We'll meet in the southern region." Chimera instructed.

They didn't leave, but stared at her squawking and looking irritated that they couldn't get to her. The stones remained pressed in her ears.

"Do you have more?" she asked impatiently.

"They killed half our flock." a second harpy complained.

Chimera looked at them, letting her gaze rest on each one a moment. She knew from her time in the pit what had probably happened. They would not have her sympathy.

"You were told to locate the girl, not attack them." she groaned. "It is on your shoulders that they are gone." She growled and they screeched in reply, lifting themselves into the sky.

The first one yelled down, "Linaphese will not like this."

"Then do your job and no more." Chimera called after her.

She quickly made her way back to the minotaur village, instructing them to meet in the southern region, then she sprinted off. It would be several days before the harpies and minotaurs would reach Parthens, and she needed to keep an eye on Samantha and her companions.

As she ran she thought of her dream, of Chartis. She had always felt she had been given a gift from the gods with her heads and extra abilities. She had seen other four-legged creatures, but there was nothing unique about them. It was partly out of joy, as much as it was necessity, that she used her skills. She'd breath her fire on man, and Chartis would tear into them, whether their heart still beat or not. She was honorable, only hunting those who would first chase her into the mountains, or track her to her cave. The only time she hunted for sport was to feed, but even then men managed to interfere. Traps laid out with living beasts, but they insulted her intelligence. She'd free the animal, and hunt the man instead. She was never sure which they were afraid of most, Nova, Chartis, or Paphene. Paphene was always ready to fight, willing to sink her fangs into deserving flesh and watch their colors change as her venom soaked through their veins. Chartis would always know where to hunt, and when they needed, where to hide. The heart of Chimera beat in Nova's chest, and she was the most emotional, letting her anger drive her, only harnessed by Chartis' logic. They considered her the most beautiful among themselves, and they depended on her the most to make the final decision on things that could put their lives at risk.

Now Chimera was led by the overwhelming thirst for vengeance. It had been too long that no one had paid for the loss of their sister. But now someone would pay, and Chimera would not lose her chance.

20

Samantha's wounds were healed by the time the fog cleared ahead of them. Rudy rode on Kuma's shoulder, trying not to complain too much over the bears heavy footsteps that shook his little body and pained his wing. No one else seemed to have any serious injuries. Samantha wouldn't talk about her wound, she refused to surrender to any suggestions, no matter what evidence was provided, until she had her memory back. But she could feel her heart pounding with relief and fear at just what all the facts were telling her.

She wished there was something she could do to help poor Rudy. It didn't seem fair that she should hold her spear in her arm so quickly when the owl couldn't even lift his wing to fly. She hoped there was someone in Parthens to help him, too. They traveled along the same road. It didn't make any sense to stray since there was no forest to cover them until they had passed Parthens. Only the heat from the light overhead surrounded them. They would be seen no matter where they walked. Every eye was watchful, every hand ready near their weapon.

Samantha looked towards where she had thought Phoebe told her the city was, but there was just a sea of green. She thought maybe it was over the horizon on the other side of the hills. But as they drew closer, she began to see small homes come into view. They were made of small boulders and dirt with grass roofs. Some were put together with stripped trees, the bark mixed into the clay that held them together. They couldn't be any bigger than a one room house. As they arrived at Parthens' border, the buildings looked the same, but some stood taller than others, some longer. Moss covered the walls and gave the air a forest aroma. It wasn't what Samantha had thought the city would look like at all. She had imagined a city like Athens. But there were no resources here to build a city like that.

Creatures of all sorts roamed the streets, even humans. Samantha hadn't seen another human being since she arrived in Arguris. No one paid them any attention as they made their way further into the city. Samantha looked around and was relieved when things started feeling a bit more like Chraimyth. There were shops set up along one road; bakers, a blacksmith, clothiers, jewelers. As she browsed the goods, she wondered where they came from, who made them, and she realized she had a lot to learn about Arguris still. They traveled a few more roads until they were in the center of Parthens. There stood the largest building she had seen in all of Arguris yet. A perfect replica of the Parthenon. Beside it stood an enormous statue made of wood. It held a spear in one hand, a shield in the other. It was Athena.

Phoebe looked at Samantha and smiled, "They still pray to you, and ask your guidance." She gestured to the people walking up and down the stairs of the building, some were kneeling at the bottom of the statue, their eyes closed in prayer.

"Some pray for their freedom." Kuma added, staring in a different direction. They followed his gaze to a small minotaur peering around a corner watching them. "I'll meet you at the lodge," he said as he carefully helped Rudy to Pans shoulder then turned and disappeared down an alley.

"Yes, so will we," Pan said, "Rudy needs a doctor, I'll help him find one."

"Thank you, satyr. I'm sure I know the right doctor, but I'd appreciate the escort all the same." Rudy said, trying to hold himself up tall. He didn't enjoy depending on them, but he was thankful they were there. Someday he might be able to say so.

Samantha still wasn't sure how much trust she was willing to put into Pan, but she knew if Rudy was willing to trust him then she shouldn't object. Samantha and Phoebe walked on a few roads until they came to a building with the same symbol hanging above the entrance as the lodge in Cyrene.

Kuma was the first one to return not long after they had settled into their rooms. "The brat will be quiet." he said. At first they didn't understand what he meant. Then they remembered the young minotaur.

"You didn't cut his tongue out did you?" Phoebe teased. Samantha gave him a look to which he responded, "No." And that was all the answer he gave.

They rested for a few hours while they waited for the satyr and owl to return. When the light outside began to fade they decided to go to the tavern. They chose a dark corner to sit in and no one paid them any attention. They couldn't help keeping an eye on the room, noting every person and creature that left and entered.

"Why would humans be here," Samantha wondered out loud. "You don't see yourself as a creature?" Phoebe asked, and Samantha felt scolded. She hadn't thought of herself that way, but she supposed Phoebe was right. "Yes, I suppose I am."

"Plenty of human creatures were created by the gods, including yourself." Phoebe went on.

Samantha knew the story of Athena's birth, and it did make sense the event should be seen as a creation. Athena was a creature no different from the satyrs, ogre, harpies, or any of the others. But Samantha was just a simple human. One with an incredible dream she'd soon wake up from and share with Celeste. That was easier to believe than remembering the wounds she just watched heal on her shoulders. She wanted to talk more about the topic with Phoebe, just to talk, to change the conversation and enjoy a meal with her friends. She'd love a moment to forget about Chimera and the harpies. But just then Pan walked in with Rudy. Phoebe waved them over.

They all stared as the two approached the table. Pan was grinning like a fool, and Rudy folded his wing in front of him as though he were a king being presented to his subjects. Samantha's jaw dropped as Pan helped him onto the table. Rudy smirked as they all observed his wing. It was clear he wasn't suffering anymore. He looked down ever so proud of himself. Samantha leaned forward to get a closer look at his wing. It looked normal, but there was something different. She thought she saw something glimmering underneath. She reached out to move one of his feathers, but he spread his wing open, revealing a shimmering metal brace.

"What kind of job is that?" Phoebe asked.

"The grandest of them all." Rudy said as he continued to hold his wing up for them to admire.

The brace was no brace at all. In fact, each and every feather on his wing was now lined with sharp daggers.

"May I?" Phoebe said, reaching out to touch one.

"Careful, they're sharp," Pan said, holding up his finger to show a cut on the tip.

Phoebe rolled her eyes, and ran her finger across the edge of one of the long blades at the bottom of the wing. She suddenly jumped and pulled away. Blood dripped from her finger and she stuck it in her mouth, staring wide-eyed at Rudy.

"Yeah, let them come for me. I'm one of the scariest things in the sky now," Rudy rested his wing and plucked berries from a plate that Kuma had been eating from.

They all shared their meal, as they had come used to doing on their travels.

"So who are we looking for here?" Samantha asked. She remembered the funny looks they gave each other when Pan first mentioned coming to Parthens. She wanted to know more about the person they were looking for.

"It is only a rumor that such a person lives here. If you ask around, no one could help you find her. She finds you. Don't ask how. No one knows. That's why it's just a rumor. It's just a story to share." Rudy said.

Samantha looked aggravated, "You wouldn't risk your life or anyone else's life over a rumor. Don't lie to me. Who are we looking for?"

Rudy turned away from her, refusing to give her anymore answers.

"She lives alone. That's all we know," Kuma offered. He pulled the last few berries away from Rudy and tossed them in his snout. Then he lifted up a large beer stein, ignoring Rudy's glare, and swallowed the contents. "If we ask around long enough, she'll find us."

As Kuma spoke, Samantha stopped listening. She had caught the gaze of a tall man who had just walked into the tavern with two other men. He looked around the room for a table, and when he saw her he stopped. Samantha quickly looked away, leaning back to hide herself behind Kuma. But the man made his away around the room, keeping his distance, stopping when he could see her a little closer. He stared at her as if he knew her. The others saw what was happening and they all rested their hands on their weapons, staring at him in warning. He lifted his hands up to his waist and stepped back. He began to walk back to his friends, looking back to Samantha frequently, his eyes twinkling and his mouthed curled in a smile. He didn't seem to mention anything to his friends as they sat down, but he seated himself so he faced Samantha.

"Who is that?" Samantha asked.

"I don't know." Phoebe said, and the others shrugged.

It was dangerous for her to be noticed, but she found herself enjoying the strangers smiles. He was handsome, with long dark hair that fell to his shoulders, dark eyes that laughed at her. He was muscular, and simply dressed, definitely not ready for any battle, though he had removed a sword from his side at the table. But everyone in Arguris carried a weapon, at least that she had seen so far.

She tried to ignore the man and finish her meal. But she could feel his eyes on her, and she was drawn to look at him again. When she did look up, Pan was standing over the man, glaring at him as he spoke. Samantha hadn't even heard him leave the table. She couldn't hear the conversation either. She grabbed Phoebe's arm, "We don't need this right now," she said. "That goat is an imbecile." she said through gritted teeth as she looked back at Pan.

"Somebody might die tonight." Rudy said. He was tapping his wing against his side, and the daggers played a quiet tune. The man's face suddenly looked grim as he got up from his seat. Kuma was already halfway on his feet as they watched Pan follow the man to the exit. Pan turned and motioned for them to follow. They left their coins on the table and quietly followed.

Outside, the sky had darkened. The road was lit with torches and many of the creatures had gone home for the night. Pan and the stranger continued to walk down the road, then they suddenly turned and disappeared. They hurried after them, following road after road until they found themselves standing at the foot of the Parthenon. Pan sat on the stairs catching his breath, but the man was gone.

"Pan, are you okay? What happened? Where did he go? Who was he?" Samantha rushed to Pan's side and looked him over. The satyr laughed as they caught their breath. "Slow down. Everything is fine, so long as he is who he says he is. I just don't know how exciting it will be for you." Pan looked at Samantha and waved to the top of the stairs.

The man emerged from behind a pillar and slowly made his way down to them. Kuma and Phoebe drew their weapons and watched for any sign of a trap.

"I assure you I will do no harm." the man raised his hands, and they noticed his sword was gone. Pan held it up for them to see. "I could never harm the Current of my heart." He held his arms to his sides and smiled again, walking toward Samantha. She didn't know what he meant and backed away. Phoebe blocked the path and Kuma approached him slowly. "The satyr told me you don't remember who you are," he continued. Samantha gave Pan a disapproving look, to which he shrugged in return. She would be sure to scold him later and remind him he was supposed to be helping her learn to trust him again, not break that trust more. She wondered what else he had told the stranger.

"You might not be able to remember anything, but I can help bring that all back."

Samantha was confused. She was sure the others had said the creature they were looking for was a female. This was clearly a man. And now that he was standing in front of her, her heart beat fast. The moment of truth was upon them. She would learn if she truly was the goddess Athena and be able to free them all, or if she carried some other unknown path. She didn't want to disappoint them if she wasn't who they thought she was, but she wasn't sure she was ready for such a responsibility either.

Phoebe and Kuma lowered their weapons and let him approach Samantha. She stood frozen, just staring at him, not sure what to say or do. They hadn't even begun to ask around for him, so how did he find them? He reached for her hand and kissed it gently. Something didn't feel right. She wasn't sure if it was how soft his lips felt and the electricity it sent through her body, or if it was the darkness that surrounded them in the night, but she suddenly wanted to be very far away from him.

"How do we do this?" Samantha asked quickly.

"Kiss me." the stranger said. He leaned in, closing his eyes and grabbing her waist. When he began pulling her in close she felt herself lose control. She pulled her closed spear from the hidden pocket she had made in her clothes and opened it.

The sound made the man jump and he took a few steps away. "I don't want to be kissed. I want to know who I am." She said sternly. The others joined her with their weapons raised. They stepped toward him, walking him up the stairs until he tripped and sat down.

When they all had their weapons to his throat Samantha asked, "Who are you?"

He looked frightened for only a second, then smiled again and said, "I'm the god of dusk, father of the four winds."

Kuma lowered his halberd and leaned in close, studying the mans face, then taking in his scent.

His eyes went wide and he took a step back.

"He's who he says he is." Kuma reassured them.

"How do you know? Have you met him before?" Rudy chimed in.

"Yes," Kuma said, eyeing Samantha, "And so has she."

21

They reluctantly followed the man into the Parthenon, where he led them down a candle lit hallway, down a flight of stairs, a maze of more candle lit hallways, until he pushed open an old wooden door and motioned them in. There were no windows and the air was heavy. They were underground, under the Parthenon. Kuma nodded for the man to enter the room before him, then he stood guard in the doorway. Samantha was thankful. The last thing she needed was to be imprisoned in a smothering dungeon where no one would find them. The room wasn't quite a dungeon though. Or at least it looked like a comfortable one. The furnishings were simple. A cot with a couple thin blankets and large fur, a wooden table with two chairs, and a bookshelf with what Samantha assumed was the man's few belongings. Dust covered everything and she wondered how often he actually came to this room. It was no place to live. She noticed a table setting with unfinished bread on the plate and the goblet next to it was still half full of wine. No one sat, but circled the table and waited for what the man had to say. They studied him, and he studied them. His gaze rested on Samantha mostly. The sparkle in his eyes made her uncomfortable and she wished she hadn't noticed it at all.

He took a seat at the table, looked at them all with a smile, then pound his fist on the table.

"My name is Astraeus." he began. The others looked at each other for a moment, as if trying to decide if the name was familiar. Only Kuma seemed to have no reaction. Samantha couldn't recall any significance to the name. He went on, "I've been living in Arguris under the name Minko since the beginning. When Athena sent the winds, my sons begged me to go. I was in some trouble of my own and they feared I'd be imprisoned for eternity. So they carried me here and I've been quietly waiting for this very day."

Samantha was confused. She still didn't understand who he was or how he had anything to do with her. Pan saw her confusion and explained, "Astraeus is father to the Anemoi, the four winds. When you, er, Athena, sent the winds to gather all of us, it was his children, the four winds, that carried us, and him. They were the ones that brought us here. He's been in hiding."

Father of the winds. She wasn't sure what that meant still, but she was slowly putting the pieces together.

"And how do you know Athena?" she asked.

Astraeus stood up and rounded the table to where she was leaning against the wall. That twinkle in his eyes again. And the way he was smiling at her. She was uncomfortable again. She stood straight and walked next to Phoebe. She didn't like being so close to him.

He chuckled and said, "You and I were great lovers. It was our love that became my trouble. The reason my sons asked me to

join all these other creatures in your great sanctuary. You have done a great work here, but I am happy my eyes can rest on your beauty again. It has been far too long since my heart has beat this way."

Samantha looked to Kuma, hoping he could offer some further explanation. He nodded and said, "You were to be married. I didn't know he was here all this time." He sounded like he was apologizing. Samantha didn't want him to apologize for anything. She was about to speak to him when Astraeus approached her again and gently laid his hands on her shoulders.

"Do you really not remember me?" he looked deep into her eyes, as though he were searching for her though she stood right in front of him. Chills went down her arms and legs when his hands touched her shoulders and her throat felt dry.

"I'm sorry," she said stepping away, "I don't know who you are. And please, we have not proven I am who you all think I am. I may not be your *great lover* at all."

As she said the words she imagined his lips grazing her cheek, her neck. Then she scolded herself, knowing she shouldn't be daydreaming about a strange mans lips at all.

"It was nice to meet you, Astraeus," Samantha held out her hand.

Astraeus looked at it a moment before shaking. Satisfied, Samantha looked at the others as she made her way to the door.

"Wait, please, I have so many questions."

"No one has more questions than I do. You may be someone's old beau, but I have no memory of that. And until I do, I'd ask you to leave me alone." She said as she squeezed past Kuma and made her way down the hall, trying to remember where they had turned.

Astraeus chased after her, grabbing her hand and spinning her around when he caught up.

"Maybe I can help. I've lived in Parthens a long time. What are you looking for?" she felt he'd follow her no matter how many times she'd turn him away. Something told her it was pointless to argue with him.

"We're looking for someone who can help me get my memory back," she explained.

"I don't know anyone like that, but I can ask around," he offered, giving her that sweet smile that was frustrating her, "You should remember me, I'm offended that you've forgotten us," he teased.

"Yes, please do that. Go, ask," she said and he laughed as she pushed him down the hall.

"I think I make you uncomfortable, goddess," he called back. Samantha grunted and looked back to the others, who to her surprise were all giving her mischievous stares. She rolled her eyes at them then they followed Astraeus back out into Parthens.

"I will see what I can find out. You know where to find me now." Astraeus said when they had reached the stairs. He approached Samantha, but she stepped back and he stopped. He waved to the group and disappeared behind a building in front of them.

Samantha let out a sigh of relief. Next to her Phoebe and Rudy laughed while Pan and Kuma stared at her quietly. "What?" she threw her arms out then stomped down the stairs.

They made their way back to the lodge for the night. Samantha laid on her cot and tried not to think of Astraeus. *Great lovers. That was his trouble.* She wondered what kind of love two people could have that would cause enough trouble that he'd need to hide for thousands of years. She remembered the story of Romeo and Juliet. She wondered if it was something like that. She could understand his children wanting him to come here to hide if his life was in danger. She certainly couldn't see herself drinking poison for anyone though.

She drifted off to sleep still thinking about him, the twinkle in his eyes, that smile she wanted to surrender herself to, and his playful voice. She tossed and turned, unable to get comfortable as he raced through her thoughts.

The next morning the companions began asking around for the person they were looking for. They had agreed if Astraeus had found anyone, they would let him find them. None of them wanted to go back to that little room and its thick air. They split up in pairs, with Rudy flying over head to practice using his armored wing and keeping a lookout for trouble. Phoebe and Pan started on the west side of Parthens while Kuma and Samantha went east. From there they split the streets up. Samantha went North while Kuma went South. Not everyone was willing to stop to speak to them, but those that did had no help to offer.

Samantha found a beautiful fountain made of boulders and moss in the middle of a court yard where several of the roads met. She sat on the edge and watched the creatures. She wondered how anyone could be so powerful to just take so many from there homes and drop them in a strange place, expecting them to give thanks and live in peace. Many of them were born here and watched family die here. And just as many were immortal creatures, sent here for there own safety.

Samantha wondered why Athena had the privilege of making that choice. Was it a quick decision? Or did she speak to any of them before sending the winds? More questions ran through her head as she watched satyr children throwing sticks at each other with an impatient mother chasing after them. Several human-like creatures wondered the streets and she wondered if they were all gods and goddesses like Astraeus. What had brought them all here? Then she dared to ask herself, *could I have brought them here?*

She thought about all the time she spent with her uncle when he was home, her time spent with Pan. She loved all his artifacts and stories. She considered the possibility her interest and love had bloomed from the connection she already had to those things, the places, the time. But that was impossible.

This was all impossible. *For heaven's sakes, I created a talking bear!*

She laughed out loud and a deep voice asked, "What's so funny?" startling her to her feet. It was Kuma. She had not heard him approach.

"I was just thinking about all of this, all that you believe of me, and how silly it is to think I could be capable of all this, or even of you." she watched the water fall down the boulders. The sound was soothing, though it was barely heard under the sound of the busy city. "I just keep expecting to wake up, Kuma. To see all of this, and you, and Phoebe, and Rudy, and Pan, Chimera, the harpies, all of it; go away."

She saw the look of pain in Kuma's eyes and she was sorry for what she said. She didn't mean to hurt his feelings. But it was easier to believe he didn't exist. That none of them did. She just needed to wake up. "I'm at war with myself. Sometimes I want to believe in the possibility that I am her. Other times it's just impossible, and I can only help but think none of this is really here. It's all a part of my imagination." She got up and began circling the fountain, rubbing her forehead, trying to keep to ignore the palpitations in her chest again. She felt her legs numbing as her anxiety grew.

"Samantha, please," Kuma reached out for her as she passed in front of him, but she pushed him away. Phoebe and Pan had just entered the crossroad and Rudy flew to a dry boulder and Astraeus walked in not far behind. They all watched Samantha as she sat down and buried her face in her hands. Then she lifted her head and let out an exasperated scream. The street became quiet as everyone stared at her. Whispers floated among them as they pointed. Phoebe stood in front of Samantha and leaned into her ear, whispering, "You have got to get yourself under control," then grabbed her arm and led her down the street. The others followed and they turned down an alley toward the lodge. A small ornamented woman stood next to a stand filled with dried flowers and bottled spices. She stepped into the road in front of them and folded her arms as they approached. Gold discs covered her hair and gold piercings decorated her ears and face. Her hands were stamped with beautiful pictures and her garments smelled of lavender.

"Please, she is distressed, come with me and I can help."

"Thanks, but we're fine," Samantha retorted and tried to push past her.

The woman grabbed her arms, looking up at her, "No, you are not. And I'm not going to wait for you to come around again. Let's go."

The others exchanged looks then followed the woman down the road.

Astraeus followed behind quietly, heeding the warning looks Kuma was giving him.

The woman led them a long way through town, not saying a word, but only looking back every few moments to look at Samantha. When they found themselves at the edge of Parthens they stopped.

"Where are you taking us?" Kuma demanded.

"There," the small woman pointed to a shack about half a mile up the hill. Everything surrounding it was dead. Beyond that everything was green and lush and they could see the trees in the distance. There was nothing inviting about her home. Samantha had no desire to go with the woman and she looked at Kuma.

"We're all here with you," Phoebe said from the other side of her. She felt her hand on her shoulder. She turned and gave her a weak smile.

"Please," the woman said, feeling their uncertainty, "I'll tell you the story over tea."

They followed her up the hill to her cottage. It was surrounded by dead grass and dry, cracked dirt. Smoke came out of the ground and there was a low buzzing in the air. There was a pond behind the house. The water was boiling and it was surrounded with dead brush. The house was covered in dead vines and the trunk of a dead tree lay against the side of it. It was small and it was hard to tell if it was made of dirt, wood, or stone. A white fungus spotted the walls and the windows dusted over. The woman held a small, narrow door open for them. Kuma had to crouch and turn sideways just to fit in. Samantha's first thought was *alchemist*, and her second was *witch*. The walls inside were covered in dried herbs and flowers, pots, and cups. It was surprisingly cleaner than the outside. She turned to look at the woman but almost collided into her. She was standing right in front of her, staring at her with a calm and reassuring expression.

"Please sit down, all of you. I will make you a lavender tea and you can tell me why you're here." she said as she walked over to one side of the room with a counter and a pile of fresh cut flowers.

"Well, we...," Rudy began.

"No, her," the woman turned and pointed to Samantha. Samantha didn't really want to say anything. She just wanted answers.

She began telling the woman everything, beginning at the rehearsal dinner party and included every detail that she could. The woman handed them all a cup of tea, not interrupting and everyone sat quietly as Samantha recalled the events that brought them to Parthens.

When she was done, everyone was silent for a moment. Their cups were empty. Astraeus sat his down next to him on the floor and leaned forward, "You were engaged?"

The woman shushed him and quietly stood, making her way to a cupboard on another wall. She shuffled around a moment until she found what she was looking for. She brought something wrapped in cloth over to them and carefully unwrapped it. It was a beautiful gold goblet with a wooden handle with root like twists along the side of the cup. It was beautiful. She put it down in the center of them then looked at Samantha and said, "I am Nemi, and this is for you."

Samantha looked at her, confused. "Nemi, it's nice to meet you, but I don't understand. Why are you giving me this?"

Nemi smiled and leaned back in her seat, "It was always meant for you. I didn't know that until just now though."

"Well, thank you Nemi, it truly is beautiful, and I will enjoy it, but we really need to be on our way." Samantha said and reached for the cup.

Nemi reached forward, too, and swatted Samantha's hand away. "Child, your way is here. This is where you need to be. I am the memory healer you seek."

Everyone straightened and Rudy's wing jingled as he hopped closer for a better listen.

"You are the goddess who provided me this safety, and you have lost your memory. I can return it to you, if it's what you truly desire."

All eyes stared at her intently. This was what they had come for. She wanted her memory back. To know who she was and where she came from. But now that the moment was presented to her, she wanted to run. She looked around the room at all the creatures that had helped her get this far. They had protected her and fought for her. And she had so quickly wishing them out of existence. Guilt made her sick to her stomach. But if they were all a part of a dream, then they would always be a part of her anyway, and she could see them in her dreams again. At least she would hope she could. She wondered if she had friends just as great in her life before she lost her memory.

She owed it to herself, and to them to find out who she really was. And if this was all just a dream or not. She closed her eyes and took in a deep breath.

"Yes, it's what I truly desire," she replied.

Nemi snatched the cup back and stood up and looked at each of them. Rudy stood tall with his armored wing, ready and waiting for instructions, for anything to happen that might give him an opportunity to show how capable he was. Pan looked on nervously, his hooves shaking under him as he rubbed his sweaty palms together. Phoebe stared ahead, her dagger laying in her lap. She was ready for anything the little woman might pull. It didn't occur to Samantha until then that this woman might be sent to kill her. But even in that event, Samantha would wake up, and it still meant this was a chance she'd have to take. Kuma stared at Samantha and she could hardly hold

his gaze. She couldn't look at the large beast with that pain in
his eyes. She had hurt him and she hadn't meant to.

Nemi stood over Samantha and held out her hand.

"Come, we have work to do."

22

Everyone watched as Nemi thoughtfully took things from cupboards and drawers and wrapped them in individual rags, tying them with twine, then piling them in a corner. She pulled down all of her dried flowers and herbs and piled them in a basket. They filled the air with a wonderful aroma and they all watched her curiously, wondering what she was doing.

"Is there anything we can do to help?" Astraeus asked. Samantha didn't really want him there. She only allowed it because Kuma confirmed his identity. He was Athena's fiance. If she was Athena, she guessed he'd be the first person she'd want to see when it all came back. He could be good for her.

At least she hoped. So far she wasn't sure what Athena could see in him. She was still curious about the trouble he was in because of that relationship. She may not have to ask him about it at all.

"No, these are my errands. Please sit patiently and wait." Nemi spoke softly as she bounced from one side of the room to the other.

Samantha thought about the possibilities, of her getting her memory back and being Athena, or realizing she's someone else completely. Either way she'd still be in Arguris. Only one way would give any of them a way out of it. She looked at everyone around her and wondered what they would do if she wasn't who they believed she was. Would that be enough to convince them she wasn't Athena, or would they take her throughout Arguris until they had uprooted the entire place in search of the answers they desired.

"You may step outside if you wish, I might be a minute," Nemi paused with a handful of clay pots as she crossed the room in front of them. She motioned to toward the door with her head, shooing them out.

They filed out the door and stood in front of the house, staring at the dry ground and dead brush all around them. No one said anything for a moment. In fact, no one looked at each other. How could they share the fear and hope that raced through their minds. Samantha most of all. She looked around at the creatures that surrounded her. They had all put their lives on the line for her at one time. They had lied to protect her and Arguris. They left their homes and put their faith in who she is.

Samantha looked at Phoebe, she was staring up toward the haze above them. She wondered what was on her mind. She had almost lost her life, twice, and she never would have been in that position if Samantha had never been placed in her care. She never did find out how she came to her home in the first place. But Phoebe had been by her side every step of the way. She had been a true friend. Samantha wanted to be Athena for her. She wanted to see her satisfied face when all her memories came back. To see her friend happy, to be able to repay that to her for all the risks she had taken to get them this far.

Kuma grumbled and Samantha looked over at him. He was lost in thoughts, probably hadn't even noticed he'd made a sound. His mother, Samantha thought about it again. How strange it would be to feel it so normal to have created such a fantastic creature. She wondered what her memories would feel like when she could acknowledge their unique bond. One she had created for them and only them. What did they share together? What else had Kuma protected her from? Samantha looked at the others. Pan patted dirt from his fur then looked at her. They stared at each other a moment.

Samantha was filled with a mix of emotions again. The uncle she loved and adored. The satyr that lied and kept secrets. She still wasn't sure if he deserved her trust or her scorn. But he had made sacrifices the same as the others. He had lost things because of her, and he had every proper reason for his actions. She could only hope that after everything was said and done her heart would be in the place to give him the justice he deserved. Whether it punishment or forgiveness, she would leave it to the fate of this day to decide.

"Are you having second thoughts, my Current," Astraeus asked. He stood at her side watching her. She hadn't even noticed him walk over.

"Don't call me that, and no, I am sure of my decision," she responded. The way he looked at her, like he could read her every thought and he found every one amusing. She wondered why he always had to smile at her like that. It wasn't comforting at all. It was distracting. Perhaps Athena adored that about him. A goddess would need a handsome distraction. A god with a smile like that could definitely do the trick.

"I will be here for you, no matter what the outcome," he assured her.

"Thank you," was all she would say. Everything about them would be sorted later. If she was Athena, a happy couple

293

would be reunited. If she remained Samantha, he could go on his way freely.

There was a sound of wind chimes as Rudy landed on a boulder. He had been flying overhead, admiring the reflections his armored wing shone on the ground. Samantha hadn't learned much about the bird during their time together, but his loyalty and determination to serve them reminded her of a loyal dog. She would never tell him that. She supposed comparing any of these creatures to the normal animals of Chraimyth would only be offensive. Still, Rudy had proven himself reliable when it seemed he could have left them at any moment.

Samantha suddenly had questions for Rudy, but decided it was too late. From here on out, everything would be left to whatever Nemi could do for them.

Then Samantha had another thought.

"What if I'm not Athena," she looked around to each of them as she asked the question. "People look alike all the time. What if I'm just a regular girl who happens to look like her. You haven't seen her in thousands of years. Maybe your memory of her has gotten hazy. I just happen to have this weapon. You," she pointed to Kuma, "just happen to feel a protective instinct toward me because that's just the kind of being you are, and," she continued quietly, sorry for what she was saying because she did not mean to hurt their feelings, but felt it had to be said, "and you are just filled with wishful thinking."

She held her hand over her eyes, ashamed.

"I'm sorry, I'm just worried where we all go from here if I'm not Athena. Wouldn't it make sense for us to have a plan?" Samantha looked at them, hoping they'd understand.

"A war has begun over you. No matter what the outcome is, there is no turning back to how things were before Speranta opened and let you in." Phoebe said as she walked over. She stood in front of Samantha, inches away from her face. It was easy to see she was irritated by Samantha's words. "If you are just Samantha, you will have to fight this war with us anyway. We may walk out of this knowing who you really are, but to Chimera and the army she raises, you are still Athena anyway. And since there is no way out of Arguris," she shot a glaring glance at Pan, who looked down at his hooves and kicked the dirt, "You don't have much choice but to play the part."

Phoebe was right. Whether she had her memories back or not, Samantha had already become Athena to parts of Arguris. Chimera would not be convinced, and the harpies had shown no interest in finding out for themselves who she really was. They only seemed interested in the sport of killing. Samantha didn't know anything about Chimera, or her anger. She didn't know how to bring her comfort or reassurance that she was not who she thought she was. But if she was, Samantha would certainly soon understand the source of her anger. She'd be better prepared to face Chimera, and the harpies, and anyone else who were preparing to fight them.

Samantha walked out several steps until Parthens was in view. She looked at the city and toward the path they had come from. She looked into all the parts of Arguris she could see in front of her. To every distance, every hill, tree, city wall and building, and to Nemi's small hut sitting in the middle of the dead ground. Then she looked at all of her friends. Her heart, for the first time she could ever remember, was filled with purpose, and motivation to fulfill that purpose. Everything about her life before now seemed pointless, like it didn't matter what her memories told her. This is where she was now and there was reason for it. There was meaning to it.

This was her destiny. This was fate. This was her adventure. "No matter who I am in the days ahead, I will fight by your side as you stand by mine. If not as Athena for the freedoms deserved in Arguris, then as I am now, for the peace maintained in Arguris." Samantha took out her golden trinket and opened her spear. She pounded the ground and knelt before them, bowing her head to the ground. She heard a moment of motion in front of her, then silence. She slowly looked up. Everyone knelt before her, those with their weapons stretched them out on their hands, those who had left theirs in the hut held their fist against their chest.

Samantha stood and walked closer to them, holding her spear out ahead of her. She stopped in front of them. Phoebe looked up first, then stood and held her sword over the spear. Astraeus wasted no time placing his sword on next. Kuma's hand came next, then Pan's. Finally Rudy flew over and landed on the spear, resting his armored wing at the center of the hands and weapons. As they looked at each other, each with their own expression, they could each feel the strength of the bond that had just been made. Samantha had an escaping moment where her thoughts went to the three musketeers and she wanted to yell, "One for all, all for one!", but she knew they wouldn't understand the reference. Still, as she looked at them, even at Pan, she knew she had found her family. Nothing beyond this day could change the bond between them.

Nemi stepped out and walked toward them. She held a small glass vial that looked like it had been broken and mended several times. It was filled with a dark substance and she held it tightly.

"Please, come with me now," she walked between them and they followed her to the small pond.

She sat at the waters edge and waved her hands over the surface, chanting for a moment, then she sat back and looked at them.

"Let me explain how this works," she began. She motioned for everyone to sit and they all sat down on the dirt.

"I was not brought here by your doing. I came of my own accord. I made sure to be where the wind tunnel would at just the right moment and let it take me away." Nemi told them, "When I came here, I had a large jug of this liquid." She held up the vial for them all to see then continued, "I used this liquid, this potion, to keep trespassers away from my home. Alone, it is deadly. She stretched her arm out, motioning to the land around them.

"You can see what it does. Like an acid, it kills. It kept my home safe out there, and though it has not been necessary," she shrugged, "it has kept my home safe here, too, I like to think."

They all exchanged glances, not sure where the woman was going with her story. She held the vial out.

"This is how you get your memory back."

Samantha was confused. Nemi had just explained how the potion in the vial meant death. Was the woman crazy? Had they just wasted their time coming out here with her? She looked at the others and could see they were thinking the same thing.

"What do you expect her to do with your death potion?" Phoebe asked grimly.

"Let me finish explaining," Nemi insisted. "I have held on to this vial in case one day it became important enough for me to use it for its true purpose."

She looked at Samantha and gave her a tired smile. "That day has come, and so has mine."

Nemi looked to the pond a moment, a sadness sweeping over her face, then she looked at Samantha. She pulled out the goblet she had shown them earlier and gave it to Samantha. Then she took the vial and pulled the cork out and spoke another chant. She looked at Samantha again. Samantha hoped she wouldn't pour that vial in her cup. She wasn't sure she could risk death for all of them, even though she had just promised her life to them.

"This vial is for me," Nemi went on, "I will drink this vial, then I will submerge myself in the water, which contains the remaining contents of the potion I had originally brought with me. When I do so, the water will absorb me, and with my body, my power. You will be able to fill your cup and drink."

They were all looking at each other uncomfortably now. Samantha didn't think she could hear any more stranger things from her being considered a thousands of years old goddess. Now a little woman would kill herself and ask her to drink her death from an acidic pond. How did any of this make sense? Nemi could see their discomfort. "When you drink, you will be drinking in my power, and your memory will be restored."

She paused, holding her finger up before anyone of them could speak, "The more memory there is to bring back, the more painful it will be. You will all need to be by her side. She will feel like she is dying, but I assure you she is not. You will have to be patient," she looked to Samantha, "and you will have to be strong."

"So you are telling us you drown yourself in acid and I get my memory back?" Samantha stood up and looked over the pond. The buzzing around them suddenly seemed louder, more threatening than it had before.

"It is much more honorable than that," Nemi laughed. Samantha studied the woman. This stranger would sacrifice her life so quickly just so she could remember who she was. "Why?"

Phoebe held her sword to the woman's neck. They all stood up and though Samantha didn't agree with Phoebe's action, she still wanted to hear Nemi's reply.

"I am the memory healer. And to be eternally remembered in the story of the freedom that is to come to Arguris is the greatest honor I could ever expect in my life. It is my choice, just as coming here in the first place was. I am happy to serve the sweet goddess." Nemi smiled at Samantha and eyed Phoebe, who was still holding the blade to her throat.

Phoebe lowered her sword and turned to Samantha, "I don't like this. There must be some other memory healer."

Samantha considered it a moment. They all watched her, waiting.

It was murder. How could she watch this innocent woman take her own life so she could regain hers, no matter what it turned out to be.

"Nemi, I can't," she said hesitantly, "I can't let you do that."

"You don't give me my permissions," Nemi barked, standing up. "We are equals in our being and we control the other no more or less. I can do as I please with my gifts."

Samantha hadn't meant to upset her. She only wanted to reassure her that they were willing to find some other way so she didn't have to put her own life at risk over an uncertainty. Before she could say anything more, Nemi put the vial to her lips and tipped it up, emptying the contents into her mouth. They all rushed toward her but she swallowed it before anyone could touch her.

"Wait until I am gone, then drink." Nemi said quietly. They all stood silent as they watched her disrobe and step naked into the pond. She disappeared under the thick surface quickly. They all watched as nothing happened at first. Nemi was just gone, like that. Samantha stared at the murky water. *Why had she let that happen*, she wondered to herself. Then the water began to boil more, the dark color becoming light, sparkling clear. The plants all around them sprang to life. Grass grew under their feet, flowers bloomed from the

previously dead bushes. The boulders were covered in moss and trees grew quickly all around them. The fungus on the house disappeared and bricks made from mud could be seen below vines of pink and purple flowers. The tree that laid against the house fell back in places as it's roots grew into the ground. The branches bloomed with leaves and pears.
They all stared in awe.

There was no sign of Nemi. Her body was gone. When the water finally settled down Samantha found herself unable to move. Kuma took the cup from her hand and walked over to the pond, filling it with the water, then brought it back to her. "Her sacrifice should not be for nothing. Drink." he ordered her.

Samantha held the cup. The liquid inside was clear, odorless. The buzzing around them had vanished. It was quiet. The silence felt like a thousand pounds sitting on her shoulders. She looked at each of them one more time, then closed her eyes and put the cup to her lips and drank.

23

Samantha didn't feel any different. Was she supposed to?
Nemi was gone as soon as she entered the water. Would it be
just as quick for her? She felt the panic building as she looked
at the water, then to the cup in her hand. This was crazy.

She looked around at all the faces staring back at her. They
were watching her intently, waiting, unsure what to expect.
Samantha looked to the sky, half expecting thunderous clouds
to being rolling in. But nothing was happening.

Something had to happen, though. Nemi had just given her
life for this moment of truth for all of them. She had to know

303

the truth. She looked at the cup again, there was still a small drop in the bottom. Perhaps she had to drink every last drop. She lifted the cup to her lips, and as soon as the last drop touched her tongue she fell to her knees.

The world began spinning. Her companions disappeared, and so did everything else. She thought she felt herself stumble, but she couldn't be sure. She suddenly couldn't feel anything. Maybe she was floating. She lost all sense of her physical body as images flashed before her eyes. So many, so fast. She knew each one well, every person, every emotion associated with the image. Every bit of knowledge shocked her, both in wonderment that she knew such a thing, while at the same time disbelief that she could ever forget such an event, or person, or thing.

There were muffled voices around her, but she couldn't tell where they were coming from. The images just kept moving before her eyes. Hundreds at a time in just a few seconds. A long scream came from somewhere, and only when she gasped for air did she realize it came from her. She tried to be physically aware of herself, but her body seemed lost somewhere. Suddenly there were images of Kuma and Astraeus. She cried out again. And she felt the pain in her chest and the tears on her cheek. There were images of others from long before even them. Memories of war and of friendship.

When she thought maybe the images would go on for eternity, they seemed to slow. Memories of her father, she remembered every detail of his face, the deep rumble of his voice, and how his eyes could twinkle and dance, or burn fire with rage. She saw his anger, at her. She saw the darkness, such a long time of darkness, then she saw the forest where she looked for the nymphs.

In the very next moment she was on a beach. It looked familiar. As she looked around she realized it was the same beach she had dreamed about so many times. She circled around, unsure what to do, and when she came back around Nemi stood before her. She jumped, startled, and Nemi smiled at her, reaching out her hand.

"Don't be afraid," she said. Samantha took her hand. She couldn't feel her. She looked to make sure she was really holding her hand, then to Nemi's face for an explanation.

"This is where you decide who you're going to be," Nemi told her. Samantha still didn't understand.

"You have been given your memories. They are yours and only yours, and they are many, it has taken a toll on your physical self and you will need time to heal. What you have to decide now is if you heal as your true self, or as only the girl you remembered yourself to be when we first met."

Nemi looked at her as she waited patiently for an answer.

"Why would you give your life for mine?" Samantha pleaded.

"It is my choice. Now, what will you choose?" Nemi put her arms to her side and her smile was peaceful, serene. Samantha admired her commitment and courage. Her faith in what she couldn't have known before.

Samantha closed her eyes, let her mind rush through the hurricane of memories that now filled her once empty mind. Then she straightened herself, opening her eyes, and looked at Nemi without blinking.

"My true self, and the girl I remember myself to be, are the same. She is I, and I am she. I will wake as Athena, as I am named, and therefore carry my power and wisdom through every day ahead. Justice will be served, and peace will be restored. Your sacrifice will be remembered forever and your name will be spoken among every mouth in Arguris who would know how you helped to free them," Athena spoke for the first time as herself in many years.

As she listened to her voice she almost thought it was someone else speaking through her. She sounded nothing like the half-confident Samantha she had been the past several years. She knew who she was, what she had to do, and those she had to beg forgiveness from. Those who needed justice, and those who needed to be held accountable for their crimes. Nemi nodded and looked at Athena a moment, her face full of life as she grinned and her eyes sparkled.

"Remember what I told you. When you drank from that cup, you consumed my powers. When you are feeling yourself again, you may still feel something new as well. And don't worry, your heart will tell you how to use it." Nemi cupped a hand over her chest.

She turned quietly and walked down the beach until her image disappeared.

As it did, Athena felt a pain in her head. She closed her eyes tightly and held her hands to her temples. Her forehead felt cold, then something wet drip down near her ear.

"Samantha, can you hear me?" came Phoebe's voice.

"Let her rest, don't rush it." Rudy's voice said.

Athena rubbed her forehead and the pain began to go away. Her memories were settling, though there was still some shock to all of it. She knew who she was. She remembered. And she had Nemi to thank for that. She had all of them to thank for that.

She slowly opened her eyes and realized they were in the dusty room Astraeus had taken them to before.

Astraeus. Where was he? It had been so long and the last time she had seen him she didn't know herself and had treated him so poorly and he had taken it so well. Now she remembered him and wanted his arms tightly around her.

"Slow, take your time." Phoebe said as she helped Athena sit up. Athena opened her eyes and looked at everyone crowded in the room.

Phoebe was still patting her forehead with a cloth. She gently took it from her as she smiled at the ogre. Everyone sat and stood in front of her. They all waited quietly but anxiously. They wanted to know if she was who they had all so loyally reminded her she was the past several months. It had been a long time since she had such loyal friends, anyone she could trust and depend on. She hoped in the time ahead they would continue to walk at her side. There was so much to be done and she would need their help if they were happy to give it. She would demand nothing more of them though. They had already given enough. More than any of them ever needed to give.

Athena looked at Kuma. The connection he had told her about at Raftik's camp, she felt it. It had always been there, but as Samantha, she didn't know how to acknowledge the feeling or understand it, but now she realized it had never left. The pull they had to each other. She was his mother, and he her child. He was her loyal guard and they exchanged a love that allowed them to cherish each other through the most unbreakable bond ever formed among living things. Kuma had a different expression on his face than he had worn in the months before. She knew she didn't have to tell him. He already felt it. He was aware of every part of her.

Astraeus shifted in his seat behind her. Athena turned and looked at him lovingly. When he saw her expression he sprang from his seat. He would have pounced on her then if the room hadn't been full of creatures, but he waited for her to say the words, to tell them all what they were waiting to hear.

"I know who I am now," she smiled at them. Everyone stood, waiting to see what fate lay ahead for them.

"I am Athena, goddess of wisdom and war, daughter of Zeus and Metis. I have remembered the justice I intended to serve and the war that I have now begun. If you will continue by my side as my loyal companions and advisors, we will end the tension Chimera has created in Arguris and maintain the peace that has been self-sustained."

Athena watched them stare at her. No one spoke. The men looked stern, almost uncertain, except for Kuma who held his halberd to his chest. There would never be any question of his loyalty. Phoebe was grinning from ear to ear, probably lost for words. Then suddenly they all erupted in a loud cheer. Phoebe and Astraeus threw their arms around Athena while the others clapped and hollered. Rudy shook his wings, letting his armored wing cling in celebration.

Kuma knelt behind them. And when the others saw, they all
did the same, just as they had done outside Nemi's hut. She
held her hands before her face and bowed before them.
"My friends, I thank you for your unfailing faith in me. Your
loyalty has earned my trust," Athena paused. She wished the
moment could last longer, but they couldn't waste time.
Chimera was still pursuing her with an army, and they'd have
to be prepared. She knew Chimera had more of a grudge
against her than just Arguris. If she could not make peace with
the creature, then Chimera would have to be laid to rest.
There would be no other option. Chimera was created to be
monstrous. Athena had hoped the loss of part of her would
change the creatures heart, but it had not. Instead the creature
held her grudge well, and would carry it to her grave.
Athena went on, "We have a war to fight, but we must make it
only with those who have no desire for peace. Everyone else
will be under our protection and welcome to fight by our
side."
They nodded in agreement.
"We have to visit the satyrs. I think they will join us." Pan said.
Athena didn't respond right away. She remembered the
rustling in the woods, the slow footsteps coming up behind
her. She remembered feeling for her spear in her pocket,
ready to turn and fight whomever was trying to attack her from
behind. She remembered standing in the forest before she had

been taken to the orphanage. This was all happening this way because of him. His mistake had cost Nemi her life, and the life of the centaur. She reminded herself of the reasons he had shared and decided for now it was best to look over his faults and accept the allegiance he persistently tried to give.

"We'll head there in the morning. We need to keep distance between us and Chimera. We don't know when she will show. It's best to keep moving and recruiting who we can," Athena assured them.

When they had agreed on a time to meet the next morning, they left the room and made their way to the inn.

"My Current," Astraeus took Athena's hand and pulled her aside as the others entered the inn, "can we share this night together?"

"Does the night belong to only one of us right now" Athena teased.

Astraeus smiled at her and led her through the streets of Parthens until they were at the courtyard with the fountain. They sat on boulders next to each other and stared at each other a moment.

"It was hard to bare you not knowing me as you did," Astraeus caressed her cheek and leaned in close to her face.

Athena placed her hand on his heart, and leaned toward him, "It was unbearable knowing you had vanished without a good-bye. I never knew where you had gone, only that you had."

she explained to him. "I'm sorry you were deserted for so long."

Astraeus wouldn't let her speak any more. He pressed against her lips and she felt herself once again lose sense of her physical body. She let herself become lost in his arms and the touch from every kiss. She knew they could both stay right there for months locked in an embrace, but they had to keep space between them until Arguris was set in order. They couldn't distract each other from the task at hand. Athena pulled away and stepped off the boulder.

"We have to stay focused. Or I might have to consider you an accomplice and lock you away" she smiled at Astraeus, knowing it would be hard for him to leave her. She didn't want to leave him either, but they would have their time soon enough.

Astraeus walked her to the inn and they both paused outside the door.

"One night," he said and ran his hand across her thigh. She leaned into him and he kissed her, pushing her inside the inn. Athena turned around and led him up the stairs to her room. She opened the door and Phoebe was waiting, a small bag on her lap.

"Yep, I knew this was coming. It's all yours," she got up and made her way out the door, winking at Athena and closing the door behind her.

Astraeus pushed her further into the room then pulled the dress off of her shoulders and let it fall to the floor. Athena pulled his shirt over his head, then wrapped her arms around his neck and kissed him as he untied his pants. They fell onto the bed together and through the whole night they were tangled, breathless; satisfying each other's desires again and again.

24

Chimera's hooves pounded against the ground as she ran along the path toward Parthens. King Korauk and his minotaur army raced along behind him and the harpies flocked overhead, led by Linaphese.

The harpy had confronted Chimera earlier over the death of her soldiers. Chimera was good at redirecting her anger. Of course the beast would take no responsibility for their deaths. "They'd still be alive if we had no reason at all to gather together in the first place. You'd still be mucking in your Haken and I'd be trailing the walls endlessly, wasting day after day in this pointless, endless circle. If you want to hold anyone accountable for their deaths, turn your squawking beak to Athena. This is all her doing," Chimera had stood face to face with Linaphese, daring the harpy to disagree, Paphene baring her fangs, and Nova giving a low, rumbling growl that shook the half bird's feathers. They had stared at each other a moment, then Linaphese backed away.

Now, as they reached about a mile out of Parthens, they slowed. The harpies landed in the fields and they all waited instruction from Chimera.

"Linaphese, send a crew to scout them out. Find them and report." Chimera instructed. Linaphese called for a small flock of six and sent them toward the city.

"We need to surround the city, to be ready," Korauk suggested. Three minotaur stood at each side of him. None of them were as large as he, but they would be larger than anything in that city, and nothing would be able to overtake them, Chimera was sure of that. If Athena didn't want to open the doors before, she would have to open the doors now. There would be no mercy with these beasts if she didn't.

"Yes, but we will wait. Keep our resources gathered until we know their location." Chimera said as she watched the small group of harpies disappear into the distance.

It was nightfall before they returned. The minotaur had put up tents and the harpies flattened pads of grass. Some of them were already asleep. They woke when they heard the screeches in the sky above. Linaphese flew to Chimera's side, and Korauk stood by his tent nearby.

"Where are they?" Chimera demanded. He knew from the ill expressions on their faces that they didn't have good news.

"We looked everywhere. We spread out and waited, watched every road, every corner, every building. There is no sign of them." one of the harpies stepped forward, mostly eyeing Linaphese, as though she weren't aware that Chimera's wrath would be much worse. "They aren't there." she finished. Chimera roared in frustration. Where could they be? Where else was there for them hide?

"Are you sending my warriors on a fools mission, beast?" Korauk groaned. All the minotaur stood, grabbing their weapons, waiting for their king's demand. Chimera had not sent them on a fools mission. This is where the harpies had said they would be. If they had moved on they wouldn't be far. She could send harpies out again to search for them, and this time detain them. But she had already tried that once and it failed.

She paced back and forth as she felt Korauk's glare burning into her. She looked toward Parthens, and in all the directions around it. The goddess was hiding. Just as she had done before. She failed the courage to come kill Chimera herself, so she had blessed someone else to do it for her and that had failed. And now she hides once more, trapped in the prison she had made for all the rejected creations of the gods. Chimera stood still, and stared at Parthens.

"Chimera!" Korauk yelled. Chimera knew he was threatening her, and she did fear him. But she kept quiet as she stared at the city.

The minotaur came up behind her with his warriors on each side. Chimera turned around just as the king was raising a fist to bring down on her head and roared, "We take Parthens!" Korauk stepped back and his minotaur lowered the weapons they held over their heads. Chimera glared at them.

"Cowards." she scoffed.

She waited until more minotaur and harpies had gathered closer.

"We will not waste anymore time chasing after a cowardice goddess who hides in her own creation. We will run rampant in Parthens and draw her out of hiding. She will come to us. Athena would never look away from justice that needs served. When she arrives, we will capture her and take everything from her until she releases us from this eternal wall," Chimera roared into the night and the army in front of her cheered. Athena and her small group would have no choice but to surrender. Even with the centaurs at their side, they would be no match for minotaurs and harpies. Paphene alone would be enough threat to them all.

"Tonight we camp, and tomorrow, we will be the rooster's crow." Chimera said, then turned and walked into the empty field.

The minotaur and harpies alike seemed happy with this. Everyone returned to their tents and grass pads and soon the field was quiet other than a few minotaur staying up to polish their weapons.

Chimera stared at the sky, wondering what it would be like to see the stars again, to see if the moon still mocked her. She wondered how the woods she once called home had changed. It had been many years. She had never given up hope that the day would come when she'd be free. That day was finally upon them.

She was going home.

Before the first rays of light had even peaked over the green hills, all of the soldiers stood ready. It was a day many of them had looked forward to, long before Athena's return. Parthens had become a city unwelcoming to those who held on to the old ways of Arguris. Many generations had moved on and forgotten that their ancestors before them were prisoners in this place. They didn't understand that this was not home. Now they could show them Athena had returned, and could free them. An entire world they could call home was there for the taking. Today they would confront the citizens of Parthens and make that message shake them to the bone. Athena would return, and they would all demand together that she undo the injustice.

They marched the last mile to the city. As they came to the cities borders, early risers spotted them and stared, unsure what to make of the gathering. A young satyr screamed when she saw the minotaurs towering through the city gates. Others gazed at the sky as the harpies hurled into the city.

Chimera sneered as she walked along side the minotaurs and heard the screams ahead. The harpies were already attacking. As the minotaurs filed into the city they ran down every road, striking market booths, tearing down awnings and support posts. Some ran into buildings and homes and threw creatures out the doors. Everyone ran, but no one knew where to run to. Some were injured, and others lay still in the road. The harpies were grabbing anything their talons could get hold of, carrying it high above then dropping it so it collided with whatever might be below. They flew low, screeching and laughing as creatures covered their ears, running into each other and into the walls.

Chimera walked slowly down the streets, looking for any sign of Athena and her crew. When anyone drew near, Paphene would lash out. No one had dared to get too close.

Street after street she prowled, watching the minotaurs tear through buildings, dragging creatures out of the homes and slaughtering them in the road. The harpies swooped down, picking up debris and and any creature who couldn't run away fast enough. The bodies were increasing, and Chimera was growing impatient. She had not come to massacre all of Parthens. She had come to taunt.

Why wasn't it working?

Nova let out a loud roar and the warriors nearby stopped and looked at her.

"Gather outside the city, take nothing, no more." Chimera ordered.

As she made her way through the streets, an aching filled her stomach. There were young and old alike lain on the ground everywhere. Part of her didn't care. No one ever cared for her. She had been alone all these years. Not even a companion. Why should she care for lifeless bodies laying around her? Still, a sadness swelled at her throat and she wanted to console those she left mourning. She saw an elderly ogre emerge from a hut and cry out when she looked around her. Then she saw Chimera and stared. "Why have you done this?" she sobbed. Chimera lifted her head and glared, "It wasn't me that did this, it was the goddess of your ancestors that put us here. She is the reason for all this." she said.

The ogre glared as tears rushed down her face.

Chimera walked on. Minotaurs rushed ahead, continuing to destroy anything in their path as harpies flew overhead, dropping what was left in their talons.

Nova and Paphene took one more look behind them. Dust filled the air now, and only outlines of the wreckage and bodies could be seen. When Nova felt something moist on her eye she let out a roar and lashed out with her claw at the minotaur in front of her. He looked surprised and let her pass. She ran passed them until she was out of the city, then she continued to run through the large grassy fields until she felt she was far enough away. She paced back and forth, grumbling, fighting against the sobs that choked her. Paphene could only watch, confused and amazed. She shifted her wait and Chimera fell to the floor. Nova growled.

"Let me be, snake!" she groaned.

"Get yourself together, we know they've had it coming all along." Paphene hissed in her stone covered ear.

"Of course I know that. They all deserved every bit." Chimera looked away and licked her paw.

Paphene wrapped herself around Nova's neck and pulled the lions head up, then stared her in the eyes. "And don't forget it. Now get us over there and let's finish this." Paphene flicked her tongue and they stared at each other a moment. They were united through most of everything they had ever gone through throughout their life. But every once in awhile their disagreements would bring them to each others throats, which served none of them well. They finally settled that whoever should be stronger and of sounder mind should lead them. Nova was showing to be more weak than she ever had before. Paphene would have to take over, and she'd have to keep an eye on Nova until she had herself together again.

They made their way back to camp where Korauk and Linaphese were waiting. They stared at her as if she owed them some explanation.

"The point was to draw her out. But she's not there," Chimera began. "Let the survivors run for help. They'll find her and she'll come.

The minotaur and harpy looked at one another.

"And how do you expect our flock and tribe to eat while we wait?" Linaphese stepped forward, eyeing the rocks in Chimera's ears. "I don't see anywhere to hunt, and unless you want to see both our kind hunting each other, I suggest you come up with a plan."

Chimera looked at Korauk. The minotaur didn't budge, just stared at her. The other minotaur were taking off their gear, pulling blades of grass and cleaning the blood off as well as they could, but it was only smearing. Some of the harpies were flying off in the distance over the field, looking for any small prey to catch for their meal.

Chimera knew Linaphese was right. They needed to stay here until Athena came, and Chimera knew she would. But she had to keep her army content enough that they didn't turn on each other in the meantime.

"Okay," she said to the harpy, "send a small flock to the woods to bring back what they can." Then she turned to Korauk. "Send a group of minotaur out to catch what they can and make sure they don't cause unnecessary trouble." Korauk groaned and bared his teeth, but went and gave the command. The two groups left and Chimera roamed outside the camp until she couldn't see either of the two groups through the tall grass. She laid down and stared at the green blades in front of her. All she wanted was her peace back. Why did it require so much ferocity?

25

Athena leaned against a tree, still trying to sort through the many memories that had flashed through her head. She still had a pain in her head but it faded a little every day. How often did anyone relive their entire life in only a few moments. Some memories remained clear, like when she created Kuma, and when she met Astraeus. Others remained simple images with no precise point in time, she couldn't remember when they had happened. She had lived a long time, she supposed it would be natural not to remember the moment everything occurred, but to be happy to remember it at all. Which she was.

She had thought a long time about her life as Samantha, especially the part spent in Arguris. She had been awful to her friends. She didn't deserve them but they stuck by her anyway. They loved her unconditionally. She would honor them and return that love. She smiled as she thought of Astraeus. Returning that love to some would prove to have certain extra rewards. Athena giggled at her own amusement. They still had things to discuss. They hadn't settled the matter of him leaving her behind without so much as a goodbye. He left her without ever knowing the wrath that fell on her after she saved all those that she could. He sat safe under the floors of the mock Parthenon while she was...elsewhere. She didn't want to remember that dark place right now.

Athena grunted and pushed off the tree. She walked through the trees until she came to a large opening. Small houses perched several yards from each other with birch trees sprouting here and there among them. The grass was neatly trimmed and a dirt path weaved through. Satyrs trotted about. Athena and the rest of her friends occupied two of the houses, given to them by friends of Pan's. They had insisted on camping in the woods, but the satyr's insistence was more pressed and they didn't want to come off ungrateful, especially with the proposal they had to give.

Pan watched Athena approach and they exchanged smiles. They had spoken on their way to the satyr herd and she had found herself grateful to him and they agreed a clean slate was best between them both. Of them all, they were two that were starting on new ground, as new people with new goals. That common ground brought them closer and they understood each other better now.

It was amusing to see the satyr surrounded by his own. He had always seemed a bit of an outcast, obnoxious and a bit dimwitted. But here the girls tended to swoon over him. They wanted to hear his stories and were disappointed he couldn't play his flute for them. He was clearly enjoying the attention, but there was business to attend to. Athena motioned to him and he nodded, shaking the girls' hands and kissing some on the cheek. There were giggles and blushes as he tore himself away.

Phoebe and Kuma didn't need to be called. They were already waiting for her. Rudy was off on his usual look out. He would return in a few hours with his report. His armored wing had proven not only a source of strength, but a new source of pride and boasting for the bird. Athena loved him, especially now that she could remember his long ago relative before him that accompanied her everywhere, just as he did. He made his ancestors proud.

With all of her friends by her side, Athena approached the elders. They were a group of satyrs whose fur and hair had grayed with age and two of them bared most of their weight on tall walking sticks. They looked about as friendly as Chimera, and Athena hoped everything would go well.

Athena approached them, smiling kindly, "Would you mind if we had a moment of your time to discuss a matter of rather great importance to Arguris right now?"

They responded immediately with grunts and began to hobble away. As they were too slow to escape them, the crew followed them on all sides, so to make clear they would not be ignored so easily.

"You need to listen to her, because what is happening will affect you, too." Kuma stepped in front of them and grumbled.

They seemed no more pleased with him than Pan did the first time they had met. Kuma might as well have grabbed them all by the throat the way they shook as they look up at him towering over them.

Other satyrs began to gather and Athena stepped away from the elders. The rest followed. She didn't want anyone to think they had come to threaten their peace. They needed their help. It may be best to be quick and straight forward about it.

"We need your help. I'm the goddess Athena, the one who created Arguris centuries ago. I returned to discuss the future of this place, but first I need to calm an army, if not defeat them altogether. Chimera leads them. We don't know the full strength of this army yet, but we know the harpies and minotaur are among them. We have to assume she'll gather more and we are asking if you would give us your aide, should we find the need to fight. We hope it doesn't come to that, but it makes it easier to know we have the support of the good citizens of Arguris."

It wasn't a planned speech, but she hoped it made their intentions clear. She was a few thousand years out of practice when it came to motivating the troops.

Everyone stared at them a moment. The elders looked to each other and everyone looked to them.

"Athena, you say you are," one of the elders crept closer to her so he could examine her better. His voice shook and he whistled when he spoke. "You have been here in Arguris all this time and never made yourself known, never explained this place to those who first lived and some who live here still."

"I arrived only a few months ago. But my circumstances were different. I didn't know who I was, even though others tried to tell me," she looked to her friends gratefully.

"And even in those months you never reached out until trouble had brewed again," another elder grumbled.

Whispers arose from all around them and the satyrs looked at them disapprovingly. Athena tried to think of something to ease their minds.

Phoebe stepped forward, aggravated and impatient, "We have been at Athena's side throughout her journey through Arguris.

Some of us have almost lost our lives and Chimera has done nothing but threaten us. Athena can not help Arguris if we allow Chimera to build an army whose only purpose is to seek her out and kill her," she paused and thought a moment, then continued, "And if they do kill Athena, that leaves Chimera running rampant through Arguris with an army and all of us with no hope of ever seeing the other side of these walls again. What do you think she'll do then?"

They paused a moment. Phoebe and Athena exchanged a hopeful glance at one another then watched as the elders gathered in a small circle and spoke among themselves. Other satyrs were drawing in closer, too, as though to hear for themselves what was being said. Finally the elders stood in a line and quietly stared at Athena and her friends a moment. Whatever they were going to say, it was clear from their expressions that they were confident and wouldn't care what opinion others might have of it. Athena closed her eyes a moment and hoped they would agree to stand with them.

"You have managed this long, we are confident that a goddess with your resources will manage again. There is plenty of room in Arguris, perhaps you can build Chimera and her army another home within." the elders chuckled and hobbled away. Samantha reached her arm out and held Phoebe back. Kuma came and stood at her side and Pan looked on worriedly.

"Pan, stay if you must. You have done enough for us that I couldn't ask anymore of you, especially if it's going to cause separation between you and yours." Athena offered. She continued to watch the elders walk away. Every few moments one would look back at her.

"Let's not waste anymore time here," Kuma grumbled.

Athena didn't want to move on until she knew the next plan of action. Where else could they go to recruit warriors. She couldn't assume Arguris was filled with species ready to fight, or even able to fight, not with the generations that had passed and the little threat that seemed to have ever been present here. Athena felt she was the biggest threat to the peace in Arguris, yet she was also their greatest hope to complete freedom. They would love her or hate her. There could be no in between.

Pan approached, holding his hands steady in front of them. He was trying to stop them from shaking. His forehead was shiny from sweat and Athena looked his entire body over, wondering if he had been bit by something. He seemed incapable or reluctant to say anything.

"Pan, are you alright? What is it?" Phoebe nudged his shoulder.

"I have an idea. It may be a waste of our time, but if it means we may have a chance," he stopped and looked around him. Most of the other satyrs had already moved on, the elders had spoken, so anything else Pan, or Athena, or any of them had to say was of no importance to them anymore.

Pan stepped closer and spoke softly, "Perhaps I can speak to the nymphs." Athena thought he was joking, clearly Phoebe did too. The ogre began laughing and slapped Pan on the shoulder. He cringed and rubbed the area, scouring at her.

"How do you expect to accomplish this without your flute?" Kuma asked. Athena stepped aside as Kuma leaned down to Pan's level, daring him to treat him like a fool.

"Sometimes love can accomplish the greatest things never foreseen by man or any beast," Pan stared the bear straight in the face. His confidence and daring impressed Athena. Once he had insisted she herself was someone she didn't believe herself to be. He saved their lives and risked his own to prove his loyalty. She couldn't brush his words away without consideration.

"How far would we have to go?" Athena asked.

"The closest part of the wall is fine, I think." Pan looked at her sadly, "It's a risk, as far as the time we'll lose, and what Chimera might gain in her army. We may find ourselves empty with no defenses, or we may find our answer. It is only a possible solution as we seem to have no more."

No one argued with him. There was an opportunity. Phoebe shared her thoughts next, "We don't have to know what will happen before we get there, we just have to be willing to try."

It seemed agreed by everyone. Someone would need to inform Rudy. Athena followed where she had seen the elders wander off but didn't need to go far as a flapping and clanking of feathers came from above and Rudy flew down in front of her. He was out of breath but trying to speak quickly, choking on his words.

"Rudy, take a moment!" Athena insisted. The owl took a few deep breaths and she noted the distress written all over his face. Something had happened. She stood up and looked around. None of the satyrs appeared on guard, there was nothing in the sky heading their way, no sounds of any sort coming from any direction. What had Rudy seen?

Rudy closed his eyes and gathered his strength. His words were soft, but painful. "She's taken Parthens. Half the city is dead. The minotaurs run under the harpies." He couldn't speak anymore after that. Athena wrapped him in her arms, holding him gently. She had to make a decision. If there were any survivors in the large city, they would need protection. Chimera needed to be tied to a leash, but they could accomplish none of this without an army of their own. They had heard nothing from Raftik.

"Rudy, do you think you can seek out Raftik? Tell him to gather his warriors and meet us by Nemi's house." The owl stood tall and bowed to her. "I will not rest til they are found." A few powerful bats at the air and Rudy was gone.

"We go now. We need the nymphs, the centaurs, and anyone else willing to help us. Phoebe and Kuma, you'll sneak into the city and gather as many survivors as you can and take them to Nemi's cottage. Keep watch for Chimera and her soldiers. Stay hidden if they approach. We don't want them to know you're there, or when we're coming." Athena ordered them. "Pan, I'll come with you to the wall, let's hurry." They all headed to their huts to gather their things, then Athena heard a voice behind her.

"What about me?" Astraeus called out. He had been silent. He looked distraught and she understood why. He had probably lost friends in the city, and who knows who else. Athena wouldn't allow herself to ponder on such things right now. It wasn't the right time.

"You'll stay here and see if you can cure them of their arrogance." Athena threw on her breastplate and strapped on her scabbard. Astraeus walked over and grabbed her, pulling her in close and kissing her. The world disappeared every time she felt his soft lips. Suddenly she understood the look on his face. He worried for her. "I'll be alright," she said as she pulled away and touched his face. "Come to Nemi's house tomorrow, whether you've had luck with this bunch or not." Astraeus nodded at her instructions, "I'll be there as fast as I can my Current." He looked at her a moment longer then disappeared.

Pan waited for her outside. Phoebe and Kuma were already disappearing over the hill ahead in the direction of Parthens. Pan fidgeted with his armor and wiped sweat from his forehead. Athena peered out at him and imagined he had never been under so much pressure before.

"You're just as brave as the rest of them, and you've sacrificed so much more." Athena touched his arms and looked at him gently. He took a deep breath and relaxed, showing her a weak smile.

"Well, I'm prepared to die if that's what I must do to make things right." Pan looked around the satyr village as he spoke. No one paid them any mind. It was as if they weren't there at all.

" Let's go. Astraeus will have a few words with the elders. I'm sure he'll sit them down to drinks and have a chat." Athena said as they passed houses.

Together Pan and Athena walked out of the village and disappeared into the trees. After an hour of walking Pan began to hum a song. She recognized it as one of the romantic tunes he used to play on the flute. The forest had grown so thick she hadn't noticed they had come right to the wall. It was overgrown with brush and weeds. She reached out to pull it away so the wall was bare and visible, but Pan stopped her. He motioned for her to stand and wait as he continued humming.

Athena had a feeling she was about to witness a magic she hadn't witnessed in thousands of years.

26

Pan sat nestled in the brush, his legs folded beneath him. His arms flowed over the leaves around him and he hummed. He kept his eyes closed and a gentle breeze pushed his hair from his face. He had been humming for hours. Athena had tried to convince him they should move on, head to Parthens and see how they can help the people, but he insisted he could get their attention. Athena considered leaving him behind, but she couldn't see how that would do him any good. She needed to be there.

She sat against a tree behind him, gazing at the wall. She had ordered them here.

The day it all happened was as clear as though it had happened yesterday. She couldn't understand why the nymphs wouldn't answer him. They must know she was there. What was the purpose of their reluctance? No matter what Pan had done, her own presence should be enough. She wondered if so much time had passed that even the nymphs had forgotten her. She never intended for them to be trapped so long. Only safe and comfortable while she pleaded their case to her father and the other gods.

Arguris was never supposed to be a prison.

"Pan, let me speak to them. I'm the one that had ordered them here in the first place, maybe they'll listen," Athena offered.

"No, they didn't open the wall for you the first time, remember. They'll only respond to me, and I have broken my agreement." Pan stood up and didn't look at her. He stared at the wall.

She was about to argue about the doors that had opened for her but then he began to cry.

"I know I've broken your heart, and I have killed what I have loved, and I have broken our agreement," he put a hand on one of the branches in the wall and wept through his words. He winced and blood trickled down as thorns pierced his palm. He refused to budge, but kept speaking, "This is bigger

than all of that now. Athena is back. You can see her here.
Right there!"

He spoke louder and reached out an arm in Athena's
direction. She stood and stared at the branches intertwined
that made up the wall.

"Please," she chimed in, "Please help us. There is an army
killing innocent creatures. Aside from the centaurs we're
searching for now, we have no help to stop them. I am not
telling you to bring down the wall. I know we can't do that yet,
but I am asking that you send help so that soon we can."
Athena walked to the wall and reached out her hand to touch
the wall next to Pan. She felt the branches, the smooth, cool
surface of the wood. Suddenly there was a soft-like skin
texture running under her palm. It enveloped their hands until
the wood itself looked like hands. Pan and Athena stepped
back and the wood moved forward with them. As it separated
from the other branches they could see the form of a woman
emerge. The forest echoed with sounds of wood creaking,
then water flowing as it changed form. The woman continued
to take shape, her skin was fair, without blemish. She wore a
vest made from bark laced with gold, with leaves hanging from
a vine around her shoulders. Her skirt flowed around her, its
dark green fading into the wind, glistening with gold. Leaves
hung here and there, swaying with the sheer material. Her eyes
were the brightest of greens, beautiful, calm, sincere. As the

last of the branch withdrew from the wall, her hair formed into a long flowing dark brown with a headdress of autumn leaves. Still holding onto their hands, she looked at each of them, then bowed her head.

Pan knelt to one knee and bowed, Athena looked at the nymph before her and smiled.

"Analie, it's been some time, I have much to ask forgiveness for my friend." Athena took the nymphs forearm in greeting and they pulled each other close, resting against each others forehead.

"We have served you well, and we understand your circumstances. We are happy to see you understand our reluctance." The nymph stared down at Pan and pulled her hand away. She walked a few steps into the forest, resting her hands on the trees that she passed. Each tree would shiver and she'd raise her head and smile.

"The nymphs have been dormant too long. I don't know how many I can make available to you, and as the walls are so far and long, it will take some time to gather who I can. We may need a few days at least." Analie continued to walk about, touching the trees as she went along.

"Is there anything we can do to help?" Athena asked.

"No, Eudora is not here. No one will be willing to listen to you," she gave Pan a disapproving look, and he stared at his hooves, a tear falling from his eyes. The nymph smirked and turned to look at them both.

"You will have your nymph army. And when Chimera and her army have been defeated, we will return home. It will be up to you to care for the creatures we have protected for you for so long." Analie waited for their response.

Athena ached to think of giving the nymph any news that would diminish her hopes of returning home. She had seen the world as it was now. All her memories showed her the trials she went on to find Arguris. The nymphs would not want to return to that world. It would destroy them.

"Analie, thank you for your help. I don't want to bring you this news, but at least take it as a warning," Athena touched the trees as the nymph had, though it didn't shiver at her palm. She looked at Analie and shared her concern. "The world is not the same. Home is no longer home, it has changed. You won't be happy their anymore."

Analie looked toward the wall, her expression sad, angry, confused. Athena slowly approached her and reached out her hand. "I'm so sorry, Analie," she said.

"No, don't be. If that's all true, then we would have moved on centuries ago anyway. We'll find a new home," Analie accepted Athena's hand and nodded her head. "I will leave you now, where should I send the soldiers?"

"To the once dead hut just outside of Parthens," Athena pointed in the direction and Analie nodded.

The nymph walked back to the wall and did not stop. The sound of creaking filled the forest again as she reached her arms in front of her and transformed. She crept like a vine through the branches, weaving in and out of the tangled wood. They watched her until she was gone.

"Let's go Pan, we need to see if Astraeus had any luck with the satyrs, and we have to reach Parthens quickly." Athena turned, ready to sprint away until she heard creaking coming from the walls again.

As far as they could see, branches flowed from the wall, taking human-like shape and filling the forest around them with nymph soldiers. All of them dressed as Analie, with their bark vests and flowing skirts. They wore different headdresses, several marked with gold vines wrapped around their flowing hair. The wall continued to thin, and for a moment Athena thought Analie was bringing down the wall entirely. She watched, waiting to see how thin the wall would become. As she observed, she noticed as the nymphs emerged from the wall, other branches took their place. The wall wasn't thinning, the nymphs that remained were expanding themselves further. Athena smiled.

Pan looked around anxiously as the nymphs gathered around. Most of them ignored him and looked to Athena. Others

folded their arms and frowned at him. The satyr took shelter
behind the goddess. He watched the beautiful creatures come
into formation in front of them.

He held his hand to his heart, feeling the pounding as he
became reminded of the years he spent chasing after them,
then Eudora. Life had been so simple. And so had he. He was
filled with shame and regret. He stepped forward, holding his
hands together in front of him, glancing from one nymph to
another. His body began to shake as the tears poured
uncontrollably from his eyes. He fell to his knees and
stretched his arms across the grass toward them, his head
tucked between his shoulders and the sobs muffled over the
grass. When he spoke, no one could understand what he said
and the nymphs just looked at each other.

Athena knelt beside him and rested a hand on his back. She
was about to say something but a soft, sweet laughter filled the
air. She remembered hearing it before, on their travels
through Arguris. The ladybugs. She stood up and looked
around. Pan was still sobbing, speaking incoherently, and
couldn't hear the sound. The laughter came again, closer.
The nymphs who had been watching the scene Pan was
putting on before them turned their heads and looked behind
them. There was a sound of rustling leaves as they parted,
making a path.

Pan fell quiet as he lifted his head and looked to see what was happening. He stayed on his knees, with Athena beside him. Everyone watched as a cloud of dirt and feathers and flowers floated towards them. As it came closer it began to take more solid form. A hand swayed at the side of the cloud as though next to a walking body. Then another on the other side. Then the arms and torso took shape, a beautifully armored gown produced itself from the neck down. Pink carnations and white daisies creating a loose belt that fell off one side of a hip. Bare feet appeared, stepping softly, quietly on the ground. Athena looked to Pan. He was staring at the creature forming in front of him as though hundreds of other nymphs hadn't just taken shape in front of him a moment before. He stood slowly, stumbling as though his knees were too weak to hold his weight. Athena grabbed his arm and helped him keep his balance. They both looked at the nymph as she brought herself together and stood before them. She stared at Pan, a soft, gentle expression on her face. Her eyes were a pale blue and her skin a soft earthy green. Her hair flowed behind her, showing no end, just disappearing into the air behind her. Vines were tangled throughout with leaves the colors of autumn. Pan stood frozen, a tear running down his face. His shock slowly changed into joy as his lips stretched into a smile. "Eudora," he finally said. He didn't dare reach out to her out of fear she may disappear. As if knowing what he was thinking, the nymph lifted her hand to him and waited. Pan smiled bigger and took the hand gently, bringing it to his lips and placing a soft kiss on her fingers. Pan laughed and cried as he rubbed her hand gently.

Eudora laughed and pulled her hand away, looking at Pan with playful eyes.

"You've changed, Pan. I'll miss the fool you once were," she said. Pan didn't understand her meaning. He knew he had changed some, he had indeed learned a great deal. But he feared a fool was something he could never escape being. But he didn't want to argue. He wanted her to speak more, so he could take in the bird-like sounds of her voice. Every word seemed to be lifted into the air and carried away into the forest like a whisper. He wanted to remember the sound forever, and to hear it every morning when he woke. He wanted to provoke her to speak more, but he didn't have the chance. Eudora reached her hands around Pans neck and stepped forward. For a moment Pan thought she may have fallen and quickly wrapped his arms around her waist. Then he felt lips on his, and his body tingled. He knew he was being kissed by the most beautiful creature he had ever seen, but he sensed the entire world in her lips, as though he were kissing every nymph and tree and flower throughout every bit of land right to the oceans shores. It confused him and he pulled away.

"You have our protection now, always. You've earned it, my sweet fool." Eudora said the last words playfully and she stroked Pan's cheek. He cupped her hands in his, his eyes twinkling. He couldn't remember the last time he had been so happy. Not even when Samantha had shown up in Chraimyth and had given him hope. Remembering why they were there, Pan took Eudora's hand and pulled her with him as he stood next to Athena. He wasn't sure he'd ever let go of her again, at least not for as long as she would bare it.

Athena smiled at them both, then looked out over the multitude of nymphs that were still gathering. They were coming from all directions now, even stepping right out of the elm trees surrounding them. They stood patiently, bowing their head to Athena, then waiting.

Athena felt hopeful. If the nymphs continued to come, there may be hope for them discouraging Chimera's threats. If the satyrs and centaurs both brought their armies, they would certainly be ready to fight, but she wanted to avoid war altogether if she could. She wasn't holding hope on the satyrs, but she did hope Kuma and Phoebe were finding survivors in Parthens. There were hundreds who needed help and healing, too.

"Dryads!" Athena called out. The nymphs stood in formation, ready for her command. "Parthens is in destruction and all beings there need our help! A couple of our companions are already there gathering any survivors, but they are not enough to help the injured and dying. I need a troop to go into Parthens and let them know they have not been forgotten, we are not going to leave them to suffer. Help everyone you can, comfort those you can't. Stay there only until it wouldn't be offensive to leave, then join us at at the dead hut."

One of the nymphs cried out and a hundred responded, disappearing into the nearest tree, or stepping back into the wall. The nymph bowed to Athena.

"We are pleased to serve you again, Athena."

"Your service has been long and I will find a way to show how much I appreciate this loyalty and friendship." Athena said softly, and she meant it.

When the hundred nymphs had gone, Athena looked out at the still growing mass spreading through the forest. She could no longer see how many were still coming, but she could hear them. The soft rustle of leaves, and the creaking of wood as they continued to emerge. The new crowd stared on, waiting for their instructions.

"Please, help me make sure everyone gets the message," Athena asked a nymph standing nearby. The nymph came and stood at her side.

Athena spoke loud so as many as possible could hear her words, "We will move to the hut, Nemi's hut, and wait as long as we can for the centaurs and any satyrs that will show up. It is not our purpose to engage in war, but to show we have the ability, with every intention of protecting the good of Arguris from both the threats within your walls, and further on in a world they aren't ready for. Chimera must come to this understanding. Peace will be maintained. Justice will be rightfully served. The future of Arguris will be for everyone to decide."

She looked to the nymph who seemed to be waiting for further instruction. "Will you make sure all those that are still arriving get this message?"

"They already have." The nymph looked to the ground, where roots were retracting from the ground and disappearing into her feet.

Athena smiled, "Thank you."

"Of course," the nymph smiled back and bowed before stepping away.

Only the sound of leaves could be heard as the nymph army turned in the direction of Nemi's hut and began making their way through the forest. Pan and Eudora walked hand in hand. The satyr could barely take his eyes off of Eudora as they walked. He tripped on a rock, not watching where he was going, and Eudora caught him, helping him up. As he looked at her gratefully, she laughed, making his cheeks red and his smile stretch from ear to ear.

Athena watched them go, walking alone behind the army and united couple. She wondered what other reunions there might be once Arguris no longer had a wall around it. What reunions were no longer possible. She looked out to the sea of dryad nymphs that moved in front of her and thought of their great sacrifice. What would they have been if she had never interfered? Her own guilts and regrets would have to be sorted later. She adjusted her thoughts to Astraeus with the Satyrs, and Rudy finding Raftik. She hoped they were both successful. She hoped they would all be successful.

She agreed with Chimera that she needed to answer for leaving them here for so long. She had never meant to, it had been out of her hands. None of them could know what happened after they arrived here. They had no idea what went on in the rest of the world after that. If she had an opportunity to explain, they may have more patience with her and be filled with more hope. She's here now, she knows who she is now, and she wants to help them all now. Hopefully that would be enough for them.

27

Rudy flew over the thick mass of trees below him, looking for the centaur that had promised to seek aide for their army. He knew exactly where he would be, and made his way to a clearing two days north of Parthens. There were only a few places the centaur made their home. They preferred the forests to the open sky. He never understood why. The harpies never attacked the large creatures, and there were no other overhead predators. The sun shone from behind the wall, so not even the light was a threat. Still, they kept to the forests, among the tall trees and sloping hills. They were never seen much around other parts either, not even the smaller towns like Cyrene. They valued their privacy, and they were allies of peace.

The owl flapped his wings and pushed himself higher so he could see farther. He had always been a strong flier, even as an owlet. There were no strong wind currents through most of Arguris, and to fly a long distance and great speed took strength and endurance. With his new armored wing, he needed to rebuild his strength all over again. He showed off to his friends like a proud beast given a gift from the gods, but the burden weighed on him. He couldn't share his pain with his friends. They depended on him, and no one had ever done that before. He wanted to be out flying, to practice using his wing, make it stronger, and to test his skills with his new daggers.

He was certain there were no other armored birds in Arguris, and he wanted to show greatness with dignity and honor. If there were to be a war, he would fight. And if he died, Arguris wouldn't tell his story as the poor bird with a broken wing. They would tell his story as the great owl with a wing of daggers that helped fight the foolish beast that dared challenge them. As the thoughts crossed his mind he twirled in the air, wrapping his feathers around him so he shot straight ahead like an arrow. Then he opened his armored wing, slashed at the air, then opened the other wing as he turned on his back and looped around to steady his flight. Pleased with his move, he tried again, with more force, then again. Instead of opening his other wing this time though, he slashed his armored wing a second time into the air, then wrapped it around him and shot toward the ground. The tops of the trees came closer and closer and he was seconds away from colliding down a tree of thick branches. He glared and smirked at the leaves just under him as he stretched his wings and glided right over the tips of the trees. He reached a claw under him and pulled the highest leaf from a tree, then lifted into the sky above, flapping his wings hard until he looked below and the trees had become specks.

He let go of the leaf in his hands as he held himself in the air, flapping hard and watching the leaf float quietly, gently to the ground.

"The next thing that falls from these talons won't fall tenderly." Rudy said as he glared off into the distance, looking back to Parthens where his friends waited for him.

He smiled and chuckled in their direction before pressing forward. This was certainly a more fulfilling task than what he'd been spending the years before wasting his time on. *Rudy, that scoundrel owes me money, go take what's mine and take what you're owed for it too. Rudy fly here, Rudy fly there.* He was a messenger in flight. Like a trained hawk, only he could speak. That didn't always please those he was sent to visit. It didn't matter, so long as he got what he came for and got paid.

But now things have changed. He's a key member to events that will go down in history, he was sure. He was happy to help Athena and the rest of the group. They asked him to keep a look out, and he was good at it. He got a view of Arguris most of its citizens had never seen. His reports helped determine their next move. Essentially, he amused himself, he was in control of the whole situation. But he wasn't that sort of creature, even if he did like to amuse himself with eccentrics. Athena had returned. Everything would soon change and he appreciated the opportunity to play such a role in it all.

Rudy's thoughts were interrupted as the satyr camp came into view above. He flew over and looked for any sign of Raftik. This camp was much like the other. Tents gathered in a clearing, surrounded by trees. Children ran with wooden weapons and shot arrows into the woods. Centaurides worked near the tents and stood near the children. The centaurs were scattered, most of them certainly out hunting. There was no sign of Raftik, and Rudy decided to wait in case he had gone out hunting, too. If he wasn't here, he'd return to the other camp and search him out there. He'd rather not take that extra time. There were important matters that needing tending too and and it wouldn't help matters the longer it took to build their army.

Rudy found a close branch where he had a good view of the tribe and could hear their chatter.

The centaurs could be fierce and brave soldiers, intimidating even. But when left among themselves, they were carefree and vibrant souls. The females smiled at each other and the children laughed. The men who stayed behind wore proud faces. Life for them was good. Rudy was beginning to think perhaps Raftik hadn't made it this far after all. He thought they should look a little more distressed if they had heard news of Chimera, and if he had shared any suspicions about Samantha. Raftik would not know she had gained her memory back, so anything he'd share would be opinion and possibly not taken to heart. Rudy chose to continue waiting, at least until the men returned so he could be sure the centaur was not here.

He spent the next few hours watching the tribe and eating bugs that crawled on nearby branches. At one point an arrow flew through the leaves above him and as it fell to the ground he caught it, snapping it in half in his talons before throwing it at the boy who stared at him below.

"Hey," the youngster called at him as he gathered the pieces and ran to show his friends.

The small group galloped to the tree and stared up at him with what he assumed were supposed to be looks of irritation or intimidation. He thought they looked more like pigs with wrinkled snouts. He saw them lift their bows and place their arrows, aiming at his branch. When they pulled back on their strings, Rudy chuckled and turned away, bounding to a branch on the other side of the trees wide trunk. He could here grunts below and hooves slapping the ground as they circled around to find him. He hopped from branch to branch, higher and higher, until the boys had given up circling and began shouting up at him. One of the mothers rode over and scolded them, pulling them away from the tree. They tried to argue but she grabbed the ear of two boys and led them inside a tent. The others scattered and quickly found other entertainment.

As Rudy made his way down he spotted one of the male centaurs near the large tent watching him. He pretended to pick something up off the branch and flew to the other side of the camp, out of the centaur's view. Satisfied he wasn't looking for him, Rudy sat in his new spot and continued to wait. The light was beginning to dim, which meant the sun was going down. The men should be returning soon.

Just as the thought passed, Rudy saw movement in the trees across the camp. Raftik was the first to emerge, along with who could only be the tribe's chief. Twenty or so centaur followed behind them as their women and children ran up to greet them. They handed their kill to the women who gathered together to skin the carcasses while the men roughed with the boys and gave gifts to their daughters. Rudy enjoyed watching them, their way of life, but he was most happy to see Raftik. There was an army to build and time could no longer be wasted. He spread his wings to take flight but pulled himself back as a centaur ran to Raftik and the chief.

"Is it settled then? Do I have my bride?" He was insistent, impatient. He looked back and forth between Raftik and his chief, waiting for an answer.

"You will be satisfied soon. Wait." The chief told him, then gave Raftik a stern look. Raftik folded his arms and raised his chin.

"I have told you, Zeira has no desire to marry and this rule is not a part of our custom, no matter how much you want to push it. Morlai should have no trouble finding pleasure with another female from either of our tribes." Raftik made his way to one of the tents but was stopped when the chief grabbed his arm and pulled him back.

"Friend, my dear friend," it sounded more like a warning than a decree, "I am chief here, and my tribe will not see me pushed around by an outsider that has no respect for our way of life."

Raftik brushed him off and they stared at each other. Rudy watched from his branch.

"Tip, I came here because I need your help, your numbers, and your skill. This will have to wait until these greater matters are handled." Raftik waited for the chiefs response, irritation growing on his face and his fists clenched at his sides. One of his hooves impatiently stomping the ground.

Tip responded by stomping his own hind legs and rearing up at Raftik, who only flinched a muscle.

"You need my numbers and skill? There will be neither if my men do not have their heads straight. He has a right to companionship. And she has an obligation."

"An *obligation*? In your tribe it may be an obligation, but among my people it's a mutual desire and understanding. Your men will have none of our women. I'll find help somewhere else. Yours is clearly misplaced and therefore useless to our cause." He was ready to run out of the camp but reared up as Rudy flew in front of him, flapping his wings, his armored feathers glistening from the fire burning in the middle of the camp.

"You should both stop acting like a couple of asses and listen," the owl perched on a thick pole standing outside the nearest tent with several bunches of herbs and flowers attached to it. The two angry centaurs looked at each other, then to him. Rudy filled them in on everything that had happened since Raftik had shook hands with Kuma and left camp. Raftik's expression softened and turned to delight and Rudy announced Athena's memory had returned. Tip looked confused, and angry. He looked Rudy over then turned away and waved him off.

"I've seen you, bird." He sounded like a drunkard from the inn looking to pick a fight. "Flying here and there above the trees. And you want to swoop down here and tell me you come from his camp to ask for my help. This fool can't even manage my help, but you think you'll have better luck?"

"Well, why not?" Rudy was happy to debate the issue if the beast felt so inclined.

"Because there's a way to things. You both have a demand, I have this one request," he waved toward Morlai who was standing in front of his tent next to another male. Both with arms folded and grim expressions.

"Yes, well, that being the case and all, I guess the only way to settle this is with a fight of our own, right here, tonight. There is not time to waste and we need to keep moving forward." Rudy rustled his feathers, down falling to the ground and the centaur look at them, then up to him.

"And who are you supposing should fight who?" Raftik asked, sounding almost amused at the idea.

"Bring the eager man, he'll fight me. Whoever lives will satisfy the other tribes demands, no backing out or you'll have to retreat as cowards and forfeit all your unwed women to the other tribe." Rudy was proud of how convincing he sounded, since he was making it up as he went along.

There was silence as the two chiefs considered his proposal. Morlai approached slowly, followed by his friend. Another centaur joined him and as Rudy watched them he wondered if Morlai might be next in line to lead the tribe.

"We'll fight," Morlai called over as one of the centaur handed him a staff. "What's a bird to a centaur anyway?" He laughed with his friends.

Rudy smirked. Just the type of fool he thought he'd be. This will be so easy they might call it murder. Rudy scolded himself at such a thought, but his regret was short lived as he reminded himself what he was fighting for. They needed to settle this matter so they could move on to much more important ones.

Tip held out his arm to Raftik. Raftik looked at Rudy for reassurance. It was clear he had no more faith than the others that a small creature as himself could defeat a mound of muscle like Morlai.

Rudy grinned at him at bowed. Raftik took Tips arm and they shook. Tip led them outside the camp and the others followed with torches. Some of the women stayed behind and kept the children back. Rudy flew overhead, then landed in the center of the circle they had made. They pushed the torches into the ground, closing them in.

Rudy studied Morlai, who entertained his friends with confident laughter, twirling his staff above his head.

"Is it playtime, boy?" Rudy taunted. "Is that why she doesn't want you?" Rudy laughed, knowing it would aggravate him quickly.

It did. Morlai quickly changed his body language and reared up, holding his staff high above his head, crying out as he charged toward Rudy.

Rudy didn't move, but watched his hooves, their speed, their beat. He hunched down, waiting for the right time, holding his wings only partially away from him. When Morlai began to bring the staff down over his head, he launch himself forward, twisting his body and letting his wings follow effortlessly. He could feel his armored wing make contact, and he heard the centaur cry out. He opened his wings and flew around, landing at the center of the circle, watching Morlai prance on three legs, the fourth spurting blood. There was commotion in the crowd and Rudy hunched down again. One of the centaurs tossed Morlai a sword. He smirked at the owl as he twirled it in one hand, hold is injured hoof off the ground.

When Rudy saw the beast aimed to throw the sword at him, he waited until it had just left his palm before lunging forward, spinning again, almost passing the centaur, until his wing brushed his back hoof on the other side. Morlai cried out again as he fell to the ground, laying on his side.

Rudy flew into the night sky, then turned and dove toward the wounded centaur. He saw him cower just before he spread his wings and landed gracefully on his shoulder. He looked over to Raftik. He smiled approvingly at him, then to his friend. Tip was angry and Rudy could almost see the daggers shooting from his eyes. He looked back to Raftik, "Is it going to be this fools end, or will the night find peace another way?"

Raftik looked at the centaur laying there bleeding, helpless, cowering. "It is the centaur way," he glanced over at Tip as he spoke. "It is the centaur way that only the strongest survive. He has lived his last day."

Rudy didn't ponder the chiefs words, and as muffled protests filled his ears, he gave one last spin and blood poured from the centaurs neck. In a moment Morlai was dead, and Rudy was covered in his blood. The crowd was silent, staring at him. Raftik broke the silence by grabbing a torch and grabbing one of the dead beasts arms. "Come, he deserves a proper burial. And once that is done, we will make plans to leave camp at first light."

At first no one moved. They only stared. They were clearly not pleased with the defeat of this young centaur, but if an owl with one armored wing could defeat him, what sort of leader in battle did they think he'd be?

Finally Tip stepped forward and took the other arm. They dragged the body into the woods and the others followed. Rudy was stopped by two centaurides who placed a bucket of water on the ground next to him and began cleaning the blood off of his feathers. They carefully wiped the daggers that covered them, and even cleaned his beak and feet.

They were easily irritated, but they were honorable. Rudy had accomplished what Raftik couldn't, and he was glad to be able to contribute more to the progress of all the change that was coming to Arguris.

This army would make them stronger and closer to defeating Chimera.

When the body had been buried they all returned to camp and the centaurides fed them. Raftik and Tip ate at opposite ends of where the males had gathered together. Rudy perched on a branch above and tore at his chunk of meat, watching each of them. The two chiefs looked at each other, then looked away, staring in the fire. Tip ripped into his meat with his teeth as though he were killing it all over again. Raftik stood up and made his way over. He reached out his arm without saying a word. Tip stared into the fire a moment, glaring into it, pondering his next move. He knew what it meant. He looked over at the females and they watched him as they hushed the children. They knew what it meant, too. He looked back to Raftik then stood up and faced him straight on.

"It seems that our friendship may be nearing its end, but our honor will always hold us together and our tribes at peace with one another. It was a fair fight, and I honor our agreement. You will have our numbers and our skill. We will gather in the morning and go where you send us." With that, he took

Raftik's arm and they shook. It was agreed. Nothing could undo it now.

Both of the centaur tribes would fight with Athena. Rudy knew he wouldn't need to interfere anymore so he flew to a quieter area of the woods that was still close enough to camp. He rustled his feathers, letting the down fall to the ground, then closed his eyes.

28

"Why didn't you ever tell me," Phoebe grunted as the ogre and bear made their way through the soft plains to Parthens. "Tell you what?"

"That, you know," she didn't quite know how to put it. Saying he belonged to her didn't sound right. Referring to the goddess as his mother seemed more accurate, but still didn't seem to quite describe their relationship. After a short pause she settled with, "about your special bond with Samantha, I mean Athena."

Kuma stared ahead as they strolled. He was quiet, thoughtful. Phoebe waited for an answer, wondering if there was something more to their relationship she didn't know. They had a long history together. She had only known either of them a short period of time in comparison. Of course there was something she didn't know about their relationship. There was a lot she didn't know. And it wasn't her business, she knew that. Seeing that Kuma wasn't offering an answer she decided to let it go. But Kuma cleared is through and in a low, deep rumble, saying, "You don't push the gods. She is my mother. I wanted her to remember me and the life she led on her own terms."

Phoebe agreed to his logic. As Samantha, the goddess had been put under a lot of pressure from the moment she set foot in Arguris. She had been just as lost and afraid, and even as frustrated as they all had been when they first arrived.

Phoebe decided to dig deeper, try to understand what life was like for Kuma as the bodyguard to the goddess of war.

"Are you happy she's back?"

Kuma eyed her as if she were being rude to ask. "Of course I am."

It was all he said.

They walked quietly most of the rest of the way, talking here and there about what they thought they might find in Parthens, and discussing battle strategies for capturing Chimera, arguing whether she should be kept alive or killed on the spot.

"Athena brought her here for a reason. She thought she deserved a chance just like the rest of us. We should hold her, give her a chance to come around." Kuma argued.

"Yes, but a creature like that was to be destroyed for a reason. It was created for destruction. It can't be trusted." Phoebe insisted.

As Parthens came into view they both quieted. There were no sounds, not one. No birds, no bugs humming in the grass. No echo of the city bustle lingering in the air. It was the voice the death.

When they came near the city walls they saw bodies lying along the path and on either side. People trying to flee. They didn't make it. They examined the bodies, looking for anyone that might still be living but they were all deceased. They crossed the wall into the city, welcomed with a strong stench of blood. Phoebe covered her nose. Pools of blood were scattered all over the road, and smeared on the walls. Buildings lay with walls smashed in, few doors were closed. Lifeless bodies were every where.

"Hello," Phoebe called out. She and Kuma looked at each other. She figured they must have been thinking the same thing. He looked as hopeless as she felt. She called out again, "We're here to help. Please come out if you can here us." There was nothing. They continued to walk the streets, stepping over dead bodies. Calling out to whomever might hear them but no one responded. Finally, when they neared the Parthenon, they spotted two children huddled together on the steps. They froze when they saw the ogre and bear approach.

Kuma raised his large paw, "It's okay, we're here to help." Their eyes grew wide when he spoke and they jumped up, running inside the building.

They followed the children, listening to the sounds of their running footsteps down the winding hallways. They saw candle light dancing on the wall down one of the hallways and slowly approached.

There were quiet hushes and children complained and something fell on the floor. Phoebe stopped just outside the door and calmly called into the room, "Please, it's okay, we're here to help. Look, my weapon is down. So is my friend's." She looked at Kuma. He shook his head. She glared at him. He glared back, but lay his halberd down where she lay her sword in front of the doorway so they could be seen from inside the room. "You are safe for now, but we need to get you out of Parthens," Phoebe continued, "May we come in?" There was a pause, then a female voice, "Yes, we trust you. Don't disappoint us."

They slowly entered the room. Phoebe was immediately disappointed, hoping there would be more survivors than this. "Are you the only ones that survived the attack," she asked.

"We don't know. We gathered who we could and came here," the voice belonged to a young satyr, practically a child.

"I understand. Are any of you hurt and need help?" Phoebe looked over the room. They were mostly children, a few elders. An old man in the back slowly raised his arm. He lowered his other to reveal a bleeding wound on his stomach that hadn't been tended to.

"Don't waste your time with him. It's fate that found this one," a woman said crudely from another part of the room.

"And should it be your fate, too?" Kuma stared down at her, to which she quietly eyed him before folding her arms, leaning against the wall and staring at the floor.

Phoebe knelt down in front of the old man and examined his wound. "Why don't they care for you old man?" She removed one of the leather tassels on her skirt side and grabbed a torch from the wall, running the leather over it at few times.

The old man smiled weakly, barely able to look at her. "I think she loves me," he laughed only briefly, before coughing, blood covering his lips and dripping down his chest. Phoebe glanced back at the woman who was watching them. She immediately turned away, staring to the floor, kicking at the dirt.

Kuma approached and gestured Phoebe to move.

"Old man, I don't believe you will survive. Do we leave you to suffer your death, or would you like us to let you find peace now?" Kuma towered over him like a giant. The little man nodded and waved him forward. He pulled a dagger from his belt and showed it the man. "May you find peace with the gods, and may those you leave behind find peace with your passing." The old man nodded, then laid himself down along the wall where he sat. Phoebe watched as most of the creatures in the room looked away. Some of the children looked on in awe and the ogre waved at them so they would turn away. The old man rested both his hands on his stomach just above his wound. Kuma placed one large paw over them, then quickly and quietly aided the dagger into the mans heart, holding it there until the old man passed on. He closed his eyes a moment then removed the dagger. Cleaning the dagger on the mans tunic, he then walked to the door way. Everyone watched him.

"Those of you who are able and willing, we ask you come with us. Parthens was attacked because the creature Chimera is looking for the goddess Athena."

There was commotion, and a mix of confused, frightened, and excited expressions.

"Who's Athena?" A small boy asked.

"She is the one that brought us to Arguris long ago," Phoebe answered. "And it is true, she has returned. We have seen her. She wasn't quite herself when she first arrived and she had to," Phoebe paused, looking for the right word again, "heal."

They exchanged glances, unsure what that meant.

"And did she *heal*?" the woman by the wall asked.

"Yes." Kuma responded. "She is building an army to fight against Chimera and maintain the peace that has been in Arguris for so long.

"Peace?" the woman stood straight and walked to the bear, staring at him with her hands on her hips. "Do you really call this peace what our ancestors have lived through and have, with no choice, left us to live as well?"

Kuma was not sure how to answer. He had come to help, not argue with this woman.

Phoebe offered, "If you do not wish to fight, I suggest you help bury the dead, then leave Parthens soon."

"I'm not burying anybody. I don't need any part in any more activities dealing with *gods*. I'll leave Parthens." She moved to the doorway, then looked back into the room. "If you're leaving then come with me. We'll be better in a group."

Half the room emptied, mostly the female creatures and their young, some of the males who pushed their families out the door. Two of them returned, having said their goodbyes.

Kuma and Phoebe examined the rest of the room. There were satyrs and humans mostly. Mostly humans. A couple ogres stood in the dark part of the room. Phoebe wondered why.

"We need to gather all the weapons we can and bring them with us. Arm yourselves with whatever you are most skilled with. If you are not skilled, gather them anyway. Arm yourself with at least a dagger, something easy to handle. We will meet outside the city by the wall." Phoebe followed Kuma to the door then stopped when they heard someone from the back of the room.

It was the ogres. One was tall and bulky, a long beard falling thin to his waste. "We don't want to leave. We will stay in Parthens."

Phoebe looked at Kuma, then to the ogre. "That is not safe. We don't know when Chimera might return with her army, or if she plans to at all. It is safe with us and the army Athena is gathering."

The ogre bowed his head, "We appreciate the rescue, but we have already decided to remain here. We will not fight, nor flee."

"Then go well." Kuma said and disappeared into the hallway. Phoebe wanted to argue more but they didn't have time for that. She looked at the ogre once more then followed Kuma into the hallway. Those that remained filled the hallway behind them. Once outside, Kuma split them up, giving groups of two or three an order, directing them again to gather weapons and arm themselves suitably. The smallest children stayed behind, clinging closer to Phoebe than Kuma. She did her best to wrap her arms around all of them at once. She couldn't imagine what they had witnessed. It was enough trauma walking through the streets to get them out of the city. Kuma watched her try to comfort the children, then he looked back into the city, at the state the creature had left it in. Perhaps Phoebe was right. Perhaps it was time Chimera be given to the after life. They could decide the peace she deserved.

They began to gather weapons around them, the children following close behind Phoebe. Some of them helping by running ahead and pointing where the weapons laid. A few creatures emerged from the closed doors and cautiously approached them. Phoebe and Kuma shared what they knew and gave them a choice. Most of them stayed and gathered weapons, the rest left, picking up a few on their way. Phoebe and Kuma gathered what they could carry and waited for the creatures nearest them to do the same. They made their way to the gate and waited for the rest to arrive.

Phoebe picked up a long heavy sword and examined it. Swinging it in the air she spun then brought it down into the ground where it sunk in deep. She let it go, leaving it sticking out of the ground.

"I wonder how Athena and Pan are doing? It would have been good if the satyrs had been more agreeable." Phoebe walked over and stood next to Kuma. She looked behind them at the children left behind. They had been orphaned, most certainly. She couldn't imagine any of them had ever been outside Parthens walls. She wondered what would happen to them. They'd follow them for now. But they'd have to find someone to take them in, away from Parthens and the armies.

Kuma walked over and grabbed the long sword, pulling it out of the ground. He looked it over and ran each side over his leg, then held it to the light above, examining it from every angle. Satisfied, he held it to his side and looked at Phoebe. Lost in his own thoughts, he said, "We'll be fine without the satyrs."

29

"Come on, Rhystas!" Astraeus picked up his mug of ale and gulped, drops dripping down his chin. Some of the elders cringed at his table manners. One stared at him, unmoved. "You know the stories. You know I was there! Sure we'll be fine without you," he continued on, shoving cooked goose and turnips in his mouth, "but where does that put you when it's all finished?" He dropped a bone onto his wooden plate and leaned toward Rhystas, "Alone? Is that really what your people want? Have you asked them? Because I think they want to fight."

They eyed one another, the table filling with low commotion among the other elders. Rhystas raised his hand, keeping his eyes on Astraeus.

"Elders, what do you say? Do we let the village determine our path?" He looked to each of them slowly as he spoke. They looked at each other silently.

"I believe those who have seen more of our world than we have might know a bit more of what the generations that follow us might desire," one elder said. He was fat, and it was a funny thing to see a fat satyr. Astraeus grinned at him, though he was mostly trying not to laugh at the curiosity of how his goat legs held him up.

There were a few nods around the table, Rhystas tapped his fingers on the arm of his chair as he considered his words.

"It is true. We have kept to this village for too long. It is our safe haven within this world created for the created. When we become fertilizer for the trees, our young will still be growing with a thirst for the world. I can not ignore this. It is our responsibility, while we are still alive and looked up to, to establish a path for them to follow. A way into Arguris, and through the walls and beyond."

The elders began to squirm in their chairs, all grinning, as though they had been waiting for this moment a long time. Rhystas frowned at them, then pound his fist on the table.

"However," he called out over the chatter that had begun, "if the people choose their peaceful life here, then we will be left alone, and you will not call upon us again to fight in any other war."

All eyes were on Astraeus now. It was an easy agreement. Either way they got the numbers, and the satyrs would be free to choose what they wanted to do with themselves when it was done.

"So it is agreed, you fight, then you go whatever way your village decides." He held out his hand to Rhystas. He looked at Astraeus as though he had been caught in a trap.

"I believe something was misunderstood," he pushed his chair back and stood up. "My people will not be taken for fools."

"But they were your words, we all heard them," Astraeus motioned to the other elders who all chimed in, "Yes," "Your words". Rhystas looked at them, then at Astraeus. He was quiet for a moment then reached his hand out and they shook. The elders clapped and Astraeus noticed the satyr that had been serving them was watching with a wide smile. The god tapped his now empty mug on the table, smiling to himself, and thinking of the satisfaction the news would bring his Current.

The following day the elders introduced Astraeus to the village hunters.

"These men will be our most skilled participants. They can shoot their arrows with accuracy hundreds of yards, even through the trees." The archers stood tall and stared at him and Astraeus knew the look. Men had tried to intimidate him many times. He smiled at them, once again trying not to insult them with laughter. There were not as many as he had hoped. Only a small handful actually. But they needed as many as were willing.

"I need you all to be ready in an hour. We have already lost too much time. We have instructions to meet outside of Parthens, where hopefully we will be met by others who have come to help." Astraeus shook their hands to show his appreciation, and his strength. He knew Athena would recognize his behavior and disapprove, but he couldn't help the fun of seeing the large beasts try not to wince from his grasp.

The next hand he shook belonged to a bulky satyr that towered over him several more feet than the others. His muscles bulged, making the skin around his arms look like it was too small a fit. He smiled and looked into his eyes as he held his hand in a strong grip. The satyr gave no expression, instead he tightened his own grip, surprising Astraeus. It wasn't painful, but he could tell the satyr understood. He winked at him then moved to greet the next satyr.

"Are we to be insulted right before we give our lives over nothing but uncertainties," the bulky satyr called out. He looked from Astraeus to Rhystas.

"What do you mean," Rhystas was talking to the other elders and turned to see who had spoken.

"Brokin, how have you been insulted?" Rhystas asked.

"Have we all not felt the reminder of where we are ranked in the hands of this man that calls us to war?" Brokin said the word man is if it were a disease and looked Astraeus up and down like he was a filthy rag.

Another satyr stepped forward, "We have." One by one the others stepped forward in protest of the gods actions.

Astraeus sighed and rubbed his forehead. *Such children*, he thought. He had forgotten what type of creatures satyrs were. He should not have teased them. He would have to maneuver this carefully or else he'd lose the numbers he hoped to bring to Athena.

He made his way through the crowd of archers and stood in front of Rhystas. "Yes, I was wrong. I should not have intimidated you like that. It is a behavior I know is frowned upon and yet I find myself in trouble over it again and again. I do not mean it personally. I am inconsiderate and rude and I apologize to you all."

Rhystas raised his walking staff and hit Astraeus on the arm.

"Hey!" Astraeus looked shocked as the elder hit him again, backing him into the crowd of archers. They circled around him and Rhystas lowered his staff.

"You do not sit at our table eating like a hog and ask us to fight for a goddess who has not proven herself. You do not insult the men who feed us and offer their skill to an army that has no certainty of strength or power." the elder shook his staff as he spoke, and Astraeus knew he had lost them. He tried to speak but the elder stopped him. Brokin stepped to his side, daring Astraeus to disrespect his leader. He knew they couldn't harm him, but he had to keep in mind the importance of their political relationship. They didn't have to be friends. They just needed to be allies.

"We will not fight," Rhystas declared. As if to settle the argument, the archers raised their bows and positioned their arrows, everyone aimed at Astraeus.

He held his hands up in surrender, "Okay, I understand. I should have thought better of my actions. I will leave you to your village, and I will not bother you further." Astraeus inched passed the arrows as they followed him, making his way through the crowd of tense satyrs.

Athena will not be pleased to hear about this, Astraeus thought to himself. He made his way to his hut, Brokin following not far behind, as if waiting for the god to irritate him more.

He went inside and grabbed his weapons and cloak. He sat on the chair next to the door a moment, thinking of any way to salvage their agreement. If not the satyrs, who else could he recruit. There weren't many villages outside of Parthens. There never had been. Anywhere else he considered was simply too far away and he didn't know how much time they had.

He grabbed his things and headed to the door. No sooner had he stepped one foot out that screams were heard from somewhere in the village. He peered around the door to question Brokin but the satyr was gone. Astraeus quietly made his way around the huts. The screams grew louder, and numerous. He pulled his sword from his waist and crept forward, ready to attack. There was a scream from one of the huts near his left and he quietly made is way to the nearest open window. When he peered inside he saw a large creature holding one of the elders against the wall. It was a minotaur, larger than Brokin, or even Kuma. He held a double-headed axe in his other hand. He let go of the elder and stepped back, holding his weapon in both hands, bringing it behind his shoulder as the elder looked on helplessly. Astraeus quickly circled the hut to find the doorway, and as he rounded the corner to the entrance he heard a soft groan, then a thud. Something scraped along the floor and Astraeus hid behind the corner. The minotaur walked out of the hut, and when

Astraeus thought it was clear, he peeked around the corner. He froze when he saw the minotaur heading straight toward him. He carried the satyr in either hand, one hand the human half, the other the animal half. His bloodied axe was strapped to his back, still dripping blood. He saw Astraeus and dropped both parts of the body, quickly pulling out his axe has he ran toward the god. Astraeus dropped everything but his sword and weaved around the huts as the massive creature chased after him. He was familiar with the minotaurs. They were vicious, destructive, hungry murderers, and bastards of creatures to kill. As they ran through the village, Astraeus spotted more minotaur, and dead satyrs chopped in half. Goat legs lay discarded along the walkways and inside doorways. The human halves were being piled near a hut at the edge of the village. Astraeus knew he couldn't keep running. He had to come up with a plan to save the satyrs that he could, and get them to leave the village.

Then he wondered, *Why are they here? Has the war already come and passed? Are they storming all of Arguris?* He heard a loud angry, "Hah!" and felt the wind on his neck as the minotaur swung his axe at his back. They wouldn't need to cut him in half. He was entirely what they enjoyed, human. Except he was a god and he didn't want to think of all the years he'd lived only to become a foul creatures stew.

Astraeus leapt and landed on the rooftop of a hut. The minotaur growled at him, raised his axe, and brought it down on the hut, cutting right through the roof. The angry beast pulled his axe through the wall and Astraeus ran the short distance to the other end of the roof. Another hut was close enough that he was able to leap over, barely escaping another blow.

The satyrs on the ground below continued to scream and call out for their loved ones. As Astraeus continued across the rooftops he spotted a tree with a wide trunk that he hoped would hold against the minotaur so he could do what he needed. It had been a long time since he had been called to use his godly gifts for the good of anything. It was typically fun and games. He wasn't a god anyone really admired or looked up to. Many in Arguris didn't even know he was a god. Those who did weren't impressed.

Today he'd put his powers to the test. He was needed and he had the means if he used his abilities the right way. He made his way to the tree, jumping onto the nearest branch and pulling himself up each one until he reached the highest point he could steady himself on. The minotaur watched him in the tree a moment, then a satyr made a run for it from his hiding spot in a nearby hut and caught the beast's attention. Astraeus was left alone, giving him a moment to consider his next move. He looked at the sky, at the trees, the huts, the minotaur, and the satyrs. He pressed his back against the tree and when he felt securely balanced he reached both his hands to the air in front of him and closed his eyes. He felt the wind wrap around his hands, the speed increasing, growing larger. His hair blew away from his face and his cloak stuck to the tree as the current blew its force. Leaves were pulled from the branches and some of the smaller branches broke off, falling to the ground below. He pulled his hands apart, separating the gust into each hand and looked at the minotaur below. He had to be sure he wouldn't harm the satyr, but he had to consider the risk of being too careful. He saw two minotaur slowly approaching four young satyrs that were huddled together near a well by where Astraeus had met with the elders only moments ago. They were far enough apart that he knew they'd be safe. He thrust one arm in front of him and a burst of wind shot from the current flowing around his hand. It only took a second to reach the minotaurs and they both fell. He watched to see if they would get up. There was no movement. He waited a moment longer to be sure it had worked. When they still didn't move he looked for more. He aimed again and again, each minotaur falling to the ground, lifeless. After the last one had fallen he scoured the village for signs of anymore he had missed. Satyrs cried and held each other, and the hands of their deceased.

Astraeus released the current, ready to climb down the tree until he noticed one of the minotaurs moving, trying to stand up. And then another. Slowly, they were beginning to pick themselves up from the ground. Most of the satyr had already gathered near the well and Astraeus knew they were even easier targets sitting in one place, and he had to do something quickly, and permanently.

He pulled the wind in again. He pulled and pulled until the wind circled his entire body, carrying him away from the tree. He leaned against the pressure of the wind so that the current carried him and he drifted toward the nearest minotaurs. They watched him, raising their axes and swords, ready to fight. With a quick gesture of his hands, Astraeus sent the wind tunneling around him. He spread his arms out to either side and the tunnel widened. The sound grew loud as the tunnel grew larger and moved faster. A roof top got caught in the current and was ripped from the hut. It was instantly torn to shreds. Astraeus leaned and drifted closer to the angry minotaur. They turned and ran, yelling to the others. Astraeus leaned more, allowing himself and the tunnel around him to move faster, faster than the minotaur. They couldn't escape the tornado, each of them picked up, flailing about uncontrollably. The god continued forward, picking up every minotaur in his path, making sure not to come to close to the satyrs now huddled close together at the well. The minotaur blew like dust in the wind, some of their bodies colliding, making sounds like trees falling in the woods. The lifeless bodies continued to crash into other minotaur as they were pulled into the tornado. Astraeus made his way through the village with great spee. Only a few minotaur escaped. The rest lay lifeless in the tunnel around him. Certain the satyrs were no longer in danger, he drifted into the woods, away from the village. He dropped his hands to his sides and watched as the tunnel slowly faded away. The bodies fell to the ground, landing with thuds and cracking sounds as more bones broke. He held a gust to his torso, pressed against it, and let the current carry him back to the village.

When he had landed in front of the discombobulated satyrs, they could only stare and hold onto each other. He didn't see any of the archers, or the elders. Hardly any of their men for that matter. At least not alive. Halves of satyr bodies lay strewn everywhere. There was no one to fight for their village, or for Arguris.

He looked at the women and children huddled together, then at the homes he had destroyed in his pursuit of the beasts that chased them. They no longer had a home.

"Please, there are some that got away, and after witnessing my display they will likely be back with more. They will seek revenge on whoever they can get their hands on. Come with me and we can protect you and help you bury your dead and rebuild your homes. But for now we need to leave."Astraeus pointed towards Parthens, and the hut where Athena had told them to meet.

A satyress stood, letting go of a child's hand that clung to her tightly.

"We do not need to sit aside while you win a war and show us pity. We are just as skilled as our archers. Who do you think taught them when they were young?" The satyress looked back to the other women who listened intently. "You can take us to your goddess, to your army. But we will be shown the same respect and given the same opportunity as any other creature who has gone there to defend their peace. Now lead us, wind god, take us to your leader. Take us to this war."

She finished and the satyresses stood, confident and strong. In a moment they went from frightful, fragile things, to fearless, determined creatures Astraeus knew he'd be proud to take into battle alongside him. He knew Athena would, too.

They were still only a handful, even less than when the archers were ready to fight with them. But these satyresses had something to fight for, and they claimed to have skill. While it had yet to be seen, Astraeus could not deny them the opportunity to fight for justice.

30

The nymphs continued to arrive in large numbers. Many more than Athena had expected. They glided through the trees and across the meadows they passed. Aside from the soft rustling of grass and leaves, only the thud of Pan's hooves could be heard. Athena had amused herself watching him stare at Eudora. He spoke to her softly, sweetly. She remembered when she and Astraeus would be alone in one of the hidden caves below Mount Olympus. They would burn candles and caress each others cheek. He would speak just as softly to her as Pan spoke to Eudora. Athena was happy for Pan. Seeing him this way made her feel even more forgiving

toward him. If Eudora loved him just as much, he would need
to be allowed to be himself in every way he found best for the
nymph.

As they made their way over a hill top, Parthens came in view.
Nemi's hut was not far away and they made their way along
the city wall. They could see the dead, and blood streaming
down the path. Athena clenched her jaw as she looked for her
friends, but it looked like they had already moved on. Several
nymph began to disappear into the ground. Unsure where
they were going Athena turned to Eudora.

"They will make the lives of the deceased forever a part of this
place. They will become, in a way, like us." Eudora looked
into the city with an expression Athena didn't understand. She
wanted to question the nymph about it but stayed quiet.

They continued on their way while the nymphs that stayed
behind emerged from the ground within the city walls and
began to approach the bodies of the creatures who had died at
the hands of Chimera's army.

One nymph approached the first body, that of a centaur still
grasping a human baby in her arms. The nymph looked next
to them and saw a woman laying with her face in the bloodied
mud. She laid her hands on both the baby and the woman and
closed her eyes. After a moment she looked at the woman and
watched as roots wound around her, rolling her over with ease
so that her face looked toward the sky. The nymph gently took

387

the baby from the centaur and carefully laid it in the woman's arms. Around her, other nymphs were doing the same thing. They approached every corpse, returning corpses of children to the corpses of their mothers and fathers if the bodies were near, laying mangled bodies respectfully on the ground. Some of the nymphs searched the buildings, carrying the deceased on a bed of roots that hovered behind them as they led the way back out to the street.

One of the survivors who chose to remain in Parthens stepped into her doorway as a nymph was about to enter.

"Who are you? What do you want?" the startled ogre demanded. Her eyes were wild and she shook a shovel beside her in warning.

The nymph studied her a moment then turned around and approached the next building.

"They're all dead. What are you looking for?" the ogre followed the nymph, the shovel still at her side. She stopped when she saw how many other nymphs were there, carrying the dead, moving them from one place to another.

"I want answers. Who are you," she demanded again.

The nymph looked across the court yard behind her and eyed another dryad nymph who finished laying down the corpse of an old man and approached the girl. The first nymph moved on and the girl held her shovel in front of her.

"You won't have me, I swear. This is my home. Those are my dead to bury. You need to leave," the girl swung her shovel at the nymph approaching her. Roots shot from the ground, wrapping itself around the neck of the tool and flung it over the building behind the frightened ogre. She stumbled backwards and landed in the mud. She looked at her bloodied hands, then at the nymph still slowly approaching. She shielded her face with her arms and began screaming.

Other nymphs stopped what they were doing to see what had the girl frightened, but quickly returned to their task.

The nymph knelt down in front of the girl and placed a hand on her shoulder softly. The ogre flinched and curled herself into as small a ball as possible.

"We're here to help you bury your dead. This is too great a task to do on your own, and we will help you honor them, I promise," her voice was sweet and flowed like a gentle stream over rocks that had been smoothed after centuries of water running over them.

The young girl uncovered her eyes and studied the nymph, who gave her a gentle, reassuring stare.

"Follow me, you can help us complete our task," the nymph instructed her.

The ogre followed her past other nymphs and corpses and to the next street. It looked the same here, too. Corpses and blood. She began to sob as she recognized faces of friends and neighbors.

"What is your name," the nymph asked.

"Buika," the young ogre sniffled and wiped tears from her eyes with a small clean spot on her shawl.

"That's a beautiful name, Buika," the nymph said as she grabbed a corpse bent over a wine barrel. Half its leg was gone and the neck was broken. Buika looked away as the nymph laid it on the ground so that it lay more peacefully.

"My name is Physlyn," the nymph moved on, looking over every corpse, making sure they were lain on the ground gently. Buika did the same once she was able to hold in her tears. A few other survivors emerged from their homes and helped once they saw what they were doing. They cried as they cleaned the faces of the deceased and looked for missing body parts. A woman with her daughter clinging to her belt found a leg and stumbled as she sobbed, holding it in her hands, looking around, speaking incoherently.

Buika approached her and reached out for the leg. The woman cried as she handed it over, sobbing.

"That's my husband's shoe," she pointed to the leather sandal wrapped around the foot. Buika nodded and made her way back to the body Physlyn had laid down earlier. When they reached it, she looked at the leg still attached to the body but there was a calf-high boot covering the foot. Buika squeezed her eyes tightly, telling herself not to cry as the woman fell against her. "Where is he," she cried. Buika dropped the leg and wrapped her arms around the poor woman. She understood her pain. She herself still hadn't found her loved ones. But she had been looking much longer, and she knew the ache of that loss never went away. She looked at the little girl watching her mother. She didn't seem to understand what was going on. She was quiet, expressionless. Buika thought she must be in shock and understood if she decided to shut down until it was over. All this was too much for a child. She held onto the child's mother while she cried, wishing she could help her. She looked out to the nymphs continuing their work. They wouldn't have answers either. She closed her eyes and let a tear escape, but quickly opened them again and looked ahead of her, at the rooftops of the buildings ahead. She could see bodies hanging over the edges. Bodies that had been taken by the harpies then dropped carelessly. There was no honor in their actions and Buika cringed as she remembered the sounds they made as they flew over the city, hurting her ears until she thought she could bare it no longer.

There was a mans body hanging off the rooftop of the woman's home. His face could be seen and Buika pushed the woman off her chest so she was looking at her. "Ma'am, um, is that your husband there," she pointed up at the lifeless body and the woman followed her gaze. She stood up and stumbled to her house, her daughter following close behind. Her mouth dropped open and her face became red, but no sound came out. When she couldn't breathe anymore she choked and gasped, then screamed. She fell to her knees and grabbed her daughter, clinging her to her chest and sobbed. A couple nymphs approached and looked up at the corpse above them. Without a word, roots grew from the ground and wrapped around each other. They grew up along the building and tangled themselves into a thick stalk. When it reached the corpse, they wrapped around the body and pulled it down so it rested atop the stalk. Then slowly the roots untangled and shrunk back into the dirt, carrying the corpse until it laid on the ground. The woman quickly ran over and threw herself over the body. The little girl approached slowly and Buika watched as a tear ran down her face. She understood that her father was gone. The child looked to the nymph closest to her for a moment then asked, "Are you going to make him immortal?"

The nymph smiled at her, "What an odd thing for you to know child," she said. She lowered herself so she was looking into the child's eyes. "Yes, sweet creature, they will all be immortal. They will always be here for you to say hello and good night." The nymph smiled as the child considered her words. Her mother had turned around to listen and waited to see what her daughter would say.

The little girl looked back at her father's body again, then back to the nymph, "Okay, but you have to come back when Mommy dies and do the same thing with her."

Her mother pulled her back and looked at the nymph apologetically, "Just thank the creature, Layla. They are doing a great kindness for the city, a kindness that will be remembered for centuries to come.

"And I want you to be remembered forever, too, Mommy," the little girl argued. The nymph smiled at them and stood, returning to her work.

Buika looked for Physlyn and found her another two streets over. She was standing quietly, and so were the rest of the nymphs. She looked around and noticed all the bodies had been laid down. The rooftops were clear, and all the doors were closed. Buika wanted to to speak to the nymph but it didn't seem the right time. There was something eerie about their silence. She decided to wait.

Physlyn and the others stood quietly a moment longer, then without warning began to move toward the center of town where the fountain stood. Buika followed along and tried to ask what was happening, but Physlyn didn't seem to hear her. Others followed as well. She saw the little girl and her mother and more she hadn't noticed before. They all followed quietly. They were all curious, like her.

When they reached the fountain the nymphs circled around in front of it in a huddle. They didn't say a word and the survivors looked at each other, unsure what to do.

A few moments later the nymphs dispersed, leaving Physlyn standing in her place. Buika watched as spread out strategically around Physlyn so that they were evenly apart, in several rows filling the court yard. Roots crept from the ground from the nymphs farthest away. There was a short pause before more roots made their way to the next row. And that continued on through each row of nymphs. The survivors jumped out of the way as roots wound through their feet. It finally stopped when it reached the nearest row of nymphs to Physlyn.

She looked to each of them, and as she did so, roots grew from under her and spread out toward each nymph in the row nearest her. All but Physlyn bowed their heads. Everyone else watched in curiosity. The nymph looked to the sky and held her arms out to her side. As she did so, all the roots began to shake. The dirt underneath them loosened and Buika watched as the ground slowly began to swallow the bodies of the dead. The dirt covered them until they could be seen no more. The ogre looked at the ground around her feet, relieved to see there were not roots near her and the ground was solid. She looked at the other survivors and the ground was solid under them, too. She continued to watch as bodies disappeared and the roots shook the earth.

It was several minutes before it stopped, even after the court yard was clear. Buika figured it would take some time to bury every body in the city. She thought about running through the streets to watch the bodies disappear but she was afraid she'd be buried, too. The nymphs had been mindful to leave solid ground for her to stand on.

The shaking finally stopped, but the nymphs didn't move. A soft green moss grew over the ground and up the walls of the building. Anywhere that there was blood, the moss grew, soaking it all up like a sponge until the whole city was covered in green. Buika took a deep breath and the stench of death was replaced with a sweet scent of lavender and jasmine. When the moss had soaked in all the blood, Physlyn still remained in her place. She closed her eyes and lowered her head. One of her arms stiffened so it was like wood and the hand became thin and flat like an axe. With her other hand she gathered her hair and held it out in front of her face. "*Boju vaki, et lu mal, soh'aira,*" she spoke as she ran the wooden blade through her hair. When the hair was cut her hand returned to the form it was before and she gathered the limp strands in both hands. She tossed them toward the sky above her and as she did so, the strands spun around each other until it formed a thick thread. It twirled and slowly fell toward the ground a few feet in front of Physlyn, then effortlessly disappeared into the earth like a snake crawling into its hole. The ground began to shake again, this time hard, making the survivors stumble and fall. The buildings shook and Buika hoped they wouldn't collapse.

Physlyn stared at the ground and everyone watched, waiting to see what would happen.

The ground in front of her began to separate and a large tree trunk emerged. It climbed several feet before branches stretched out in every direction. A shadow grew over them as leaves filled each branch and they continued to grow above the fountain. Flowers bloomed and quickly disappeared, fruit growing in their place. Buika wasn't sure she was familiar with it. The other nymphs held their hands cupped together towards the tree. The same fruit from the tree grew right in their hand.

Physlyn finally opened her eyes. She reached toward the tree and caught a piece of fruit as it fell into her hand. The nymphs turned to Buika and the others and offered them the fruit they held, encouraging them to eat. Buika took the fruit in her hands and held it up to her nose. It didn't quite look like an apple, but it smelled like one.

She stared at the nymph in front of her. She was probably the most peaceful, beautiful creature she had ever seen. She looked around the courtyard, at the beauty that had taken over the city. As though the massacre had never happened.

"Please, eat," the nymph said softly.

The ogre held the fruit to her mouth and bit into it. It was the same texture as an apple but had a color inside that she couldn't describe. The other survivors began to eat as well and they smiled warily to each other. Buika swallowed and took another bite. As she chewed she noticed things around her began to change. The colors of the buildings were different. They looked the same color as the fruit. She suddenly couldn't remember why she was there or when the nymphs had arrived. She looked at the fruit in her hand and tasted it again. The sweet taste covered her tongue and she ate until nothing was left but the rind. She lost all care of what was going on and she felt possessed by the beauty that had overcome the city.

The nymphs escorted each one of the survivors to their homes that were now free of blood and smelled clean and fragrant. Buika walked inside her hut and found her bed. It was beautiful. Everything inside her home was now as though she were resting among the gods she had heard stories about. She laid her head on the pillow and felt the blanket cover her, someone tucking it under her chin.

"Live well, sweet creature. You won't remember me tomorrow," Physlyn watched Buika until she heard her softly snoring, her lips curled in a smile.

She made her way back to the street where the others were gathering. She nodded to them and sunk into the ground. The others did the same as the survivors fell asleep in their beds. They re-emerged when they had caught up with the other nymphs and Athena. Physlyn found the goddess and told her, "Parthens is at peace."

Athena looked at cottage ahead, "I hope we can bring peace to all of Arguris."

Secrets of Arguris by Dianna Ortiz

Made in the USA
Middletown, DE
10 June 2021